# ROUGH TERRAIN

BY LAURA J. ELDRIDGE

# ROUGH TERRAIN

*For my great aunt Gert, thanks for believing I was going to be an author all those years ago.*

*Indian Mound State Forest*
*Ramsey, Idaho, 2009*

The last of the rain had moved out overnight and the air had come in cold, more seasonable for October in the high country, causing fog to encompass the mountain. It was nearing dawn; the only noise being the occasional drip of water from branches as they splashed off rocky outcroppings that were scattered throughout the leaf-covered forest floor. A pair of wolves trotted through the murkiness, their paws making no sound on the wet leaves, in search of an early morning meal; their thick, gray fur blending into the fog. The larger, male wolf stopped and sniffed the air, the female several steps behind. Lowering into a crouch, the two moved cautiously forward. Several feet in front of them, on the ground, was a hind leg of a caribou. Instinct and hunger took over caution as the smaller wolf advanced and began to nibble on the carcass.

The hunter swore under his breath as he looked through the scope on his rifle and centered it on the smaller animal. The wolves were hard to see through the pea soup weather but it was as close as he could get without giving off his scent. He needed a clear shot if he was going to take them both down. The larger wolf was hanging back, obviously not trusting that his meal was so easily presented. The huntsman had been tracking these two for several hours. He had figured out their likely path and he'd gotten ahead of them. They'd shown up right on cue.

*C'mon Lobo*, he willed the larger animal to move forward. Bagging these two meant that he could sell the pelts for pocket change and still take care of some unfinished business before noon.

The Chevy Blazer's headlights bobbed erratically as the vehicle navigated the steep mountain passageway. The fog was so thick that the weak light barely illuminated the ghostly shadows of trees that lined the dirt road.

In the cab of the vehicle, Amanda Whittier braced her jean-clad legs and multi-colored sneakers against the floorboards as the Blazer hit another deep crevice, causing the vehicle to bounce like a carnival ride. Pink polka dot socks peered out from underneath her cuffs.

It seemed that her father drove from memory as he tried to avoid the deep ruts created by recent torrential rains, which made the road almost impossible to travel. Being in the mountains, it wouldn't have been unusual to have to go through snow this time of year, but it had been a warm fall so far.

The dashboard's lights gave off a soft glow and the radio was quietly playing a favorite station. Stealing a glance at her father, Amanda smiled to herself. He'd worked as a game warden at the Indian Mound State Park for as long as she could remember. It had become routine to accompany him on his rounds before he dropped her off at school. Her mother had died six years before, when Amanda was eight. It had seemed like minutes from the time the lump had been found to her funeral. This park and surrounding mountains were as familiar to her as her own backyard.

As if feeling her stare, he turned and grinned at her.

"Tell me again why we are up here on your day off?" she asked.

Mark Whittier regarded his only child with amusement. Her honey-blond hair was pulled back into a French braid, showing off her mother's green eyes and heart-shaped face.

"We're up here because I left some paperwork at the tower. Knowing your uncle Peter, he'll have the place looking like a bomb went off and I'll never be able to find it again!"

Amanda laughed.

Mark's brother, Peter, was also a game warden. Amanda had been just a baby when Peter had gotten divorced and began drinking heavily. He had been sober for over five years now and appeared to be getting his life back together.

What Mark didn't tell Amanda was that he was worried about his brother. For several months, Peter had been acting secretive, disappearing for long periods of time and was constantly late for work. It might be coincidence, but it seemed that his disappearances coincided with increased poaching activity in the park.

Mark had tried to talk to his brother the night before, to get some answers, but Peter had avoided looking directly at him and had sidestepped all his questions. While he hadn't smelled any liquor on his brother's breath or noticed any blood shot eyes or other tell-tale signs that Peter had been drinking again, Mark just felt in his gut that something was wrong. Peter had the early shift this morning and Mark just wanted to check on him to make sure that he was okay.

• • •

The Blazer turned into the driveway of the fire tower: a large square wooden structure that thrust one hundred and twenty-five feet into the air. Stairs zigzagged up the middle to a lookout deck offering a three-hundred-and-sixty-degree view of the park and the mountain range that gave the park its name. On a clear day, Amanda could see a hundred miles in three directions. During the summer, she spent a lot of time at the top of the tower watching for smoke. Forest fires in the park were a fact of life. Lightning, cigarettes and unattended campfires had all taken their toll on the forest in years past. Spotting a wisp of smoke miles away could save thousands of acres of forest, countless wildlife and human lives.

A small cabin sat at the base of the tower with a battered green game warden truck parked out in front.

"Looks like Uncle Peter is already here," Amanda observed as they pulled alongside. "Hope you can find your paperwork now."

Hopping out of the Blazer, she didn't notice that her father didn't reply.

• • •

The smell of coffee and a wood fire greeted them as Mark opened the door and they entered a room that was twenty-four by twenty feet. Several desks faced each other and file cabinets lined the back wall. Locked cabinets took up one wall and a long counter took up another. A small wood stove in the corner was chasing away the dampness and chill of the morning. It was fairly warm in the room so the stove must have been burning for a while.

A man in his mid-thirties, dressed in a ranger uniform, had his back to them as they entered. He was talking on his cell phone. "It's going down just before dusk tomorrow," he was saying as they came in. He turned and looked at them. "I have to go," he told the person on the other end of the line before disconnecting. Shoving the phone into his pocket, he asked, "What are you two doing up here today?"

Mark ignored the question as he made his way over to the coffee pot.

Amanda watched as her father poured himself a cup of coffee and leaned back against the counter. Taking a sip, he studied his brother, as did Amanda. Peter was several years younger than Mark, but his blond hair was thinning and he carried an extra twenty pounds on his frame.

Peter's uniform was wrinkled, as if it had been slept in. His eyes were red and heavy-lidded, and he wouldn't meet Mark's gaze as he shifted papers around on his desk, trying to appear casual. The air in the room practically crackled with unseen tension.

"What's going down at dusk tomorrow?"

Peter sighed. "A surprise party. Stop worrying. Take Amanda, head back to town and enjoy your day off."

Mark slammed his cup down on the counter, spilling his coffee. "I'm not leaving until you tell me what is going on with you."

Amanda didn't know what to do. She had seen the brothers argue before, that was nothing new, but this situation was something she didn't understand.

"I'm going to the observation tower while you two figure this out." Grabbing a pair of binoculars, she had almost reached the door when the two-way radio on the counter crackled with life. Mark went over and answered the summons while she hesitated, her hand on the doorknob.

"Shots fired in the vicinity of the Gorge overlook," a male voice reported.

"Roger that," Mark replied into the mike. He then headed for the gun cabinet on the far side of the room. Producing a ring of keys from his pocket, he fitted one in the lock and swung open the door. Taking out two rifles, he laid them on the desk before reaching in again and grabbing several boxes of bullets. Turning, he relocked the cabinet. His movements were deliberate and precise.

Amanda noticed that Peter was staring at the map of the park on the wall. He hadn't moved since the call had come in. She looked at the map and back at him. His face had gone pale at the message and his eyes were narrowed.

"That can't be them," he muttered. He pulled out a piece of paper from his pocket and looked at it.

Mark hadn't noticed his brother's behavior as he scooped up the rifles and ammunition.

"C'mon Peter," he called striding toward the door, letting Amanda go ahead of him.

Peter snapped out of his musings to rush after his brother, who was already halfway to the vehicles. The fog was already starting to burn off as the sun crested over the mountain, its early rays trying to penetrate the chilly remnants of night.

He grabbed the truck door as Mark tried to swing it open. "Go home Mark. I'll take care of this. It's probably just some kids letting off steam before school." He grinned, yet never relaxed his hand on the door.

Mark studied his younger brother for a moment before glancing over to Amanda. She could read his thoughts.

"There's something going on with you and I want to know what it is." Brother stared at brother.

"I can do this call on my own," Peter insisted. "I don't need you to watch out for me. I'm fine. Take Amanda to school."

Mark started to argue then stopped. "Amanda and I will follow and be your backup. If everything's okay, then we'll just head on down."

Peter looked like he wanted to argue but thought better of it. Seizing one of the rifles, he headed to his truck. Amanda had grabbed the binoculars and two of the two-way radios. She watched her uncle send gravel flying as he drove off. Exchanging a look with her father, she swung up into the Blazer.

Mark pulled alongside Peter's truck in the parking lot that led to the Gorge's overlook path. The Gorge was a deep gash in the earth's surface. Jagged granite walls framed a sheer hundred-and-fifty-foot drop. Occasional small trees clung to life on a small ledge or crevice in the rock. At the bottom was a river, fed in the spring from the abundance of melting snow that came out of the higher rough terrain, along with huge boulders, worn smooth from thousands of years of water.

Peter was already out of his truck, looking at a beat-up green Dodge that was also parked in the grassy lot, its license plate caked with mud. The truck didn't look familiar, but it wasn't an uncommon thing to have hikers out this early in the morning, or it could belong to whoever was shooting.

Mark opened his door and took a hold of Amanda by the arm as she started to open her door. "You stay here," he ordered, grabbing one of the two-way radios and his rifle. He met her green eyes with his own steady blue ones and gave her a crooked smile. "Peter's probably right. It's most likely kids fooling around." He winked at her. "I'll be back before you even miss me. Here's looking at you kid."

Amanda smiled at his movie reference and his bad Humphrey Bogar-timitation from Casablanca. They had watched all the classic movies to-gether and both of them could recite most of the lines. The quote was their private game.

"Dad," she called.

He turned and looked at her. "We'll be fine. I'll be right back," he said to her unspoken plea. "I'll radio if I need help."

He shut the door and walked over to where Peter stood. "Did you run the plate?" he asked.

Peter shook his head. "I will if we don't find anyone."

Mark nodded his agreement and followed Peter onto the path that led to the overlook.

Amanda watched them until they blended into the forest. The sun's rays were still trying to burn through the lingering grayness. She rolled down the window. There was no sound except for the distant rushing of water. It was too quiet, way too quiet. Birds should be singing and squirrels should be busy gathering food for the winter. It seemed as if the forest was watching, waiting for something or someone.

A glance at her watch showed that they had only been gone for just over twenty minutes. The silence seemed to be pressing down on her like a predator stalking its prey. Not seen but felt. Picking up the radio, she willed her father to call her. She knew better than to call him. It could give away his position.

Several gun shots split the quiet and made her jump. The shots were loud, which meant that they weren't that far away. Grabbing the binoculars and the two-way radio, Amanda bolted from the Blazer's cab and headed down the path. It took everything she had not to break into a run but she knew that whoever fired the shots could be just ahead.

The sound of water became louder and the trees began to thin as Amanda got closer to the rocky overlook. Seeing movement through the leaves, Amanda slowed her pace and crept slowly forward. Hiding behind a tree trunk, she saw her father through the binoculars, lying motionless on the ground at the feet of a man dressed in camouflage. The man's face was hidden by a hat pulled down low over his eyes. In one hand he held a high-powered rifle, pointed at her uncle, who was kneeling next to his brother. Peter was holding his upper arm as blood stained the shirt under his hand.

Amanda tried to hear what her uncle and the man were saying but the sound of the river below drowned out their voices. The word "poacher" and "trick" drifted back to her but that was all.

Desperately scanning around for something that she could use to help, she looked up as her uncle shouted. He was being forcibly dragged to the rocky edge of the overlook. Before Amanda could process the consequences of this, the man pushed Peter off the edge. Then without so much as a backward glance, the man strode back to where her father lay.

Amanda's lungs stopped working as blackness swam before her eyes. Dropping the binoculars, she grabbed the tree trunk for support. Frozen in place, she was unable to comprehend the horror that was unfolding before her. She watched helplessly as her father was dragged to the spot where her uncle had just disappeared. A painful intake of air caused gasping sobs to start from deep inside Amanda's chest.

Using his foot, the murderer rolled Mark over the side of the gorge.

Amanda put a hand over her mouth to stop the scream that bubbled up as her father disappeared from sight. Her two-way radio crackled in her hand. Without thought, she pushed the button and whispered brokenly into the mic, "He shot my dad and threw him over the side of the gorge. Please help him."

She didn't realize that she had taken a few steps forward until she focused on the man's shadowed face staring straight at her. She dropped the radio as he raised his rifle.

Self-preservation made her turn and run as the bark on the tree next to her exploded.

. . .

Amanda ran without thought as her heedless flight brought her deeper into the park. Branches and brambles tore at her clothes and lashed her face. Finally collapsing against a large oak, she took in gulps of air. She needed a plan if she was going to get out of the park alive.

Forcing back the tears, she willed her breathing to slow as she looked around to get her bearings.

Her father had taken the keys to the truck so it was useless to back track.

She had heard her uncle use the word poacher and that made sense. Obviously, this man was used to killing, whether animal or human, and he had lured her father and uncle to their deaths. Since she was a witness, he would be tracking her now. He was the hunter and he had her on the run. This was his game, she realized. He reveled in the hunt; in the kill. To murder two park rangers with no hesitation showed her just how dangerous and ruthless he was.

Anger coursed through her veins and pushed back the grief. Well, she wouldn't be an easy prey. If he wanted to kill her, then he was going to have to catch her. This park was her home and she was well-versed in tracking. An old Indian friend of her father's had taught her lots of tricks. Straightening her spine, Amanda concentrated on where she was. If she went east or south, she would be trapped by the gorge. Her hometown of Ramsey lay to the west, but it was too far to walk, and he would be able to cut her off at the expansion bridge. That left only one choice. Putting all other thoughts out of her head, she set about hiding her tracks and headed north.

• • •

Amanda sat at the edge of the clearing, hidden from sight by a low bush, surveying the surrounding forest. She had been walking for hours, back-tracking several times and hiding her trail as best as she could but she knew that he was still tracking her. The clearing was full of trees that had been cut and abandoned. They were strewn about like a child's game of pick-up sticks. Eventually they would be cut up and hauled away.

In the distance she could hear a helicopter, but it was too far away to be of any help to her. Amanda took her time scanning the far trees. She debated about going around the open space. It would be faster to go through the middle and walk across the logs, therefore not leaving any footprints. On the other hand, she was much more vulnerable out in the open. Exhaustion was starting to set in. She needed to get out of the park to get some help. The fastest way to do that was to go straight across. Satisfied that no one had gotten here ahead of her, Amanda made her way into the clearing. Halfway across, she noticed that the woods had gone silent. Squatting down among the logs, she listened. His footsteps could be heard in the woods behind her, faint, like the rustle of leaves in a light breeze. Quickly, she scooped out dead leaves between several logs that had fallen to create a small opening. She jammed herself into the space and scooped the vegetation back over herself and waited.

She could feel him.

Watching.

Her ears strained to hear the slightest sound. With a slight vibration to her left, he was suddenly there, like the hawk waiting for the rabbit to bolt from the bushes. Without moving her head, Amanda could see his feet just inches from where she was hidden. Terror and panic were building up inside her. Closing her eyes, she willed herself to breathe slow and quiet. Silently, chanting a prayer that he could not hear her heart that seemed to be beating out of her chest, a crescendo waiting for its finale.

Amanda opened her eyes and peered out. He hadn't moved. He wore worn hiking boots and he had several knives hanging from his belt. She couldn't see his face from her position, but she knew that his eyes were searching for any movement. Evil radiated from his body like tentacles reaching out to pull her from her hiding space.

*Please go away*, her mind willed him to move forward.

For a moment, she thought it had worked as he took several steps. He had torn his pant leg and a tattoo peaked out of the hole. Bright colors blended but she couldn't quite make out the design. She was so intent on the tattoo that she jumped when he spoke.

"I know you're here," he called out. His voice was deceptively calm and cajoling. "You can't hide forever. I'll find you. Come out now and I won't hurt you." Silence surrounded them as his voice trailed away, echoing off the quiet forest. "I'm not alone. I'll have men watching every road and trail that you could possibly take within an hour. You can't escape from us." Us? There were more men, murderers, poachers or whatever, in the area just waiting to hunt her down? It was mid-morning and the sun was warm and bright, yet Amanda was ice cold.

"Again, come out now and I won't hurt you."

She knew that he was lying. He was a cold-blooded killer and she had seen him. He couldn't let her live. Poaching was a billion-dollar industry, every ranger knew that. Killing her was just part of business. Then there would be no witness left to worry about. He'd most likely classify her and her family as collateral damage.

Did he know how close she was? All he had to do was look down. For a second, she wished that he would. Her family had just been slaughtered. Amanda would never see her father again. She didn't want to go on living too, but if she died, then this man would never be brought to justice. He would go on killing innocent people and poaching off the land. Her father and uncle would have died for nothing. Someday, she vowed silently, she would see him pay for what he had done.

A branch snapped in the woods. Swinging to the left, the hunter headed off in that direction, noiselessly slipping into the trees.

* * *

The moon had been up for several hours before Amanda crawled from her hiding space.

Her body was stiff, and her right arm had fallen asleep hours ago. The night animals had taken over the forest and they had gone about their normal routines. If the poacher had still been in the area, she would have known it. The moon was at its zenith and would give off just enough light to be able to make her way. Using the logs as cover, she inched her way toward the edge of the forest. Reaching the safety of the trees and blending into the shadows, Amanda swiped at tears. She didn't dare break down now as she had a long way to go to get to safety. She looked back at the empty clearing before silently disappearing into the darkness.

*Ramsey, Idaho, June 2019*

Amanda's smile was bittersweet as she turned onto Main Street, shortly after sunrise. The street was empty. Memories came flooding back as she passed buildings that hadn't changed in ten years. She had not expected the deep wrenching pain that settled in the region of her heart and made swallowing hard at seeing her old hometown again. She had the odd thought that the town had held its breath, waiting for her return. Waiting to give up its secrets too, she hoped.

Since the street was deserted, Amanda slowed her jeep as she studied the buildings, passing the old movie theater that was advertising a new sci-fi movie. The marque, showing its age with burnt out or broken bulbs.

Amanda, her friend Sherry, and every teenager for miles around would show up, no matter what was playing. It had been the place to be. After the movie, the crowd would make its way to the old drugstore that stood on the corner. It was a historic landmark, according to the plaque out front, and still had a soda fountain in the back. They would all crowd in; girls dressed in their best clothes, acting nonchalant and the boys in their best jeans and shirt, flirting with the girls.

That all seemed like a lifetime ago now.

Further up the street, on the left next to the playground, was the nursing home where Amanda had sung her heart out in fourth grade with the chorus from school. It had been Christmas time and the residents had slowly emerged from their rooms to listen. One elderly woman had thought that

Amanda was her granddaughter who had come to visit. The woman kept calling Amanda by her granddaughter's name. It had seemed harmless to play along, and besides, it had made the woman happy. Amanda recalled feeling so sad that she had insisted on delivering the woman a Christmas card every year until the woman passed away. Try as she might, she couldn't remember the woman's name now.

Swinging the jeep into a parking space in front of the general store, Amanda shut off the engine and looked up at the large wooden structure with its covered porch running the length of the building. Tall windows gleamed in the early sunlight, enticing Amanda inside to with their displayed merchandise.

Closing her eyes, more memories came flooding back. She pictured her father entering the store, as he had hundreds of times before, to buy Amanda and her mother's favorite candy, which he'd bring home as a surprise. Amanda had gotten a job there; stocking shelves and cashiering. Her father had taken her out to dinner to celebrate her first paycheck. He had been so proud of her, picking her up from work every day, the summer before her world changed. She'd bought a laptop with that summer's earnings and was planning on going into wildlife management when she was old enough.

Things had been so simple then, her future bright and promising until an evil man changed her plans and altered the course of her life in a moment. The growing pain in her chest threatened to spill over so she bit the inside of her cheek and fought it. Amanda was good at hiding her emotions; good at hiding a lot of things. Taking slow, deep breaths, she cleared her mind of the past.

When she decided to return to Ramsey, Amanda had realized she would have to go undercover. There was still a murderer out there who knew she was alive. It was too risky to be herself. The police and FBI were no closer to finding the killer than they had been ten years ago. It seemed as if he and his band of poachers had disappeared from sight, like ghosts. Deep down, Amanda knew the only way to flush them out was to return to Ramsey and look for clues herself.

She had dyed her blond hair a deep auburn color and hid her green eyes behind brown contacts. Glasses altered the curve of her face and she hoped time had changed her looks enough over ten years to dim people's memories of her appearance. They must be fooled. Using her mother's middle name of Leigh and the last name of Doane, taken from some distant relatives of her father's, she had applied for a ranger job at the Indian

Mound State Park. With her new position secured, Amanda was coming home as Leigh Doane.

Shadoe, her white shepherd, sat up in the back seat. He'd been sleeping since they had left the hotel in South Dakota very early that morning. With a small whine, he nudged her arm as he stood between the front bucket seats before licking her face.

"I know, you want to get out," she patted his head and ruffled his ears. "Let me just get the key to the house and some supplies, then you can go run."

Shadoe seemed to understand and turned to lie back down on the rear seat.

• • •

The general store hadn't changed since she had last been inside. Canned goods still lined three aisles of shelves down the middle while on the right wall were shelves of glassware and cooking pots. On the left wall, jeans and other items of clothing were neatly folded on rough wooden shelves. The old store smelled of herbs, wood smoke and leather, just like she remembered.

The business had been in constant operation since the early 1800s. It was also on the historical register and had a descriptive plaque on the front of the building. Not much had changed in the past hundred years, except that the merchandise had been updated. The floor's original wide wood planks had worn smooth over the years, and every inch of space was utilized for displaying wares. Hurricane lamps, axes, camping gear and coils of rope hung from the rafters. Behind the long counter, which ran across the front of the store to the left, were cases of rifles and ammunition.

"If the general store doesn't have it, you don't need it," Amanda's father's words echoed in her mind as she looked around. Some basic things were still needed in these modern times. This high in the mountains, the weather and wildlife could be unpredictable. To the right of the front door was a wood stove with chairs surrounding it; a favorite place for the locals to gather and chase away a winter chill. The chairs were empty on this warm summer morning. In fact, the whole place appeared to be deserted, the only noise coming from a radio in the back of the checkout counter. The announcer was enthusing about a popular restaurant's virtues.

Bracing herself, Amanda headed toward the back of the store, her sandals making no noise on the wood beneath them. Grabbing some milk and butter from a standing cooler, a modern upgrade from the wide, chest coolers of her childhood, she turned and bumped into an elderly woman.

"Oh! I'm so sorry Jes….," she started to say before snapping her mouth shut.

*Great! I'm not even in town ten minutes and I almost blow my disguise.*

Jessie Sweeney barely reached five feet in her stocking feet. Despite her decade's absence, Amanda still recognized the store owner, whose face was lined with wrinkles, and her short, cropped hair now white. It was town lore that Jessie had been around since the first settlers because no one seemed to know her true age. Amanda had laughed, years ago, when Jessie had confided in her that she had started that rumor herself. There was a sharp mind behind the blue eyes that were studying Amanda now.

Silence hung in the air as Amanda fumbled for something to say. "I'm sorry, I didn't see you there."

"Not many people look down far enough to see me! You must be Leigh?"

Amanda nodded down at penetrating eyes that twinkled up at her. The woman had a booming voice for someone so tiny.

"Jessie, we spoke on the phone." She reached out and shook Amanda's hand. "I feel as if I already know ya." Jessie's gaze never left her face, and she seemed lost in thought for a moment, before shaking her head and continuing. "Well, you'll be wanting the key to the house, I guess."

Amanda let out the breath she hadn't realized she had been holding, afraid that she had been recognized. Jessie radiated boundless energy, like a hummingbird flitting from flower to flower, never slowing the speed of its flight. Turning, the storekeeper headed toward the front of the store.

Amanda would need to be more careful in the future, especially when meeting people she knew. From now on, she had to become Leigh Doane, mind body and soul, and forget about her life as Amanda Whittier.

"I stocked the house with plenty of food items. You'll just need to get the perishables."

Jessie's voice floated back to her.

Grabbing a few more things, Amanda headed toward the large, front counter. Setting the items down, she looked at the jars of candy in front of the counter, and closed her eyes.

"Please, dad. Can I get caramel creams and butterscotches? I promise I won't eat them all today! I'll make them last all week!"

Her father would smile at her, reach into his pocket and pull out several dollars. "Here you go. Get a few of those chocolates your mother likes too."

Some of the memories of her father had faded with time but at that moment, looking at those candy jars, she could see and feel her dad's presence beside her.

Amanda's eyes felt dry and she swallowed hard, trying to hold back the tears that wanted to burst forward. Grief had threatened to consume her over the last ten years, but she had never given in to it. Anger had kept her together and made her feel stronger. When she decided to return to Ramsey, she had known she was going to have to face her memories, but she hadn't realized just how vivid they would be.

The sound of a clearing throat brought her back to the present. Across the counter, she found Jessie studying her. Amanda wasn't sure, but she suspected that Jessie could read her thoughts.

"Here's the key to the house and I've drawn you a map on how to get there. The phone is hooked up and that number's on the paper as well," Jessie said, smiling. "I know that all you young people have those fancy cell phones now, but sometimes the towers don't work, so you'll be glad for the landline." She rang up the groceries as she talked.

"Pretty quiet around there, except for a house just down the road, though it's not so close that you'll be bothered." Jessie paused then winked at Amanda. "Although once you meet the owner, you might just want to be bothered."

Amanda frowned as she paid for her purchases. Obviously there was an eligible bachelor living there and Jessie wanted to play matchmaker.

"I live here at the store, upstairs, if you need anything. That number's on the paper too."

Amanda thanked Jessie, then carried her bags out to the car. She shook off Jessie's comment about her neighbor; people were always trying to fix her up with a brother or single male friend. She would just have to let everyone know that she had no intention of getting romantically involved, no matter how nice-looking a suitor might be. She was in town for one reason; to find a murderer.

. . .

Jessie's rental house was a good-sized log cabin that sat at the edge of a large pond, framed by century-old oak trees. A perennial border of flowers had been planted across the front of the house creating a riotous display of color that Amanda could see the moment she turned into the dirt driveway. Pulling closer, she noticed oversized wicker furniture nestled on the large farmer's porch. Like the flowers, it was bright, painted pale yellow and sporting bright striped cushions that matched the striped hammock hanging between two trees on the right side of the house.

Parking the jeep, she opened the door and breathed in the woodsy fragrance that she remembered from her childhood. It was pure mountain air. Shadoe leapt over her and ran around the house, heading for the pond. He dove into the water with reckless abandonment. Amanda smiled as she walked down to the shore to watch him splash around. *Crazy dog.*

She couldn't imagine her life without him. It was hard to believe that she'd only adopted him four years ago, after he'd been hit by a car. The once handsome shepherd had been emaciated, filthy and suffering from a broken leg, among other things, when he had been brought into the vet hospital where she was doing an internship for school. One of the animal control officers had told her they'd been trying to catch him for a while but he'd stayed mostly in the shadows, never venturing close enough to anyone to be caught. Amanda had fallen in love with him instantly and named him Shadoe. Although he was in pain and scared, the dog had never attempted to bite her, so they'd formed a bond while he recuperated.

Amanda had been very careful, over the years, not to care about anyone or anything, but when she'd looked into Shadoe's eyes she had seen a reflection of herself; lonely, vulnerable, yet wanting so much to trust, to belong. Realizing that she needed him as much as he needed her only made their bond stronger. They'd been inseparable ever since.

Turning and surveying the house, Amanda wondered how long her mission would take and for how many seasons she would be living here. While she had always dreamed of working at the park with her father, nothing had stopped her from wanting to be a ranger. Becoming a game warden had been a way into the park so that she could look for the poacher who'd killed her family. It wasn't until she'd received the letter offering her the job that she'd really faced the truth. She wanted justice and needed closure if she were to ever be herself again.

After she'd escaped the park, ten years ago, there had been some talk of Amanda entering WITSEC, but without an arrest and pending trial of the man who had murdered her father and uncle, the witness protection program was not an option. So Amanda had been placed with a distant cousin of her mother's, who lived in Massachusetts, on Cape Cod. Celeste and Roy Clarke had been in their late fifties, with no children of their own, and they had tried to fill in as Amanda's parents as best as they could. Amanda had taken on their last name, and she appreciated the patience and love they gave her, even though they had been at a loss as to how to take care of a grieving teenager.

Amanda smiled as she recalled how Celeste would show up at every softball game Amanda played, always yelling encouragement from the bleachers, not just for her but for all the girls, no matter what team they were on.

The couple had done their best and Amanda loved them wholeheartedly but changing her identity had meant that she could never feel like people really knew her, not the real her, Amanda Whittier. All they knew was the façade of who she pretended to be. She didn't want her life to be a lie anymore. Being able to once again claim her father's name as her own had become an obsession. The poacher had destroyed everything she had cared about. For the last ten years, she had lived in constant fear that he would track her down and kill her too. Well, she was tired of running. At twenty-four years old, it was time to take back her life. Snapping out of her musings, she whistled to Shadoe before heading to the jeep to unload her belongings.

• • •

Amanda was relieved to see that the kitchen had been updated with all the latest appliances and conveniences, but where most people had replaced their countertops with granite, Jessie had kept the old wood surfaces and, in Leigh's opinion, it gave the kitchen more personality. Opening the cabinets to put her groceries away, she was amazed at the amount of food Jessie had already stocked up for her. The shelves were bursting with cans of various soups, tuna fish and boxes of pasta, among other things. There were even two large jars of peanut butter.

"Good Lord," Amanda muttered, looking over all the items, "the woman must think I eat like a linebacker!"

Moving into the living room, Amanda surveyed the massive stone fireplace that took up the entire wall to the left. Plenty of firewood had been stacked neatly into an alcove. Someone, probably Jessie, had already laid the wood for the fire; all Amanda needed to do was set a match to it. Though it was summer, nights could get cold in the mountains.

Walking over to the picture window, Amanda looked out over the back deck toward the pond. A narrow wooden dock jutted into the water to where a small rowboat was tied up. The surface of the water was smooth as glass, helping to calm Amanda's nerves. Her eyes darted to an occasional ripple, most likely from a fish.

Directly in front of the window sat a fair-sized oak table with a wine-colored tablecloth and a hurricane lamp. Three ladder-back chairs with wicker seats were pushed in around the table. Amanda could picture herself sitting here, eating breakfast or dinner, enjoying the soothing view of the water. Sunlight spilled through the window and landed on the tabletop, pooling on the hardwood floors. Shadoe had followed her into the room and gave a sigh of contentment as he splayed out across a large braided rug.

The pendulum of a tall grandfather clock sitting in the corner, on the other side of the window, swung slowly from side to side, its ticking the only sound in the room.

Amanda's eyes wandered over the display of rustic furnishings that were mostly colored in dark blue, burgundy and hunter green, giving the cabin a timeless quality. Handmade quilts and knickknacks gave it a homey feel. It was the type of room that was showcased in country living magazines, yet this was also a room that was clearly meant to be lived in. A full bath and a master bedroom completed the layout of the first floor. Stairs to the second floor revealed a loft containing twin beds and a small bathroom.

It didn't take Amanda long to unpack as she'd only brought some clothes, her laptop and groceries from Jessie's store. A glance at the clock revealed that it was past lunch time. The apple that she had eaten for breakfast was long gone so she decided to make herself a sandwich.

• • •

Balancing a plate in one hand and a glass of water in the other, accompanied by Shadoe, Amanda stepped out onto the back deck and headed for a glass table with a floral market umbrella.

Mallards were aimlessly swimming on the pond, occasionally diving to catch a late afternoon meal. Amanda had forgotten how quiet the country could be. This was exactly what she needed. The last few months had been a stressful whirlwind of organizing, packing and planning for her trip.

Shadoe, tired from the long drive and playing in the water, stretched out at her feet and promptly fell asleep.

It was too quiet. Memories started to creep in. Summer days spent fishing with her father and gardening with her mother, swimming at the lake with childhood friends. The memories that should have made her happy instead reminded her just how much she had lost. What would her life have been like without that terrible day? A tear slipped down her cheek just as Shadoe raised his head and whined. Reaching down to pat him, Amanda reassured him that all would be fine. Trusting her touch, he settled back down.

Amanda had lost count of how many times she had gone over that day in her mind, analyzing everyone's movements, each word that had been said, looking for any hidden meaning or clue. Everything had appeared normal, part of their routine, except for her uncle. Why had her father been worried about him? Looking back, it was obvious that Peter had known something. Memories of him looking at the map and saying that the call couldn't be right flittered through her head. Why had he tried to talk her father out of going with him that day?

For a long time, she'd suspected that Peter had been in league with the poachers, but why would they have killed him too? Had he turned a blind eye to their activities at the park only to have them turn on him to ensure his silence? Peter had loved his brother and niece. Amanda couldn't imagine him putting her in danger, never mind having his brother murdered, but she still believed that he'd known something.

As a child, she'd spent a lot of time at her Uncle Peter's house. She had so many wonderful memories of playing the princess while he played the evil dragon or the prince who came to rescue her. She'd even had a trunk of toys at his house to play with. He'd become distant as she had grown older, yet she had always loved him. It was hard to think that he might not have been the person she'd thought he was.

The grandfather clock chimed six, rousing her from her thoughts.

"C'mon Shadoe." She stood up and stretched, "Time to make the bed and get you some supper."

Shadoe barked at the word supper. Leigh smiled as they went inside.

• • •

Across the pond, half hidden by the trunk of a large oak tree, a man was watching Amanda. His eyes narrowed in concentration and his mouth became a thin slash as he lowered the binoculars. He couldn't be sure that this was the girl he'd been searching for.

It had been years. He had put out several contracts for information about where she had disappeared to but they had all been dead ends. That had surprised him as he had hired some of the best trackers in the world. He had figured that it shouldn't have been hard to find a fourteen year old girl who had been orphaned. However, she had vanished without the proverbial trace. Once again he had to admire her tenacity and cunning.

Several weeks ago, he had heard a rumor of a new female park ranger who was set to start at Indian Mound. Since the park was located in a small town, it was unusual for someone without local ties to request a transfer there. He figured that it had to be Amanda and she was looking for him. It only made sense that she would want to come back and seek justice. He felt it in his gut.

He needed to get closer. If it was her, then he wanted to see her expression when she finally recognized him. He wanted to savor her terror when he finally finished the hunt that he started ten years ago.

He wanted her to know that he had won.

Amanda awoke before her alarm. Peering through the bedroom window toward the eastern horizon, through the trees, she saw the sky was streaked with orange and pink clouds. The only sound in the still darkened room was that of Shadoe's deep breathing as she stepped over his sleeping form to head for the shower.

The hot water helped to chase the cobwebs from her brain. Pressing her head against the cold tile, letting the water flow over her, she thought about the day ahead.

This would be her first day working as a ranger at the park and Amanda knew she'd have to be very careful. She would be meeting her coworkers and couldn't afford to make any slip ups, like she almost did with Jessie yesterday. While there would be new people who would have no idea who she was, there were still some old-timers who had worked with her dad and uncle; men and women who'd known her since she was born and considered her one of their own daughters. How was she going to handle seeing these people again, lying to their faces? Pretending not to know who they are? Pretending not to be who she really was? The hardest part was that she was set to meet her co-workers at the fire tower and Amanda was dreading seeing that place again.

Turning off the now-tepid water, she stepped out of the shower and wrapped a towel around her damp body. Staring at her reflection in the clouded mirror she said out loud, "Hello, I'm Leigh. Leigh Doane."

• • •

Sitting at the glass table on the back deck, with a cup of coffee cradled in her hands, Amanda continued to practice her new name as she stared out over the pond. Her stomach felt queasy, yet she forced herself to eat a small breakfast. Golden sunlight was now filtering through the trees, chasing away the slight chill of the night. Birds chirped and sang from the trees, echoing over the pond as they awoke from their nests to begin the day. She tried to absorb the peacefulness of the scene, concentrating on her breathing and clearing her mind.

It wasn't going to be easy to see her father's old friends again. Leigh braced herself for what promised to be an emotional day filled with memories. Hopefully she could get through it without giving herself away. She planned to talk to them, discreetly, to see if they might recall something that she had been too young to notice or remember. The trail had grown so cold that she was desperate for any clue, no matter how small or insignificant it might seem.

Locking the cabin door, Leigh took a deep breath then headed for the jeep. Shadoe sat on the porch steps, watching as she opened the vehicle's door. He turned his head sideways as she asked, "Would you like to come with me?"

Leigh could have sworn he smiled as he bounded down the stairs and jumped into the front seat. He moved over to the passenger side and she rolled down his window so that he could stick his head out of it, as he always did. As they headed down the driveway, it appeared that Shadoe was looking forward to his first day of work, even if she wasn't.

• • •

The road to the fire tower hadn't changed at all, except to maybe get worse. Deep grooves still cut into the dirt, made from past torrential downpours, causing the jeep to bounce around. Shadoe jumped into the back seat and lay down with his head on his paws. Leigh had loved taking this route as a girl, but now, as she navigated what barely passed as a road, she tried not to think about the last time she had traveled it. There would be plenty of time, later, to give in to those memories.

As the forest began to thin out on her left, she caught glimpses of the tower through the trees. Unconsciously, she slowed her speed, but all too soon the driveway to the imposing structure was directly in front of her. She turned her vehicle into the small dirt parking lot and shifted into neutral.

Weeks of mental preparation still hadn't prepared her for the physical impact that seeing the fire tower provoked. Anxiety washed over her with the intensity of a tsunami as the jeep's engine hummed.

Her father had helped build this tower, and she had thousands of memories of him at this very spot. As much as it was painful to see it, she felt a closeness to him since this was also one of the last places she had seen him alive. His presence was so palpable that it wouldn't have surprised her to see him standing in the doorway, waiting for her, but she knew that would be impossible.

There was only one other vehicle in the lot, a jeep like hers, so she pulled up next to it and parked. Lowering her head to the steering wheel, she willed herself to breathe slowly.

Leigh needed to compose herself, but she missed her father so much at that moment that she felt a physical pain, like a band tightening around her heart and threatening to stop it from beating. This was not the time for her to lose it. There would be plenty of time to feel again, after the murderer was behind bars, then and only then could she stop repressing her emotions. *Stay strong* was her mantra, something for her to hold on to. She was afraid that if she started to feel the pain now, she would start crying and never be able to stop.

"Are you okay?"

Snapping her head up at the sound of the masculine voice right next to her left ear, she gave a startled gasp. Turning, she met concerned, blue eyes.

Her brown eyes roamed over his face. Sun-streaked blond hair was neatly cut but still a little too long, curling below the collar of his t-shirt. He seemed vaguely familiar and looked to be only a few years older than herself. A memory tugged at her. Did she know this man? Giving herself a mental shake, she looked back at him.

His eyes were filled with amusement. "Am I your type?" he asked.

"Excuse me?" she answered, frowning at him.

"Just wanted to know if you like what you see." He straightened up and put his arms out from his sides.

To her amazement, he turned slowly around, like a model on a runway. When he was facing her again, he put his hands on his hips and stopped.

*What an arrogant jerk!* She thought, snapping her mouth shut. Pasting a smile on her face, she swung the jeep door open, just missing him with it. Getting out and standing in front of him she barely reached his chin.

"I'm Leigh. I didn't mean to stare, but you look like someone I used to know, a long time ago. I can see now that you're much shorter and heavier than he is. Also, a lot older." She hoped the slight would have some negative effect on him, but it seemed to make him more amused.

"Jared McLean," he replied, offering his hand.

Shoving her hands into the pockets of her khakis, she wondered for a moment if she recognized his name. Unable to place him in her past, she turned back to the jeep to let Shadoe out.

"Are you a ranger here, Jared?" She tried to sound casual.

"Investigative photojournalist. On assignment."

Leigh's heart sank. Just what she needed, someone who would want a constant guide, asking questions and getting in her way. Hopefully the more seasoned rangers would be assigned to chauffer him around. Maybe they wouldn't cross paths too often.

"What's the focus of the article, travel or wildlife?"

Jared looked surprised at the question, then gave a dazzling smile. "You're the first person to understand that I don't just take pretty pictures and that there's an actual story that goes with them. I was beginning to think I'd have to give a lecture at the library about what it takes to be a real photojournalist."

"You mean the kind that pays the bills?" she asked, walking toward the ranger's cabin with Shadoe at her heels.

Jared fell in step with her. "Exactly."

He reached the cabin door ahead of her and stepped back so that she could enter first.

Taking a deep breath, Leigh crossed the threshold into a room that hadn't changed since she had last been there. The desks were in the exact positions they had always been. Shadoe sniffed around before lying down with a thud in front of the file cabinets. He put his head on his front paws but his eyes followed Jared's every movement.

Leigh recalled the image of her uncle, standing next to his desk, on that fateful morning. She walked over to the map of the park that was still tacked to the wall. It had yellowed with age, but she could clearly see where Peter had stared at it after the call came in. Why had he been surprised at the location of the shots? Had he known about the poachers being at the park that day?

The small wood stove hadn't been lit but Leigh felt cold and numb inside. She was grateful for Jared's presence because she wasn't sure if she could have handled walking into that room alone.

"To answer your question," Jared leaned up against the same counter her father had leaned against while he'd studied his brother, "I'm doing a piece on our National Parks and the problems they face by being under-funded. My bosses are hoping to pump some interest into the public to get some of the funding back and increase admissions."

Despite herself, Leigh was impressed. It sounded like a big assignment.

"Why did you pick Indian Mound? Why not Yosemite, or Acadia, or some of the bigger, well-known parks?"

"Precisely because those parks are so well-known. I want to highlight the smaller parks, the ones off the beaten path that people don't know much about. Make them feel as if they're hidden gems just waiting to be discovered. Virgin land, so to speak." Jared's eyes roamed over the room, then settled on her. "Besides, I like the view in this one."

The room wasn't that big, and Leigh could feel her face turning red as she blushed. Shadoe raised his head and whined. Unable to meet Jared's gaze, Leigh turned to look out the window. "Views can be very misleading."

Jared's eyes narrowed as he studied her profile. "Care to elaborate?"

Leigh was saved from answering by the sound of trucks pulling into the driveway. She would have to be cautious of spending any time with Jared. If he found out who she really was it could jeopardize her mission of finding her father and uncle's murderer.

Schooling her features, she prepared to meet the other rangers.

• • •

Later that night, Jared stared at his computer screen. He'd only been in Ramsey a little over a week and in that time, he had been very professional in his approach and questioning of the locals, but he hadn't learned a damn thing to help him with his assignment.

The only person of interest so far was Leigh.

Leaning back in his chair, he thought about the way she had parked beside him. She had looked scared, vulnerable, and there something else about her that he couldn't put a finger on. He could see that her face had been white as a sheet. Why had he felt such an overwhelming need to comfort her?

He'd turned on the charm to try to unnerve her. Most women were caught off guard and flattered and it wasn't too long before they were telling him anything he wanted to know. Leigh had been surprised but had recovered quickly; he had to give her that.

Jared frowned. Leigh had looked uncomfortable around the rangers who'd been working at the park for a long time. She'd appeared to avoid them as much as possible yet kept glancing at them, when she thought no one was looking. And why did she change the subject whenever personal questions came up? She'd definitely looked relieved when she was paired up with a younger ranger. Her behavior spoke of someone with something to hide. *But what?* Jared wondered, clenching his jaw.

Taking a sip from a can of local ale, he typed in his e-mail password. He'd send a note to his friend Matt, a private investigator, and have him do a little digging into Leigh's background. It wouldn't hurt to know who he was dealing with.

The sun streamed through the bedroom windows and fell on Leigh's face, causing her to groan, roll over and pull the pillow over her head. With a resigned sigh, she turned onto her back and stared at the ceiling. Today was her day off and she wasn't looking forward to it. The past week had been an emotional roller coaster of seeing people and places that had triggered thousands of memories and resurrected ghosts. So far, she had managed to stay busy and keep her emotions under control, but now, with time on her hands, would she be able to contain them, or would they bubble up and create a fissure that would eventually crack the veneer that she worked so hard to create?

Meeting her coworkers was difficult enough, but being introduced to Guy, the longest-working ranger at the park, had been the most difficult to face. Guy had been like a second father to her; teaching her how to build a campfire, rock climbing and shooting a rifle. It had been so hard to shake his hand while pretending to be a stranger, but somehow, she had done it. While it had been a relief that he hadn't recognized her, it had also stung. She'd left the cabin quickly, before she could burst into the tears that had threatened to spill over.

Although Guy's hair had thinned and grayed, and he had gained weight, she would have known him anywhere. His voice was so etched in her brain that she could have sworn she could hear him giving her advice throughout the years.

Shadoe padded into the room and rested his head on the bed. As always, his presence reassured her as he stared at her through expressive brown eyes.

"Okay buddy, I'm getting up. We'll go for a walk after I take a shower." Heaving herself out of bed, she headed for the bathroom.

• • •

At first, Leigh walked with no thought as to where she was heading, taking the path that circled the pond. Shadoe ran ahead, enjoying his freedom, sniffing at everything, and then waiting until she caught up to him before running ahead again. The sun was hot, but the thick foliage overhead protected her, making the walk comfortable.

Taking a left at a fork in the path, it was several minutes before Leigh realized the trail led to a main road. She navigated the steep embankment and stepped onto the pavement. There wasn't a car in sight in either direction. Staring at a black mailbox a few hundred yards to her left, she wasn't at all surprised that she had ended up here, of all places. Maybe subconsciously she'd headed this way on purpose, knowing that at some point, she'd be drawn to the place that she had once called home.

• • •

Tall grass and trees filled in the dirt road that led to the house, now reduced to a foot path. Branches caught at Leigh's clothing, as if trying to stop her from going forward, but she tugged them free and continued. Somehow the house was summoning her, silently drawing her closer, and calling her home.

Turning the last bend, in what barely passed as a road, the roof of the house came into view. It looked as if the forest was trying to reclaim the space the building was sitting on. What once had been a quaint mountain cabin was now a rundown shadow of itself. Neglect was evident everywhere. The windows had been boarded up and the front porch was tilted at an unnatural angle. Saplings were growing from the gutters and brambles had taken over the side of the house. An occasional board had rotted and fallen off a window, allowing the glass behind to be broken, letting in the elements.

A lump formed in Leigh's throat as an ache settled in her chest. This house was where she had felt safe as a child. Now it was in ruins.

It was obvious that no one had lived here since she had fled into the night, all those years ago. Someone had packed up the contents of the house and had shipped them to her aunt, who had put everything into a storage facility on Cape Cod.

She'd never worked up the courage to open the boxes and go through her dad's things. It had all belonged to another time, another life. It surprised her to realize that she hadn't thought once about what might have happened to the house. In her mind it hadn't changed, but in reality it had fallen apart.

Testing her step, Leigh climbed onto the front porch, making her way to the bay window to peer through the broken glass into what had once been the living room.

Leaves, dirt and debris could be seen scattered across the floor even though the inside was dim. Stepping gingerly, she made her way over to the front door and was not surprised to find it unlocked. There was nothing here to steal. It wasn't uncommon for a sudden snowstorm to catch a hiker unaware, even this close to town, so it was customary to leave abandoned houses unlocked, in case someone needed shelter.

The creaking of the wood door shattered the silence as she stepped inside, stopping just inside the threshold. It took a few seconds for her eyes to adjust to the gloom. The stench of mice assailed her and ashes drifted down from the chimney and into the fireplace as something scurried up the flue.

Cobwebs hung from the ceiling, draping walls that at one time held pictures of Amanda and her family. The once china-blue paint of the sheet-rock had faded and peeled and was now covered with graffiti.

Testing the floor, which seemed surprisingly solid despite its looks, Leigh ventured further into the room. Empty liquor bottles gave testament that wildlife hadn't been the only ones to take advantage of the empty cabin.

Her footsteps echoed in the empty space as she walked slowly toward the kitchen. Glancing through the doorway on her left, she noted that it had been gutted. Turning, she headed down the hallway instead. The small room on her right had been her parents' bedroom. Her mother had been so excited about the red floral wallpaper that now hung in tatters. The room next door had been her dad's office, with her bedroom taking up the end of the hall.

Like the observation tower, the office held so many memories of her father. They had spent hours in there playing games and talking. Again, Leigh realized that she had been truly blessed with having her father's undivided attention; if only she had appreciated it as much while he had been alive.

There had been a large desk in the center of the room which she hoped had been shipped to her storage unit. Maybe when this was all over, and she had her own place, she'd be able to use it. The bookcase and cabinet that had been built into the wall had been pulled from its housing, the wall behind destroyed with what looked like an ax or possibly a chain saw. The gouges appeared to be fresh. Puzzled, Leigh glanced around to see several spots had been torn up in the wood floor and in the walls as well. The other rooms had also been vandalized.

At first, Leigh assumed the teenagers who had used the house as a party venue must have caused the damage, but the more she studied the uniformity of the destruction, it appeared as if someone had been deliberately opening walls and floors as if looking for something. Kids wouldn't have been as selective. Why would someone be looking for something now? The only things of value here were her memories.

A shiver ran down Leigh's spine. *Unless someone had been looking for a clue as to her whereabouts.* Shadoe's barking outside made her jump. She crossed quickly to one of the windows and tried to peer past the plywood. A man's voice stopped the barking. She sprinted out of the room, down the hallway and through the living room. Opening the front door, Leigh barreled into a solid male chest. Arms reached out to steady her as she jumped back with a small scream.

"Whoa, slow down, I'm not going to hurt you."

The voice was familiar. Leigh stopped struggling long enough to look up meet Jared's concerned scrutiny.

"What are you doing here?" She pulled out of his grasp and took several steps back.

"I was out walking when I met up with your dog. I didn't see you and thought you might be hurt or something."

"We'll, I'm not." She brushed past him and strode outside.

Jared caught up with her at the end of the porch. "What were you doing in the house?"

Leigh glanced sharply at him but he only showed mild interest. The sunlight had helped to calm some of her nerves, but she had to remember that Jared was an investigative reporter. If he thought for a moment that there was a story here, then he wouldn't hesitate to use it. Wasn't it all about ratings with journalists? Her aunt Celeste had tried to shield her from most of the publicity of her father and uncle's murders, but she remembered that the story had spent months in the headlines.

"Just looking around," she shrugged. "Looks like the place has been abandoned for a long time."

"About ten years now. I'm sure you heard the story about the Whittier family tragedy?"

As if by some silent agreement, they had fallen in step together and were headed back down the overgrown driveway. Shadoe trotted behind them, stopping to smell a bush every few feet.

Leigh's pulse jumped as she took a deep breath. Here was a chance to find out what people knew about the poachers. "No, who were the Whittiers?" she asked in what she hoped was a normal voice.

Jared looked surprise. "Really? I would have thought you'd have heard the story about Mark Whittier, a park ranger who lived in that house with his teenage daughter, Amanda."

Leigh feigned ignorance with a shrug.

"Well, his brother, Peter, was a park ranger here too. About ten years ago, Peter asked Mark and Amanda to meet him at the Gorge overlook early one morning. The brothers must have got into a serious argument," he paused to pick up a stick and throw it for Shadoe, "because Peter shot and killed Mark and Amanda and then threw their bodies over the side of the Gorge.

Her blood turned cold. Leigh stopped walking. "What?"

"Then Peter committed suicide."

She couldn't have heard right. For the last ten years she had gone over every detail of that day. She could still see the poacher pushing her uncle over the side of the gorge and then going back for her father. She could still hear the bullet hitting the tree next to her.

Even though her uncle could be annoying, she had loved him. How had people believed that he could have done such a thing? Surely one of his friends had questioned that lie? Then she realized that everyone believed that she was dead too. Only she and the poacher knew the truth. Amanda Whittier was the only living link to tie him to the murders.

Unaware of the shock his words had created, Jared kept walking and talking. "They found Mark's body, but they never found Peter's or Amanda's. It really shook this town up. Nothing like that had ever happened here before. I was working on my school's newspaper at the time. I went to school with the daughter, Amanda, but I don't remember a whole lot about her. She was a little younger than me. Poor kid."

Leigh struggled not to stare at him. So that's why he'd seemed so familiar! Of course, Jared McLean had been three grades ahead of her. They hadn't traveled in the same circles so he probably wouldn't have recognized her even if she hadn't been assumed dead. No wonder he was so arrogant. She seemed to recall that all the girls had been in love with him.

He paused to look at her.

Avoiding his eyes, Leigh started to walk again. "That's awful. What motive did they give for the uncle to kill his brother and niece?"

Jared picked up another stick. Shadoe chased it noisily through the leaves.

"No one knows for sure, but it was speculated that Peter, the uncle, was having an affair with a married woman. Supposedly the woman's husband was wealthy and influential. When he found out about the two of them, he threatened to ruin them both."

Shadoe had returned with the stick and was looking at Jared adoringly.

*Traitor*, Leigh thought uncharitably.

As if reading her mind, Shadoe looked over at her and whined.

"But that doesn't explain a murder-suicide. People have affairs all the time and don't go around killing their family just because they were caught," she pointed out.

"True, but it seems that Peter had gone back to drinking and gambling. Apparently, he was in debt up to his eyeballs and the husband was threatening to buy out his debt so that he could collect on it. Peter would have lost everything; his house, job and the woman that he supposedly loved. General opinion is that he killed himself and took Mark and Amanda with him so that they wouldn't have to live with the shame of it all."

They had reached the bottom of the driveway and Leigh's mind was racing. She went over what she could remember of her uncle. She had no recollections of him drinking, and she was sure he hadn't been under the influence that morning. He had looked nervous, not drunk. No, something else had been going on. There could have been a woman involved, she supposed, but that didn't explain the murder/suicide story. She began to pace back and forth. Her uncle had known something about the poachers, she was sure of it but she didn't think he would have ever intentionally involved her or her father. Hadn't he tried to send her and Mark away when the call had come in about the shots at the Gorge? As Leigh recalled it had been her father who'd had insisted that they go as backup over Peter's protests.

What bothered her the most out of this new information was there was no way that a trained Ranger could have missed the tracks and evidence of a third man at the murder site. A lump formed in her throat. What if some of the Rangers that she knew and trusted were part of the poaching gang and her uncle had found out about it and that's why they killed him? They could have concocted the story to cover their tracks. Maybe she and her father had just been in the wrong place at the wrong time and became collateral damage? If that were true then she couldn't trust anyone.

Leigh placed two fingers to her temple. Her head was beginning to throb and she felt sick to her stomach. "I need to go," she said abruptly.

• • •

Jared watched her carefully. She had that haunted look again. It was in her eyes, he decided. They carried a deep pain and something else that he couldn't define. "I'll walk you home," he offered but she shook her head.

"No thank you." She gave a semblance of a smile. "I appreciate the offer but I'm sure that you have more pressing things to do and I don't want to keep you from them." She patted her hand against her thigh. "Come on Shadoe."

Jared watched as she walked rapidly away, never looking back once.

• • •

The library, which had been built in the mid 1800s by a cattle baron, sat at the edge of town. Constructed out of brick to replace the former wooden building that had been destroyed by fire, the library had been added onto over the years until it was a maze of rooms. It was just past noon and the library was quiet. Several older women were sitting on upholstered chairs

in the front room, most likely discussing the latest Oprah Book Club se-
lection, or the latest gossip.

Leigh entered the main room where floor-to-ceiling windows were open
to let in a soft breeze and plenty of sunshine. Glancing over to the librarian's desk, she breathed a sigh of relief to see a woman whom she didn't
recognize and wondered if Mrs. Baker had retired. A pretty woman, about
Leigh's age, with shoulder-length blond hair, stood off to the side of the
desk waiting as twin girls, probably no older than seven, checked out their
books. Through a doorway to her left, Leigh could see several small children playing in the kids' room.

A tingling sensation made Leigh glance around to see that the blond-
haired woman next to the desk was now staring intently at her. She froze
in place as the stranger moved closer and lightly touched her arm. "Amanda?" she asked hesitantly, her eyes wide, voice low and trembling a little. I
thought you were…"

Leigh sucked in her breath. Damn. Of all the people to run into. Shari
had been her best friend since they were five years old. They'd been inseparable. Shari, painfully shy, Amanda being the bossier of the two, had
helped Shari to come out of her shell.

How was she going to lie to someone who had often finished her sen-
tences? She desperately wanted to hug her old friend. "I'm sorry, you must
be mistaking me for someone else," she said, extending her hand. "I'm
Leigh Doane. New ranger at the park. Started last week."

Shrewd eyes stared at Leigh before Shari took Leigh's extended right
hand and turned it over, revealing a half-moon scar on the fleshy part of
her palm. Shari then bent down to reveal a matching scar on her own knee.

The girls had been eight years old and were playing in Shari's yard when
a neighbor's dog had managed to get under the fence and made a rush for
them, growling and flashing its teeth. The large mongrel had gotten hold
of Shari's leg. Amanda, always the protector, had grabbed the dog's ear to
pull it away and was bitten in the process.

Their scars had made them feel like twins with matching birthmarks.

Leigh looked up from her hand and didn't know what to say.

Shari forced a smile that didn't reach her eyes. "Nice to meet you Leigh,
I'm Shari Dean." Hooking her arm in Leigh's, she turned to the girls. "Why
don't you two sit in the beanbags and read your books for a minute? I'll be
right back."

The girls nodded, then nestled deep into the colorful fabric-covered
beanbags.

Dragging Leigh away from the desk, Shari found an empty corner where she could still see the girls. After checking to make sure that no one was close enough to hear them, Shari crossed her arms over her chest, looked at Leigh and waited.

Leigh wasn't sure whether to keep up the charade or confide in her childhood best friend. She didn't want to put Shari and her family in any danger. How could she ever forgive herself if something happened to Shari or her beautiful girls? There hadn't been a day that had gone by that Leigh didn't regret doing something that might have helped save her father or uncle. Counselors had repeatedly assured her that she had done exactly the right thing in running away, but that hadn't lessened the pain of her survivor's guilt. Leigh had ached for someone to confide in and here was someone who knew her, Amanda Whittier, not her alias.

Feeling trapped, Leigh looked around and saw a group of teenage girls entering the library, smiling and whispering to each other. Her throat tightened and her gaze skittered away to land an older couple who were sitting in padded chairs, their hands clasped, as the man read the paper out loud to the woman. Leigh closed her eyes. She had missed so much and though Celeste and Roy had done all they could, she still felt very much alone.

Shari had waited long enough. "All right, give," she demanded in a loud whisper. "I know who you are. I thought you were dead! Start talking."

So much for the painfully shy Shari. Having children had made her tough.

"Okay, okay," Leigh took a deep breath. "Yes, it's me, Amanda, but no one knows I'm alive and I need to keep it that way. My uncle didn't shoot me or my father, and he didn't commit suicide. They were both murdered by a poacher. I escaped but he could still be out there, looking for me."

"Poacher?" Shari looked shocked.

Taking out a pen and piece of paper from her purse, Leigh jotted down her cell phone number. "I can't go into details right now. Knowing who I am puts you and your family in danger. If you know of anything that can help me, please give me a call, otherwise I think it's best if we aren't seen together."

"That's ridiculous." Shari's voice was sharp. She looked around before lowering it again. "I will call you, and don't think you can avoid me. My husband and I are going out of town for a few days but when I get back, I want to hear everything."

"Look, Shari," Leigh began.

"No, no excuses. I'll call you to set up a time."

Leigh had forgotten how stubborn Shari could be. "Alright," she agreed. "Next week."

They walked back to where Shari's daughters were engrossed in their books.

"It was nice to meet you, Leigh. I'll be calling you."

With that, Shari ushered her daughters out of the library.

Leigh watched them leave before turning to the woman behind the desk. "Do you keep old local newspapers?" she asked, smiling.

"Of course. We have the Ramsey Gazette on microfilm going back to the mid-eighteen hundreds. It contains all the local news. A lot of articles after 1995 can be found online."

Leigh had already done an Internet search and had only managed to find brief articles on herself and her family, which was surprising considering the murders had been big news at the time.

"Microfilm would be great."

The woman nodded before leading Leigh to the archives.

. . .

Going back fifteen years, Leigh stumbled across a small article that had been written six months before her father's and uncle's murders. An elderly woman, named Joan Kent, had gone to the town meeting to complain about shots being fired at various times during the day and well into the night. Her property bordered the western boundary of the park, where hunting wasn't allowed. Mrs. Kent also reported that she had seen several helicopters flying very low around her house and then landing in open fields.

The article stated that a park representative, Peter Whittier, was at the meeting and had promised to look into the complaint.

Leigh scanned the next few weeks of papers until her heart sank. Another article a reported that Joan Kent had been killed after her car skidded on a dangerous section of highway plowed through a guardrail and went over an embankment. The writer had called it a "freak accident" but Leigh wasn't so sure.

Sitting back in her chair, she closed her eyes. Leigh remembered something about a car accident and a woman dying, but no details came to mind. It must have been Joan Kent, but it hadn't meant anything to her at the time, other than just being a tragic story. Had her uncle Peter considered it too much of a coincidence, coming on the heels of Joan's complaint, or had he not seen a connection and let the whole thing drop?

Leigh was searching for more articles related to the park when she came upon the article of her father and uncle's deaths. The headline jumped off the page at her: DOUBLE MURDER/SUICIDE ROCKS STATE PARK

Bowing her head, Leigh fought back tears as she read the article, which featured photographs of her father and uncle in their park service uniforms. Her picture had been lifted from her yearbook.

So it was just as Jared had told her. The article repeated the rumor that Peter Whittier was having financial problems. Authorities surmised that he had started drinking and gone up to the Gorge to fire off some shots. He had then reported the shots on the two-way radio, knowing that his brother was at the fire cabin and would respond. The article states that Mark had taken his daughter with him and they had presumably found Peter drunk and despondent. It was not clear what may have caused the two brothers to argue or why Peter had shot Mark, then Amanda, before shooting himself.

Leigh's blood ran cold when she realized that it was her call for help over the two-way radio that morning, stating that "He shot my dad and threw him over the side of the gorge," that had been translated by authorities to mean that she was accusing her uncle of the murder.

Unable to read another word, Leigh printed out the article and left the now deserted library. Her neck and back ached from sitting for so long and her eyes were burning from studying the small print of the microfilm. She inhaled deeply as she stood on the sidewalk and was surprised to see the sun was setting and a few stars had already begun to appear in the darkening sky. Buzzing with pent-up energy, she got in her jeep and drove back to the cabin, where Shadoe was waiting for his dinner.

Unlocking the door, she let Shadoe out and made her way around to the back of the house. Not wanting to be closed in by walls, Leigh sat at the end of the dock, with Shadoe at her side, her legs dangling over the edge. A light breeze and the sound of the water gently lapping at the pylons soothed her body and her mind.

The pond was one of the reasons that Leigh had rented this particular house; she needed to be near water. Cape Cod was a man-made island that jutted out into the Atlantic Ocean, three narrow bridges being its only connections with the mainland. When she had first arrived at her aunt and uncle's house on the Cape, she had missed the mountains so much that it had been a physical pain. Leigh had never been away from her home state of Idaho before, so moving to sea-level had taken some getting used to. Eventually, she had discovered that standing at the ocean's edge, listening to the gentle waves and gazing out at the curved horizon of the vast expanse of water, had soothed her in the same way that the mountains had.

When she was close to water she felt at peace.

Unclenching her hands, Leigh realized that she was still holding the papers that she had printed out at the library. Resisting the urge to tear the articles into tiny shreds, she folded them and tucked them into the back pocket of her jeans.

The hoot of an owl, echoing from across the pond, made her smile. Like the water, it helped to ground her, as did Shadoe who was now nuzzling her hand. Seeing the headline and photographs had brought that day's horrors back to her. The fear, the pain and the overwhelming sense of loss, even though she'd heard the story from Jared earlier that day, had been unexpected. Now she knew that it wasn't an accident that they had been called to that particular site on that particular day. A cover-up of that magnitude took some planning.

Looking up at the stars, Leigh made a silent promise. Nothing was going to stop her from tracking down everyone responsible for the deaths of her family.

Nothing.

During the second week on the job, Leigh managed to either work by herself, taking tourists on guided tours, or get assignments with the newer rangers at the park. On the off-occasion that she met up with one of the older rangers, who might remember something she could work with, she would ask her questions cautiously, mixing up some fact on purpose, to see if there were any discrepancies in their corrections. Yet all of her carefully worded inquiries had turned up nothing new. Neither the rangers, nor anyone else for that matter, had ever questioned the official story.

Sitting in her living room, Leigh snapped the lid of her laptop shut before turning to glare through the dining room window in frustration. It was Thursday morning, her day off, and she was no closer to finding any clues than she had been ten years ago.

There were no reports of poachers or any other illegal activities in the park beyond the article she had found pertaining to the late Joan Kent, so there would be no help from that quarter. Leigh had exhausted the resources at the library and nothing could be found online. For all the news coverage of the incident, the same information had been recycled along with a lot of speculation. How was she supposed to find a killer if no one knew that they existed?

Heaving herself out of the chair, she decided to go into town. She had been careful to limit her time there, in case someone recognized her. Now she would have to take that chance. This was a small town where everyone knew everyone else's business, so if there had been poachers around, someone would have noticed something. There had to be a way she could jog memories without raising suspicion. The thought that the poachers were local, and the townspeople were protecting them, crossed her mind.

Would they have stood by as someone killed their own?

Shadoe looked disappointed at being left behind at the cabin but it was too warm of a day to leave him in the car and risk heat stroke. Leigh promised him that she wouldn't be long as she headed to her jeep.

Turning onto Main Street, she decided to get a cup of coffee at the café, which was the local hangout. Most of the morning crowd had been and gone by the time she arrived, yet she was aware of curious stares from those who'd lingered over their coffee as they turned at the sound of the jingling bell over the door, announcing her arrival.

The café was small but gave off a feeling of spaciousness. It had been updated with a trendier look since she had last been there. The old linoleum floor had been replaced with wide pine planks and the walls were trimmed with bead board wainscoting, painted an off-white. Plants softened the look, rustic lanterns and local artwork completed it. Even though it was called a café, it was set up like a diner where a long counter with low stools ran along one side. A wall with a hole cut into it, for serving food, separated the kitchen from the dining room. Tables were scattered around and tucked into the far corners, set up against the windows, and there were even a couple of booths.

Leigh found a stool at the end of the counter where she could see most of the room. She breathed in the heavenly aroma coming out of the kitchen. The waitress was down at the other end of the counter removing the remains of someone's breakfast. Leigh suppressed a grin when she realized that Gertie was still running the café. Glancing around, Leigh smiled pleasantly at anyone whose eye she caught.

"You must be Leigh, the new park ranger everyone's been talking about," a voice came from her right.

Leigh turned to find that Gertie had made her way down the counter and was giving her an assessing look. Even though she was in her seventies, and wrinkles had changed her features, there were still traces of the beautiful woman that Gertie had once been. Though time might have dimmed her beauty, it hadn't dimmed the shrewd mind that was now taking her measure. Her long, dangling earrings made jingling sounds as Gertie turned her head to say goodbye to a departing customer. Her sharp eyes returned to Leigh almost immediately. A unique shade of violet, her eyes were striking against her silver hair, which was tied in a braid that hung down her back to her waist. Over her tall, willowy figure, she wore a tie-dyed t-shirt with an Indian print skirt, all covered by a tie-dyed apron. Rope sandals completed her unusual waitress uniform.

Leigh could almost see the wheels turning in Gertie's head, categorizing everything about her. It was well known that Gertie and Jessie knew all the gossip and happenings in town.

They were both smart women. Asking too many questions here could cause Gertie to become suspicious.

Pasting a smile on her face, Leigh nodded. "That's right. I arrived in town a couple of weeks ago."

Gertie wiped the counter in front of her before reaching underneath it to retrieve a new paper placemat and napkin, which she set in front of Leigh. "Specials are on the board, though Mel would be happy to cook you anything from the regular menu." Reaching under the counter again, she brought out silverware and a worn, laminated menu. "Stick around town long enough and he'll have it cooked and ready to go whenever you come through that door."

Mel was obviously the owner of the voice that came from the kitchen and was trying to sing along to a country song, off key. Leigh hoped he cooked better than he sang.

"Just black coffee please. I already ate breakfast."

Gertie's eyes narrowed but she didn't ask the obvious question that if all Leigh wanted was a coffee, then why didn't she just stop at the drive-through coffee shop down the street? Leigh was grateful because she didn't have an answer to that question.

Without a word, Gertie made her way over to the coffee pot, poured a cup and brought it back to Leigh. "You let me know if you need anything else," Gertie said as she left to check on the rest of her customers.

Leigh had only met Gertie a few times, when she was just a kid, but she had heard the stories of Gertie's past. She had been a young woman when her fiancé was drafted into the Vietnam War. He'd been listed as missing in action, after his plane was shot down in combat, and then changed to killed in action when they hadn't found his body. Gertie had been devastated and had thrown herself into protesting the war, resulting in her getting arrested several times. One night, she had packed up and left, without a word to anyone. She hadn't been heard from for years when she drove back into town one day. She'd paid cash for the café; no small amount considering that there was a full apartment on the second floor. No one seemed to know exactly where she had been or how she came to have so much money. And Gertie wasn't telling.

* * *

Taking a sip of her coffee, Leigh studied the few lingering diners. One woman, probably in her early sixties, rose from her chair, said something to her companion before making her way over to Leigh.

Smiling, the woman held out her hand. "Welcome to Ramsey. I'm Edith Blaine. My husband and I would love to have you come over some night for dinner."

Leigh had forgotten the ways of a small town, where it was customary for people to drop off casseroles and food to a newcomer. She had arrived home, several times, to find food on her doorstep with a note. Also customary was the dinner invitation.

Shaking the older woman's hand, she smiled. "I'm afraid that right now my hours are so crazy that I can't make too many plans ahead of time," she answered with some regret. "I would love to take a rain check on the invitation, if that's alright with you?"

If she was going to find out information, then dinner at someone's home was the perfect chance to talk to people who might know something.

Edith's smile widened. "My son, Daniel, was a ranger at the park. He always complained about the hours when he was first hired, too. Thankfully he was transferred to another park before all the problems started."

Leigh was all ears. "Problems?"

Edith looked flustered, turned to look at her husband, but he was talking to another couple.

"What problems was the park having?" Leigh asked again, trying not to sound overly interested.

"Well, I… I wouldn't say problems really…it was just that…" Edith stammered.

"Times were tough for all of us back then." Leigh jumped as Gertie's voice came from behind her; she hadn't realized that she had been close enough to hear the exchange. "Folks had to make some tough decisions." Gertie stepped forward, putting herself between the two women. "Daniel took a position at another park, with better hours and pay. Isn't that right, Edith?" She looked pointedly in Edith's husband's direction. "You best get going as it looks like Bob's ready to head out. See you tomorrow."

Edith grabbed the lifeline she had been thrown, said a quick goodbye and then made a beeline for her husband. There were hurried goodbyes to the couple he had been talking to as she hustled him out the door.

Leigh wanted to rush after them, to find out what the problems were that had made Daniel Blaine leave the park, but she doubted she would get much more out of his mother. Edith's swift departure had confirmed for Leigh that the people of Ramsey knew much more than they were letting on.

A bus boy sauntered out of the kitchen and started to clean off the tables. Gertie took care of the remaining customers as the boy set up for the lunch crowd. Soon it was just Gertie and Leigh in the dining room.

Grabbing herself a cup of coffee, Gertie sat down on a stool at an angle to Leigh's seat so that they were face-to-face. Leigh had finished her cup long ago, yet she lingered. The hair was standing up on her arms, like there was an electrical charge in the room. Leigh felt something big was about to happen. Now with Gertie stirring her coffee not more than three feet away from her, Leigh felt edgy and restless.

Gertie's face was devoid of emotion as she cradled her cup in her hands and stared into space. Leigh was beginning to think that Gertie had forgotten she was there when the older woman began to speak.

"I grew up in this town. Sometimes I thought I'd go mad here. Finally, I couldn't take any more of the gossips andbusybodie, so I packed my bags and hit the road. Was gonna make a name for myself. Stop those god-awful wars."

She paused to sip her coffee, as if she was forming the words in her mind, before she continued.

"I made so many mistakes and bad decisions that I figured I could never show my face around here again. Wondered how I was gonna go on and fix the mess I'd made. Then I realized that I couldn't fix what I had done; just had to let the past go and do my best to become the person I knew I could be."

Looking at Leigh, her expression once again unreadable, Gertie leaned forward.

"We can't change the past, no matter how hard we wish we could. Bad things happen and we have to learn to let go and move on. It's for the best."

Leigh's heart started pounding and her breath caught in her throat. What exactly was Gertie trying to say? Before she could ask, the café door opened and the bells jangled.

"Jared!" Gertie smiled and got up off the stool. "I've been wondering where you've been. Haven't found someone else to serve you breakfast, have you?"

Jared gave Gertie a devilish grin. "No one could serve it to me the way you do, Gertie."

Leigh rolled her eyes.

"You wouldn't be able to keep up with me," Gertie bantered right back. "You just sit down right there and behave yourself. You want something to eat? Coffee?"

Jared shook his head and took the abandoned stool next to Leigh as Gertie shuffled off into the kitchen. Leigh wanted to call her back and find out exactly what she knew, but she had a feeling that Gertie had said everything she was going to at this point.

"I've been looking for you," Jared said, grinning at Leigh. "There's a county fair coming this weekend. I was hoping you would go with me."

The invitation surprised her. "Me? Why?"

"One, because I believe I would enjoy your company. Two, I thought you might enjoy seeing a Midwestern county fair. Three, I didn't think you'd have anything better to do."

He had ticked of his reasons on his left fingers, looking relaxed, as if her answer was of no importance to him. Her first reaction was to say no, but she hesitated, which surprised her. What harm could there be in going with him to a county fair? It might actually help her in the long run. The more she was seen at local events, then the more people would learn to trust her. Besides, she hated to admit it, but he was right, she didn't have anything better to do.

"Alright," she nodded.

"Great, I'll pick you up on Saturday at six." He hopped up off the stool. "I'm running late but I saw your Jeep outside. Figured now was my chance to ask you. I'll see you Saturday."

Gertie came out of the kitchen just in time to wave goodbye to Jared. Both women sighed as the door closed behind him.

• • •

The carnival was in full swing when Jared and Leigh pulled into the parking lot. It appeared as if half the county had come out to the midway. Jared grabbed Leigh's hand and pulled her through the throngs of people as they headed toward the ticket booth.

The Ferris wheel was full, and the screams of the roller coaster riders brought a smile to Leigh's face. The rides were set in the middle of a field, with food booths running down one side, game booths running down the other. Neon lights were lost against the bright sky, but Leigh knew they would create a magical atmosphere after the sun went down. Carnivals always seemed more mysterious and dreamlike at night.

A dance floor made of wood planks had been built on the grass in front of a bandstand on the far end. Paper lanterns swayed in a light breeze as dancers twirled colorfully to a lively beat from the band.

"Let's get something to eat first, then we can walk around and see what rides I can talk you on to," Jared suggested.

"Talk me on to?" Leigh pretended to be insulted. "I'll have you know that I've ridden some of the biggest roller coasters on the eastern seaboard with my hands in the air the entire ride."

It pleased her when he laughed out loud.

"Okay, if that's true then I am impressed, but I'll need proof of such a claim. It's been my experience that women just aren't that brave when it comes to carnival rides."

"You're on, and may I suggest that you hang out with a better class of women?" Laughing, Leigh punched him in the arm.

Jared had shown up on time and even complimented Leigh on her appearance. It had taken her hours to decide what to wear. Since this wasn't a date, she had wanted to be casual yet still dress up a little, finally deciding on jeans, high heeled boots and a blue gauze blouse. There had been a slight thrill of satisfaction when she saw the appreciation in Jared's eyes as she opened the door.

Jared bought Leigh a hot dog at one of the food booths.

"It's surprising how much better food tastes at a carnival," she remarked. "I never cook hot dogs for myself but that was delicious. Now I just need a snow cone, fried dough and some cotton candy."

Jared laughed. "Well I certainly don't want to disappoint you or leave you hungry. Do they need to be in that order?"

Leigh blushed. "No, I think we can start with the fried dough and work in the snow cone later. I'll probably take the cotton candy home to eat. "

• • •

Leigh enjoyed her fried dough as they strolled through the tents of crafts, produce, baked and home goods. Everything from jams to quilts was on display. The prizewinners sported colorful ribbons and Jared discussed with Leigh how someone could have grown such a perfect rose or made such a beautiful quilt. Leigh liked his observations, and how he brought up points that she hadn't thought of herself. He made her look at things from a different perspective, without pushing his opinion, and she found herself slipping into an easy rapport with him.

Walking down the aisle of game booths, vendors called out to them, trying hard to entice Jared to come play their games and impress his girl.

"Would you like me to win you a prize?" he finally asked with a grin.

"Honestly, I'd rather you save your money."

He grasped his chest and groaned. "Ouch! You don't have any faith in my abilities! I'll have you know that I was the Carnival Game Champion of The Year in my younger years."

Before Leigh could respond, a voice interrupted them.

"Well, I see the prodigal son has returned to his roots."

Turning, Leigh looked up into an aristocratic face that was surrounded by short, jet black hair. He looked amused as he glared at Jared through cold, grey eyes. The man's watch probably cost more than Leigh made in a year and his clothes looked tailor made. She felt Jared stiffen next to her but doubted anyone else noticed the tension between them.

"Cole, I should have known you would still be here, living off daddy. How is the Senator anyway? Still giving in to special interests while over-taxing the little people?"

Jared spoke the words in such a flippant way that Leigh was surprised when Cole began to laugh.

"My father is doing just fine. I'm sure he'd love to argue with you regarding those special interest groups. He'll be home next week. I'll be sure to let him know of your concern."

His eyes turned to Leigh with calculated interest.

"I don't believe that we've met," he said taking her hand, which she quickly withdrew.

Jared was forced to introduce them.

Leigh immediately recognized the name although she had never met Cole in person. Cole Langford was three years her senior and he had gone to a private school. The Langfords had summered in the area but had moved into their ranch permanently about twelve years ago.

"So, this is the new park ranger." Cole smiled. "The descriptions of you don't do you justice."

Leigh couldn't believe that she was blushing.

Amused, Cole continued, "I'd like to invite you over to see my ranch. I have several horses and we could go for a ride. It's under construction right now, but some day it'll be one of the finest ranches in Idaho."

Leigh knew the Langfords owned the property that abutted her father's home, but she had never been there. Security had always been tight, with Cole's father being a senator, and visitors were discouraged, unless they had been personally invited. Cole would have been around seventeen at the time of the murders. Leigh wondered if he had seen or heard some-thing that could be of use to her. It wouldn't hurt to talk to his father and any workers who had been around at the time.

"I'd love that," she replied. "My schedule is always changing so I'll have to let you know when I'm available."

Cole pulled out a business card from his wallet and handed it to her.

"Call me any time."

With that, Cole exchanged a look with Jared and wandered into the crowd.

Leigh almost laughed out loud. He actually thought she was interested in him on a personal level. *What an arrogant jerk!* She knew that if she hadn't been with Jared, Cole Langford wouldn't have even looked her way, and she certainly wouldn't have looked his. Turning, she smiled at Jared but was startled to see that he was scowling. "What's the matter with you?"

A mask seemed to slip over Jared's face as he shot her a nonchalant grin. "As you just heard, I did a piece on some shady special interest groups that Senator Langford was backing. The groups and the Senator have corruption written all over them, but I can't prove it. Not yet. I'm convinced that Junior there doesn't fall too far from the tree. You might want to remember that, when you're out on your ride with him."

Jared tucked his hands into his pockets. "Since you don't want me to show off my skills at the game booths, I guess you'll have to prove to me that you can handle the rides."

Leigh laughed. "You're on! Good luck keeping up with me."

After daring each other to go on the scariest of rides, Leigh and Jared spent over an hour dancing before Jared suggested they get something to drink to help them cool down.

* * *

Leigh took a sip of her lemonade; the real kind, freshly squeezed from lemons with lots of ice. She savored the blend of tart and sweet as she watched dancers moving to the music. She was sitting beside Jared at a picnic table, with a few inches separating them, yet she could feel the heat coming from his damp shirt. Despite herself, she was enjoying his company and didn't want the evening to end.

Stars were appearing in the night sky and the moon was low on the horizon, visible only through the trees. A warm breeze caused the white lights that hung over the dancers' heads to sway back and forth, as if they, too, enjoyed the rhythm of the night.

"So, what made a woman from the east coast come all this way out to Idaho?"

Jared asked before taking a long sip of his soda. "Seems like a big move for someone to make alone. Especially someone who doesn't have family in the area."

Twirling her cup, Leigh had anticipated the question. Jared had been hinting all night that she was a mystery to him. Being an investigative journalist, it was only a matter of time before he got around to the questions.

"What's so strange about it?" The breeze caught her hair and blew a few strands across her face. Brushing them back in place she glanced away from him. "My family was killed in a accident when I was fourteen. I didn't have any close relatives, so I was placed with a distant aunt in Massachusetts. I love the ocean, but I've always wanted to see the West. Seemed like being a park ranger was the best way to do that. Applied to several parks, and was thrilled when I got the letter saying that I was hired here. For the record, I'm not alone; I have Shadoe."

Holding her breath, she waited for him to reply. Could he tell that she was lying?

Jared studied her for a moment before looking back at the dancers. "Indian Mound is such a small park. Why not Yellowstone or someplace more exciting?"

Leigh remembered that she had asked him the same question and what his answer had been.

She peered at him in the dim light. "What's wrong with working in a smaller park?"

Concern flashed in his eyes before he looked away for a moment. Then he shrugged. "There's nothing wrong with small parks, just seems that most rangers are looking for better pay and more experience that a bigger park could give them. Besides, Ramsey isn't a swinging hot spot for a single female used to the bright city lights. Most of the kids can't wait to leave this town the minute they graduate high school. I know I couldn't."

The band finished a rowdy country song and began a soothing ballad, causing the dancers to slow down and drift across the dance floor in a unified sea of color.

Although the music had slowed, Leigh could feel her heart racing. There had been a look in Jared's eyes, a minute ago, and she could feel that he wanted to tell her something. What was troubling him?

"So what about you?" she countered. "Why is an investigative photojournalist hanging around Ramsey for so long? What story are you really looking into?"

Leigh didn't expect him to laugh. "Sorry to disappoint but I have no big secret. I picked this park because it's in my hometown and I was a little burned out after my last assignment. Figured I could rest while I still brought in a paycheck." He leaned in close. "Unless you know some secret about the park that you'd like me to check out?"

Not daring to look away, she smiled sweetly, "How would I know any secrets? I just moved here a couple of weeks ago."

Leigh relaxed a little when he nodded and looked back at the dance floor.

• • •

It was late when Jared pulled his vehicle into the driveway of Leigh's cabin. Parking behind her jeep, he got out and walked around the front of his truck to open her door. Escorting her onto the porch and to the cabin entrance, he stood back as she unlocked it.

Shadoe trotted out and around the side of the house as Leigh turned to Jared and held out her hand. "I had a great time tonight. Thanks for inviting me."

Encompassing her hand in his, Jared gently pulled her close and leaned down until his lips were just mere centimeters from hers. There was a brief hesitation, as if he was waiting for her to pull away and when she didn't, he closed the small distance. His lips grazed hers and she felt lost in the delicate sensation. Small sparks of electricity bubbled from her throat, reminding her to breathe. Leigh pushed away to stare at Jared with wide, confused eyes.

"I don't want to get involved with anyone." Her voice sounded weak, even to her own ears.

He grinned, took several steps back and then his grin faded. "Be careful of Cole. He'll take a woman like you and eat you for breakfast."

With that cryptic message, he walked back to his truck and drove away.

• • •

Leigh watched the taillights of the truck disappear before calling to Shadoe to head back inside the cabin. *What was she doing?* She had felt something shift within her chest as Jared leaned towards her, but she couldn't afford to let him in. Not now. She had erected too many walls after her father's death. Walls that kept her focused on revenge. She was in Ramsey for one reason. To get emotionally involved with someone now would only threaten her mission. Leigh knew she couldn't afford any distractions, no matter how tempting they might be. She had simply enjoyed a beautiful summer night at a fair with a friend. This relationship with Jared was just temporary. Once she claimed her life back, she'd be moving on.

• • •

The next day was Sunday. Not having to go to work until later that night, Leigh took the opportunity to clean the cabin. Glad for routine chores to help keep her mind off Jared, it was lunchtime before she glanced into the refrigerator and realized how empty it was. Grabbing her purse, she and Shadoe headed to town.

• • •

Jessie was bagging up a lone customer's purchase but as soon as the woman left the store she made a beeline for Leigh.

"Hear you went to the Fair with Jared. Knew the two of you would hit it off. That boy needs someone to help keep him in line and you need a strong man to come home to at night."

Jessie wasn't one to beat around the bush. "Also heard you accepted an invitation to go riding with Cole Langford, at his ranch."

Leigh shouldn't have been surprised because Jessie knew everything that went on in town. It was just amazing at the speed at which she received her information. Leigh longed to ask Jessie about the poachers but Jessie wasn't stupid; she would be able to fit all the pieces together and figure out who Leigh was in no time. She couldn't risk being uncovered this early into her investigation, or risk putting Jessie into possible danger. Continuing to load things in her basket, Leigh pasted a smile on her face.

"Jared and I went to the Fair as FRIENDS." She emphasized the last word. "As for Cole, I think he only invited me to get under Jared's skin. It would have been rude to decline."

Jessie wasn't one to be easily deterred. "Watch out for Cole. That boy has ambitions and I'm not so sure they're good ones. She followed Leigh down the aisle. He and his brother, Kyle, were spoiled to the core. It won't matter to Cole if you're seeing Jared, once he's taken a shine to you."

Jessie's voice boomed through the store and Leigh was glad the place was empty since this was definitely fodder for the rumor mill. It wouldn't be helpful for people to see a three-way romance where there was none. She needed to blend in, not call attention to her every move.

"I appreciate the concern, Jessie. I really do, but don't worry about me. I'm not seeing Jared or Cole, and I have no interest in dating anyone right now."

She took a deep breath. It was the truth. Until she could find out who the murderers were, she couldn't take the risk of someone else becoming important to her. Jessie must have seen the something in her face because she became unusually quiet.

Thanking small favors, Leigh finished her shopping and drove back to the cabin.

# CHAPTER FIVE

After several days, Leigh realized that no matter what she said, the town's gossip mill was alive and going full force. The phone lines must have been burning up as people discussed her alleged love life, judging from the amount of people who stopped her to give their opinion on Jared and Cole. Even though she wanted to scream, she would smile and assure them that she was just friends with the two men.

Cole clearly wasn't her type and she hadn't heard from Jared since the night of the fair. She'd bite her tongue off before she admitted that she was hurt by his silence. He'd asked her on a date, kissed her and then dropped out of sight. It just proved what she knew all along; that he wasn't a distraction she could afford to have right now.

It was for the best, she thought, as she pounded a chicken breast flat for dinner, with more force then was necessary.

• • •

Driving over to the Langford ranch, Leigh couldn't help but recall her phone conversation with Shari the night before. Laughing, she had told Shari of all the warnings she had received about Cole. Jared was definitely better liked, but he was a womanizer, according to several well-meaning elderly ladies who had stopped her at the bank.

Shari hadn't laughed, as Leigh expected she would. She had become serious instead.

"Be careful, Leigh. There have been stories circulating around for years about Dean Langford, Cole's father. They say the man is ruthless, and there are some questions on how he became a senator. Most people believe that Cole and Kyle don't fall too far from the tree."

Leigh remembered that Jessie had mentioned a brother. "I haven't heard a lot about Kyle. Was he around much?" she asked her friend.

"No, he's quite a bit older than Cole. Kyle didn't really stick around here very long. I don't expect he'll ever come back. My guess is that he was shipped off to private school at an early age, like Cole." There was a small pause. "Why are you going riding with Cole anyway? Jared seems more your type."

Leigh rolled her eyes. "Not you too," she groaned.

Shari laughed. "Come on, Jared is seriously hot. Why don't you have a fling with him and get it out of your system?"

Leigh was quiet and Shari became contrite. "I'm sorry, I didn't mean to be flip."

"No, it's okay," Leigh said slowly. "He is seriously hot but I have no intention of being just another notch on his bed post. Once I find this poacher and bring him to justice, well then I feel that I can start my life again and find someone to spend it with. Until then I'm just a fictional character."

Shari gave out a sigh. "Well I don't agree. From what you've told me, Jared seems to like you, whether you call yourself Leigh or Amanda. Any way, I'm expecting you at my house for dinner on Friday night. Show up any time after you get out of work, it'll give us a chance to talk and catch up."

Leigh agreed before saying goodbye and hanging up.

• • •

The drive leading to Cole's ranch was paved, which surprised Leigh. Most people didn't even fill in the potholes on their roads, whether they had money or not. The driveway was long and wound its way through large oak trees to end in a semicircle in front of a massive two-story ranch house. The wrap around porch ran the length of the house. Frosted, etched glass side light windows flanked the large impressive front door.

Pulling up, she saw Cole standing on the porch. He was on his cell phone and ended the call as she got out of the car.

"I'm so glad that you took me up on my offer," Cole said coming down the stairs. He was wearing riding pants and boots that made him look even more aristocratic than normal. She looked down at her jeans and sneakers, feeling self-conscious.

Cole seemed to read her mind. "We have several extra pairs of boots in the barn. I'm sure that we can find something more suitable and in your size. The Senator is always inviting friends and colleagues over for meetings, and some like to go riding. We're prepared for anything around here."

With a sweep of his hand, he indicated that Leigh should head toward the barn, an impressively large, grey structure that was set back a small distance from the house.

Stepping into the cool, dark interior, it took a moment for her eyes to adjust. Looking into the first stall, Leigh was disappointed to see that it was filled with boxes, empty feed bags and other miscellaneous items that were coated with a thick layer of dust and cobwebs.

"How many horses do you have?" Leigh inquired as she looked down the long row of stall doors that ran the length of the building on both sides.

Cole had been in the process of opening a pocket door to her left, but he turned to look at her briefly before disappearing into the room.

"I originally had forty horses on the property. Sold most of them at auction." His voice filtered out of the open door. "I kept ten, for now, but they don't have the bloodlines I need."

There were sounds of things being moved and tossed aside. When Leigh peered into the tack room, all she could see were saddles and more cardboard boxes piled up on each other. These boxes weren't covered with dust like the ones in the stall. As she stepped into the room, she accidentally brushed against several boxes that had been stacked together and the stack started to teeter. Grabbing the top box, she noticed that there was some writing on it. Leigh wasn't able to make out the words before Cole reached over her and righted the pile.

"Found a pair," he said holding up a dusty pair of cowboy boots. "Shall we see if they fit?"

Taking her arm, he quickly led her out of the tack room and back into the main aisle.

His grip was firm, yet not painful and she couldn't help comparing his touch to Jared's. Where Jared's touch had been light and friendly, Cole's had a possessive edge. Twisting slightly, she broke the contact and headed to a bench to sit down. Cole handed her the boots and leaned back against a stall door.

Slipping off her sneakers and putting on the boots, she noticed that the wood on the stall doors were beginning to rot and the hinges were rusted.

"I would have thought a ranch this size would have people everywhere," she said as she stood up. The boots were a little loose, but they would work. She made a mental note to go shopping next week to buy her own pair of riding boots.

Cole straightened and headed to the back of the barn where two horses were already saddled and tied to the hitching post. "Well, normally there would be, but we've had some lean years since I haven't been around to oversee things so I had to let some people go. My plan is to have this ranch up and running within the year with some of the best horse breeding stock in the state." He checked the cinches as he talked. "Some of my investments are about to pay off and when they do I'll be here full time. I'm going to really turn this ranch around."

Cole had picked out an Appaloosa for her to ride. Leigh had brought sugar cubes with her, and now bringing them out of her pocket, she quickly made friends with the small mare. Cole's horse was a thoroughbred and once he had eaten a few sugar cubes, he tossed his head around as if he was impatient to be off.

• • •

They walked the horses to the edge of the tree line to a path that required them to ride single file for a while, making talking difficult. Entering the darkness of the forest, Leigh closed her eyes for a moment to breathe in the familiar scents. This was her childhood playground.

The earthy smell was exactly as she remembered it. Opening her eyes again, she scanned the area.

The dappled sunlight played tricks with her eyes, creating shadows and light, causing ordinary things to take on mystical properties in her imagination. The woods had always been a magical place for Leigh. She smiled to realize that hadn't changed.

The forest was getting brighter so Leigh wasn't surprised when the path led them into a meadow. The view was spectacular from this side of the mountain. The distant mountain range looked like a smudge of darkness against the blue, cloudless sky. Closer, hundreds of miles of woods stretched before them, in various shades of green, as if an artist had brushed the strokes onto a canvas. Leigh sighed appreciatively at the western boundary of her property.

This view was in her blood.

• • •

The Appaloosa stood contently as Leigh stared out over the scenery, but Cole's mount began to prance back and forth, eager to move on.

"Wow, this is beautiful. It must be wonderful to own all of this and be able to come out here anytimeyou want."

Cole laughed, pleased.

"Well, I don't own all of this yet. Most of what you see belongs to the State but the land to your right will soon be mine." He gestured in the direction of her land. "The previous owner died suddenly and didn't leave a will, or an heir. It's been in land court for years, but I hear it should be settled any day now and I'll be the first one in line to buy it."

"Really? How lucky for you," she mumbled. Steeling her features, Leigh feigned interest as her thoughts raced. Since when had her property been put up for sale? That was impossible because her father had left a will. She had read it herself. This land belonged to her. If she had predeceased her father, then it would have gone to Celeste.

Her father's property had been secured for her by Celeste and Roy, who had disguised the property as a nature preserve, which meant that to the land could never be sold. This had been the only way she could keep her identity a secret while hanging onto her childhood home and rightful inheritance. How had it ended up in land court and why hadn't anyone told her about this?

Leigh realized that someone had gone to a great deal of trouble to cover their tracks following her uncle and father's murders, and now Cole wanted to buy her property? This was all she had left to connect her to her past with her family. She swallowed the rage that filled her belly as she fought the urge to tell Cole that this was HER land, and there was no way in hell that he, nor anyone else, was going to take it from her.

The mare must have felt her anger because it began to whinny softly and shake its head.

"It's okay, girl," Leigh assured her mount, patting the horse's neck. Turning to Cole, she said, "I guess she's ready to head out."

Cole didn't seem to notice any change in her voice as he turned the thoroughbred around and started to walk alongside the woods.

Taking one last look at the vista, Leigh swung her horse around and followed him.

• • •

They rode for another hour or so, crisscrossing the park and her land. Cole talked non-stop about his big plans for the ranch. He'd run trail rides, of course, but the bulk of his business would focus on breeding some of the country's best racehorses. When Leigh asked him how one financed such a large endeavor, Cole was evasive. All he would say was that some investments were coming due.

When she asked him what he did for a living he answered, "Public relations for my father."

"And you're happy, working for the Senator?" she pressed him.

"Sure. It's a cushy job, and it definitely has its perks. Politics is all about making connections," he paused to make sure she could hear him, "with important people who can help get things done. For me, that means rubbing elbows with the rich and famous and occasionally kissing their asses."

They were back on the single file path so Leigh couldn't see his face. It was hard to tell from the tone of his voice whether he was serious or kidding.

"That must be fun, meeting all those interesting people and living the jet set life. Why settle down here, when you could live in Washington, DC, or Hollywood?" she asked.

Cole thought about her question for a moment. "Let's just say that this town has lots of hidden opportunities, if you're willing to look for them."

He steered the conversation back to his plans for the ranch as they returned to the barn and handed off their reins to a man who came out to take the horses.

• • •

"Built in the late 1800s," Cole said, "the house has been updated several times over the years, But not lately. I'm going to gut it and turn it into an exclusive bed and breakfast." Cole continued as he lead Leigh through the back door and directly into the kitchen.

Leigh took a deep breath. She felt like she had stepped back in time. Original hand-planed oak floorboards graced the floor and years of traffic had worn the thick planks smooth. Most likely the original, a black wood cook stove dominated the back wall, a cast iron tea pot completing the scene. The stove's chrome pieces were in desperate need of polishing, and the metal body was dull from years of use, yet Leigh could almost feel the heat that must have come from the large piece as it kept the bone-chilling winter cold at bay. Power outages were common at this elevation so a stove like this one would have been invaluable.

Oak cabinets lined another wall and a long, scarred oak table with chairs was placed in the middle of the room, an ornate wrought iron chandelier hanging over it. How many families had sat at that table and had meals together Leigh wondered, sharing dreams, heartaches and triumphs? Probably generations. She felt their presence still resonating from every corner, like invisible shadows from the past.

Delicate dishes were visible through the glass in the corner china cabinet, lending a feminine air to the space. Even though it had been updated through the years, everything spoke of form and function, keeping most of the original kitchen intact. Someone had definitely cared for the character and history of the place. It wasn't hard to picture this kitchen weathering storms and providing food, warmth and comfort to its occupants.

"I love this kitchen," she turned to Cole. "Whoever updated it last knew what they were doing. That stove is amazing!"

Cole visibly shuddered. "That's the first thing that's going to go when we start renovating. I have a five-star chef ready to start anytime and he expects a top-of-the-line kitchen."

Leigh was speechless. The thought of modernizing this kitchen, stripping away its history, was painful for her, though she couldn't have said why. Stainless steel appliances and granite counter tops would make it look like every other kitchen in America, cold and without personality. She said as much to Cole.

"I'll be running a business, Leigh. I can't let sentiments take over function here. This kitchen will need to run efficiently, as will the rest of the house. Some of the world's richest people will be staying here and they will all expect the best."

"But if you maintain the character of the house, wouldn't it be a draw all of its own?" she argued. "Rich people can stay anywhere. They probably have expensive hotels on speed dial for crying out loud. Give them something more unique, like a five-star bed and breakfast that brings them back to the romance and simplicity of the old west. You can't find anything like that around. Surely people would appreciate an experience like that?"

"Who would want to go back to a time when you had to wash in a copper tub or use an outhouse? No, this bed and breakfast will be one of the most up-to-date and modern destinations on this side of the Mississippi."

Leigh could tell that Cole had no idea what she was talking about and that it most likely would be futile to try to make him understand. He lived in the fast lane, where was no room for nostalgia.

"May I see the rest of house?" she asked, sadly.

"Of course, but I warn you, it is a little rough around the edges."

They left the kitchen and walked through a dining room that had once been a parlor. Beautiful wallpaper featuring large pink roses on vertical trellises still covered the walls but was faded and tearing in places. A small ornate black wood stove occupied one wall, a relic from days before furnaces and radiators.

The narrow hallway off the front foyer ran from the front door straight through to the back of the house. A staircase hugged the right wall and ascended to the second floor. Several doors could be seen from below, but they were all closed.

Stepping across the hall, Leigh followed Cole into the living room where a huge stone fireplace took up a good portion of the far wall. The couch, which faced the hearth, was decorated in greens and browns and two over-sized leather chairs, real leather from the looks of them, were placed on either side of it. An antique writing desk sat under one of the windows to the left while a large pool table took up the space to the right. Heavy drapes, in hunter green, hung on either side of the floor-to-ceiling windows that faced the front of the house. Combined with the heavy furniture, the room had a cloying feel to it.

Leigh wasn't surprised to see a leather bar had been set up in the corner, to her right, with stools and a mirror backsplash that had fine etching around the edges. It was definitely a masculine room. There was nothing to even suggest that a woman had entered this room in the last century except that it was immaculately clean.

Bookcases flanked the fireplace and contained a variety of books, trophies and photographs. Leigh crossed the room and ran her fingers down the spines of the books, which were mostly biographies of politicians, world leaders and other influential people, some of whom were still alive. Well, that made sense, she thought. Cole had said that he was in public relations so it was probable that he would travel in the same circles as these people.

"Have you met any of these people?" she turned and asked him, surprised to see that he was still standing in the doorway.

He shrugged nonchalantly, "Some of them, but I can tell you that most of what they write in their 'autobiographies'", he made a quoting gesture with his hands, "is pure fiction."

She was about to ask him to explain when his cell phone rang.

Pulling it from his pocket and looking at the caller ID, Cole hesitated before saying, "Excuse me, but I have to take this call. I'll be right back."

Leigh turned her gaze back to the bookcase and the photographs. Most were of Cole and an older boy, Kyle, she supposed. They were holding up fish, skiing or sitting on horses; normal childhood activities captured through the camera's lens.

Looking at the photos made her smile. They all seemed to be of happy times. Several showed a woman hugging her children. Leigh assumed she was Cole's mother. Moving along the shelves, she froze as she saw a familiar face in one of the frames. Her uncle, Peter, was standing with a group of people who looked to be in a hunting party. The woman from the other pictures was smiling for the camera but her uncle was looking at the woman, whom he was standing next too. Picking it up, she studied it closer. The expression on her uncle's face was unreadable.

The newspaper had said that Peter was despondent over a woman. A married woman. Could that woman have been Cole's mother or an aunt or a female relative perhaps? This photograph brought the 'other woman' aspect of Peter's supposed story into reality. Leigh had dismissed it before as just a story the poachers had created to throw the authorities off their trail. Now she would have to consider the possibility that her uncle was indeed having an affair with Mrs. Langford, or whoever this woman was. Had this affair gotten him killed?

There was a light slam of the front door and footsteps echoed in the hallway right outside of the living room. Leigh quickly put the frame back on the shelf and moved to the other side of the hearth. Grabbing a book, she turned to see an older version of Cole step into the room.

The senator was dressed in a dark grey three-piece suit that probably cost more than her jeep, brand new, and his silk tie was so tight up against his throat that it was a wonder the man could breathe. His custom made Italian leather and his suit looked like it was Armani, or some other expensive label. Pushing up his sleeve, he consulted his watch, his aristocratic face scrunched into a frown. Gray hair, sprinkled throughout his once-black hair, framed his face, giving him a distinguished look.

Leigh cleared her throat.

Looking up, he seemed taken back to see her, but he quickly recovered.

"Hello, I'm Leigh Doane," she held out her hand as she walked forward him.

Meeting her halfway, the senator took her hand in a firm but quick handshake.

"Dean Langford," he responded. "I didn't realize there was anyone in here. I'm looking for my son."

His smile didn't quite seem to reach the eyes that were assessing her, but Leigh couldn't tell what conclusion he was reaching.

"Cole took a phone call. He said he'd be right back."

Dean nodded his head. "You must be the new park ranger. Tell me Leigh, are you from the area?"

Never having met him before, she felt comfortable that he wouldn't recognize her. "No, my family is on the east coast. I've always wanted to see the American west and your son was kind enough to show me some of the gorgeous views around here."

Was it her imagination, or did he relax with the news that she wasn't a local?

"I have to give my son credit; he can certainly find the most beautiful women."

Leigh blushed, but was saved from having to reply as Cole took that moment to step back into the room. He looked tense and uncomfortable to see his father.

"Senator, what a surprise. I saw the limo outside. The driver said that you had just arrived and wouldn't be staying long."

"No," Dean Langford obviously was used to being addressed as the senator by his own son because he didn't even miss a beat in answering. "I have a few things to attend to and then I'll be catching a plane back to the Capital. We have some important business to discuss before I leave."

Leigh noticed that neither man showed much affection to the other. In fact, they almost acted like strangers meeting for the first time.

There was a short, awkward pause before Cole turned to Leigh.

"I see that you met Leigh. I was giving her a quick tour."

The senator gave a curt nod of his head before saying, "Yes, we introduced ourselves." Then he gave a halfhearted smile. "I'm sorry that I interrupted. I'll be in the study when you're done." He bowed his head at Leigh and made his way from the room, his footsteps echoing on the wood floor.

Cole frowned as he watched the doorway that Dean had just disappeared through. Turning to Leigh with an apologetic smile, "I'm sorry. I wasn't expecting my father today. Something must have come up."

It was obvious that the senator's arrival had shaken him.

"That's okay. I need to get going anyway."

Cole looked relieved.

Turning, she replaced the book in her hand but knocked over a picture in the process.

"Sorry! I hope I didn't break it," she exclaimed as she bent to pick it up.

It was a photo of a little boy with the mystery woman, both dressed in their Sunday best, standing in front of a church.

Cole walked over and took from her hands.

"Is that you with your mom? She's beautiful."

After a quick glance at the photo, Cole put it back on the shelf. "Yes. I must have been about five or so."

"Did she come home with your dad today?"

Cole smirked. "They haven't been in the same room in a good twenty years. I haven't seen her since she walked out on us. These pictures are all I have to remember that I even have a mother."

Leigh didn't know what to say as Cole walked her to her vehicle. She could sense that his mind had already dismissed her. Reaching the jeep, she turned and offered him her hand.

"Thanks, Cole. I had a wonderful time."

He took her hand with both of his yet there was no spark in the contact.

Not like when Jared had touched her hand that day at the fair.

"I'll call you. Maybe we can get together again soon."

"I'd like that," she smiled. "I'll take a rain check on seeing the rest of the house." Leigh got in her jeep and waved as she started down the driveway. When she checked her mirror, seconds later, she saw that Cole had already disappeared into the house.

Navigating around the parked limo, she didn't notice that the curtain of an upstairs window was pulled back and a man was watching her drive away.

• • •

As soon as she reached her cabin, Leigh called Celeste. The answering machine picked up so Leigh left a message regarding the pending sale of her property.

Celeste returned Leigh's call later that night and promised to contact the lawyer who'd set up the supposed nature preserve trust. "

"How are you doing, being there alone?" Celeste asked her voice full of concern. "One of us could fly out and stay with you, if you want us too. No one would know who we are."

Leigh smiled. She appreciated Celeste's offer but it was too risky, besides she knew that this was something she had to face on her own. "I'm fine," she assured her aunt. "I have Shadoe and whether it's a good thing or not, my childhood friend, Shari, recognized me at the library the other day." Ignoring Celeste's gasp, she continued. "It's okay. She understands the need to keep my identity a secret and honestly it helps knowing that at least one person in this town knows who I am."

Celeste must have had the phone on speaker because Roy's booming voice came through. "You give her our number and if anything suspicious happens, you have her call us immediately and we will be on the next flight out of Logan."

Tears welled up and it took her a moment to reply. "I know you would Roy. I'll text you Shari's number just so you have it in case you can't get a hold of me, but please stop worrying. No one else has recognized me and there has been no hint of any illegal activity."

She hadn't told them about the murder/suicide story. If they knew that there had been a cover-up, they would insist that she return home and she would never find the man that killed her family.

Celeste sniffled and the sound tugged at Leigh's heartstrings. "Stop Celeste," she said more sternly then she meant to. "I am fine so don't go getting all teary on me."

"I can't help it," Celeste gave a shaky laugh. "I'm a worrier, you know that." She took a deep breath. "I'll do my best but it's just so hard because we miss you so much."

Roy echoed the sentiment.

"And I miss you guys." Leigh rested her head against the wall. "I promise to keep in touch and let you know if I get any leads."

Leigh felt a little homesick after they hung up.

• • •

Several days passed without Leigh seeing or hearing from either Cole or Jared. She couldn't help thinking about the way she'd felt with Jared after he'd walked her home from the fair. The gentle kiss had been electrifying. Her brain had warned danger but her body had practically melted into his. Being several grades ahead of her in school meant they hadn't traveled in the same circles so of course he wouldn't remember her, never mind recognize her ten years later, with different colored hair and eyes. She remembered him though. His good looks had earned him the hearts of many of the girls in school. No wonder he was so arrogant. *Damn, but arrogance looked good on him!* She would have to guard herself from falling for him too.

• • •

Shari's house was an old farmhouse located several miles out of town. Old oak trees helped shade the front porch and Leigh smiled to see several swings were now hanging from their huge branches

Shari's twins came running out the front door as Leigh pulled into the driveway that was on the right side of the house and parked behind a black SUV. They stood shyly on the porch as she approached them. Unlike most identical twins at this age, these girls weren't dressed alike at all. One wore a frilly dress with plastic high heels and lots of plastic jewelry. The other was clearly a tom boy, dressed in overalls and sneakers. Leigh felt a longing as she stepped onto the porch. *What must it be like to have such beautiful children? Was Shari afraid for them every day?* No one knew better than Leigh how life could change in a nanosecond. Precious children disappeared all the time, no matter how much they were loved.

"Hello," Leigh said, unsure of how to act. She hadn't been around too many children but those she did, she tended to treat the same as an adult. These girls were younger than what she was used to.

"Hi," replied the princess. "I'm Olivia. I'm six." She pointed at her sister and added, "This is Samantha, Sam for short. She's six, too."

Biting back a laugh, Leigh held out her hand. "I'm Leigh and I'm not telling you my age. I'm very pleased to meet you both."

Olivia took her hand and giggled. Samantha was very solemn as she shook it quickly.

"Mom says to bring you inside the minute you get here."

It seemed that Olivia did all the talking. Not shy at all, she led Leigh into the house, followed by a silent Samantha. Olivia kept up a running monologue as she led the way into the living room. Samantha, by some unheard command, ran to tell her mother that her guest had arrived.

Olivia was telling Leigh all about her ballet classes when Shari entered the room.

"I can't believe you're finally here," Shari said, smiling. "It's going to be just us girls tonight. My husband has to work. He needs to stay at the fire station whenever he's on call."

Turning, she addressed her daughters. "Why don't you two clean up the mess you made in the yard?" To Leigh she said, "Dinner is almost ready. Come with me. We'll have some wine while I finish the salad."

Leigh gasped as she entered the kitchen. "Wow, this place is gorgeous!"

Where Cole wanted to wipe out the character of his home, Shari had embraced her kitchen's history. Large cabinets lined the walls; not the plywood box store type, but real wood that had been painted a cream color, contrasting beautifully with the butcher block countertops. The floor was the original wide wooden planks and sunshine poured in from skylights in the cathedral ceiling.

Despite its authentic appearance, Leigh soon realized that modern conveniences, like the refrigerator and dishwasher, had been tactfully hidden behind cabinetry. Still, she wouldn't have been surprised if a pioneer woman had walked right in and started cooking on the wood stove in the corner. This stove wasn't as big or ornate as Cole's, but it looked to be just as functional.

Taking a seat on the other side of the butcher block center island, Leigh watched as Shari poured them each a glass of wine, handed her one and then started chopping tomatoes.

"Your girls are beautiful."

Shari looked up with a smile. "Yes, they are. They can be hellions though." A thoughtful look came over her face. "Olivia is a lot like I remember you were as a kid; fearless, bossy and always has to be in charge." She sighed. "Sam is following in my footsteps, painfully shy and only talks to Ben, myself , and a few friends."

Taking a sip of her wine, Shari avoided looking at her own friend. "I'll never forget the day they told me you were dead. I knew it couldn't have been true. We had a bond, as if we were twins, and I just knew that I would have felt something if you'd died that day." She took a longer sip of wine, "I stood in the pouring rain and watched them lower your casket into the ground and all I wanted to do was scream that you weren't dead." She paused, her fingers tightening around the knife she was about to chop a tomato with, "I waited for you to call me and let me know that you were all right but…" her voice trailed off.

Leigh didn't know what to say as a lump formed in her throat.

There was such pain in Shari's eyes when she finally met Leigh's gaze, "You were the one who was always so brave and I was always afraid." She drew in a shaky breath. "I wanted to die that day. I wasn't sure how I was going to go on without you."

Leigh bowed her head. It had never occurred to her how Shari would have felt about her presumed death. She'd had her own grief to deal with. Now she felt guilty for not contacting her best friend sooner.

"I'm sorry," she said.

The words seemed so inadequate after all these years, but it was the only thing she had.

"It's okay," Shari wiped away a tear. "I used to have dreams that someday you would come back and tell me that it was all just a big misunderstanding, but after all this time, I'd pretty much given up hope. When I saw you in the library, I honestly thought I was seeing a ghost." She had finished chopping the tomatoes and started on a cucumber. "I never believed the official story about your despondent uncle going on a killing rampage. I don't think too many people in town did either."

"Why do you say that?" Leigh wanted to know.

Shari thought about her answer for a minute. "You know how people like to talk. There was a lot of speculation about what happened at the park that day. One thing about being a teenager is that people forget you're in the room half the time. I remember overhearing a few conversations that didn't quite make sense to me. No one came out and said it, but there was a general sense of fear that if people said too much, they might be next. How could they be next if it was a murder-suicide between brothers? I asked Jessie about it, but she told me I was imagining things, said that it was normal for people to be afraid after someone they know dies tragically like that. After a while, no one really said anything whenever I was around."

Leigh sat back in her chair and tried to sort through what Shari had just told her. Had she been right all along? Had the town's people been a part of the poaching operation, or at the very least, did they know who the poachers were? Had they protected the criminals all these years out of some kind of loyalty or fear? She shied away from the thought that even Jessie could be protecting them.

"Is there anything you can remember that wasn't right back then?"

Shari shrugged.

"Was anyone acting odd? Were there any strangers in town? Do you know if they continued their operation in the park or if they headed out somewhere else?"

Shari put her hand up to stop the flow of questions. "After I put the girls to bed you can tell me everything that happened up there at the gorge that morning. Maybe something will jog my memory." Leaning across the island, she touched one of Leigh's hands. "We'll figure this out together. Now drink up! We'll find whoever killed your father and your uncle."

With that she called to the girls to sit down to dinner.

Leigh sipped her wine but couldn't shake the awful feeling that she was putting Shari and her family in danger just by being in their home.

. . .

True to her word, Shari hustled the girls to bed shortly after they'd finished eating. Dishes were put in the dishwasher at record speed, prayers were said and foreheads were kissed. Olivia had kept up a lively chatter throughout the meal and even Samantha got in a few words. Leigh's heart ached for the quiet girl. She remembered how painfully shy Shari had been at that age. How she had always sat on the sidelines, too afraid to join in until they had become friends. Leigh had basically bullied her into coming out of her shell. Now, as Shari sat down on the opposite end of the couch, there was no remnant of that shyness left.

"All right, girlfriend, start talking," Shari announced.

"How is it that you have six-year-old twins?" Leigh stalled. "You must have been still in high school when you had them."

Shari gave her a look that said she knew Leigh was avoiding her. "I started dating Ben my freshman year in high school. We got married two weeks after we graduated. The girls were born a little premature, but they only had to stay in the hospital about two weeks. So, now, stop stalling and talk."

It took over an hour for Leigh to relate the entire story. She didn't leave any detail out. Shari knew this area and these people better than she did.

As Leigh finished the story, Shari sat back and looked thoughtful.

"It would take an awful lot of money or power to cover up something like that," Shari mused. "There are only a few people around here with that kind of pull." She stared at Leigh. "There were a lot of people at the funeral. I know Jared was taking pictures for the local newspaper. Maybe we could ask him to let us look at them and see who was around at the time. Perhaps the shooter was there, just like in those crime shows. He sounds sick enough to do something like that. Maybe he was hoping you'd be there too."

Leigh snagged on something Shari had said. "Jared was taking pictures at the funeral?"

"Yea, I remember because I had such a crush on him at the time. He was doing an internship at the paper."

Leigh sat back and thought a moment. "We can't just ask to see them. He'll want to know why." She frowned. "I saw the newspaper article about the incident at the library, but I didn't think to look past that to any funeral information. I'll have to go back to the library this week and see if the photos were published in it."

"What I don't understand is why they had a funeral for all of you, if they only had one body." Shari winced. "Sorry, that didn't quite come out right."

"It's okay. I guess the authorities wanted to keep up the appearance of my death. It gave everyone a chance to say goodbye. That way, in people's minds, I was really dead."

"The authorities?" Shari wanted to know.

"The people who helped me to create a fake identity and sent me to live with Celeste and Roy."

"Your mom's cousin and her husband? Okay, I'm trying to keep up here."

"They told me that everyone in town thought I was dead. No one mentioned that they also thought my uncle had killed me and my father."

"So, the guy who murdered your father and uncle knows you're alive?"
Leigh nodded. "He does."

"He has to figure that you'll come back here someday to find him." Shari frowned. But I doubt he and his buddies would ever come back here, knowing that they might get caught."

Leigh appreciated that Shari was trying to reassure her but she doubted the poachers had stayed away. Edith Blaine had said there'd been some problems at the park and she had bolted when Leigh started to question her. And then there had been that subtle warning from Gertie. Something in Leigh's gut told her that this gang was local and still active in the area. Why were the people of this town so afraid of them that they'd cover up murder in their own backyard? Leigh decided to keep that observation to herself as she had already told Shari too much.

"I'm sure you're right, Shari, but that doesn't mean that I'm going to stop looking for them. I'm convinced that someone in this town knows who they are. Someday, they will let something slip."

Shari took a thoughtful sip from her almost-empty wine glass.

They both sat in silence for a few minutes, lost in their own thoughts. Leigh was the first to stir. Looking at her watch, she was surprised to see how late it was getting.

"I have to go." She gave Shari a hug. "I really didn't want you involved in any of this. I feel as if I've put you and your family in jeopardy."

"Don't be ridiculous. Like I said before, I doubt that any of those people are still around here." Shari waved away her protest.

As she drove away, Leigh wished she felt as confident as her friend did.

The brake lights of Leigh's jeep cut across the shadows on the man's face. At the end of the driveway, she turned onto the main road and the vehicle's lights disappeared out of sight. He waited a few minutes before stepping out from his hiding place. Dressed in camouflage, he had concealed himself in the overgrown rhododendron bush directly under the living room window where he'd been able to hear most of the women's conversation before moving to the thick foliage of the hydrangea bushes that lined the bend of the driveway. One of the twins had almost caught him when she'd run outside to grab a soccer ball from the shed.

Though it was true that Amanda had saved him a lot of trouble by coming back, he almost felt disappointed. He had fantasized about how he was going to hunt her down and kill her no matter how far she ran or how long it took. Prove to himself that he was still the best at tracking and catching his prey. He'd planned on dealing with her alone. However she had complicated matters by involving her friend and the children, but if he had to, he would tie up any loose ends. There was a lot of money at stake, and her timing couldn't have been worse. Damn, but he should have dealt with her ten years ago and avoided a shitload of problems. Well, he certainly intended to rectify that mistake by making sure he finished the job this time.

Taking out his cell phone, he punched in some numbers as he walked down the road to where he had left his car, his boots crunching heavily on the gravel.

"Have you seen the trophy?" he asked into the receiver. "Make sure it's what we paid for. This client is very important. I don't want any screw ups."

He listened to the voice on the other end.

"I've got some unfinished business I have to take care of. I'll be there on time."

He paused to listen again.

"Don't threaten me. You do your job and I'll do mine." Angrily, he jabbed at the screen to end the call.

Reaching his car, he yanked open the door and climbed into the driver's seat. Leaning back against the soft leather he closed his eyes. Concentrating on letting his breath even out, he tried to clear his mind. It was always like this before a hunt; he could feel the excitement at the prospect as he focused on his prey. It was a shame, really. Amanda had grown up to be a beautiful woman.

Lighting a cigarette, he took a long drag and let the smoke out slowly. Irritation rippled up from the pit of his stomach as he thought back to the day that still haunted him. She and her father weren't supposed to have been at the gorge that morning, just the uncle. Killing all of them had been the only option.

It still amazed him that such a young girl had been such a worthy adversary. Truth be told, he almost admired her skills. She was the only thing to ever escape from him. She'd hidden her trail well. Waited him out. It didn't change the fact that she was a liability to his operation; one he planned on rectifying as soon as possible.

Starting the engine, he plotted his next move as he drove away.

• • •

Jared was bone tired. He'd been getting up before dawn for the last week to take hundreds of photographs to support his cover that he was doing a photo expose on the park. Chad, his editor, was going to love some of the scenic shots. He'd had had to climb mountains to get them. After he downloaded and sent the images off, Jared would have some breathing room to concentrate on the other half of his mission.

Still damp from the shower, he'd thrown on some shorts and an old t-shirt that had seen better days. He grabbed a beer from the fridge and made his way to the Adirondack chair on his back porch, overlooking the lake. Leaning back, he took a swig and gazed out at the water. He wondered what Leigh was doing. He hadn't seen her since the night of the fair. Had he really just been too busy to even call her? Jessie made sure he knew that she had been to Cole's ranch and that she'd had dinner at Shari's.

Jared grinned at the memory of Jessie scolding him for letting her have a "date" with Cole. According to Jessie, he was going to lose out on the best thing that could ever happen to him. "Don't you want a wife and settle down?" she'd asked.

Why did women assume a single guy had to get married in order to be happy? He had to admit that he missed sparring with Leigh. They'd had a great time at the fair except for when Cole had shown up. Thinking of Cole made him frown. Things were not as they seemed with the Langfords, but he'd be damned if he could figure out what was going on with them.

Suddenly restless, Jared got up and went back into the house. Throwing the beer can into the recyclable bin he headed for the living room, settled himself at his desk and booted up the computer. There had been no time to check emails, and knowing Chad, his Inbox was probably overflowing. Sure enough, the email icon read into the triple digits. Scrolling down the list, Jared deleted all the emails that promised him anything from physic readings to male enhancing medications. What he wouldn't give to filter junk emails into the Spam folder, but he had to check every email to avoid missing something important. Most of the remaining new emails were from Chad, each one more demanding than the one before. Grabbing his camera, Jared downloaded the memory card of photos and sent them with a brief note. Next, he noticed that Matt had sent a reply to his earlier email request.

"Hey buddy, got some info on your mystery woman. Name is listed as Leigh Elizabeth Doane. She went to high school in Massachusetts. School transcripts say she transferred from Florida, but when I check out previous yearbooks and other school records, I come up with nothing. I've checked her birth certificate and I gotta tell ya, something doesn't add up with this girl. Her parents were killed in some sort of freak accident, but I can't find any of their names in any data bank. Almost seems like she didn't exist before she surfaced in high school. Her paperwork looks like someone who doesn't want their past to be found. But I'll keep digging."

Jared sat back in his chair. Well, it seemed that Leigh was more mysterious than he thought. So, what was she doing here? Working in a national park wasn't exactly hiding. People from all over the world visit the park every year. She was bound to run into someone who knew her, eventually.

He scowled. What if she was part of the poachers' operation? Being a ranger would give her the perfect cover to find out where the rangers were going to be at any given time. This would help the poachers get in and out of the park undetected. Since the Whittier brothers and Amanda had been killed, the poachers had temporarily moved their operation to other parks and game reserves, but for some reason they always returned to this park. What he needed to find out was why. What was so special about this particular park that kept drawing them back?

Jared ran his fingers through his hair in frustration. He didn't like the thought that Leigh was involved, but if she was, then she was the first solid lead he'd had in over five years.

Leaning forward again, he typed a quick reply to Matt, thanking him for the intel. As an afterthought, he asked Matt to send him a copy of Leigh's yearbook picture.

Hitting Send, he stared at the screen and sucked in a deep breath. There was one email left to open. He had noticed it earlier, but he'd saved it for last. His supervisors weren't going to be happy that he hadn't turned up anything that wasn't already public knowledge. With a resigned sigh, he opened the message.

Sure enough, they were considering scraping the entire operation.

"Give me a little more time," Jared wrote back. "The trail here is ten years cold but my sources are certain that our suspects are heading back in this direction. Word on the deep web suggests that something big is about to go down. I'm already established here. They all trust me. Let me and my team figure out when and where the next operation is going down."

Jared's finger lingered over the keyboard as he reread his reply. His team had spent years following leads, most of them dead ends, in hopes of finding any information on the poaching outfit that had been plaguing most of the parks in the Northwest. It was only by going high tech, and delving into the deep web, that they were finally able to start piecing together the movements of the poachers they had been searching for. This was the part of the internet that didn't appear on a Google search. Special software was needed to access it, and to keep the user anonymous. It was full of dark websites. A way for crooks, serial killers and thieves to find each other. Perps could hire hitmen, buy illegal weapons, or watch someone being tortured, among thousands of other deranged fetishes. Recent chatter on some of the poaching sites had hinted that a big gig was being planned for Indian Mound. This was the reason Jared had talked his supervisors into letting him come home and set up shop, so to speak. Now they wanted to just pull him out?

With a confidence he didn't feel, Jared hit Send.

So far, it was the hottest and driest August on record in the area. This made the rangers nervous because with thousands of acres of dry timber, forest fires were a real threat. Lightning, a spark from a campfire, or a carelessly thrown cigarette butt could wipe out miles of forest in such conditions. People in town, never mind the state, were on edge, hoping that rain would come soon and bring some welcome relief.

Leigh was at the top of the watch tower, having come to work early to potentially spot smoke or any glow of a fire in the dawn light, before the sun rose over the mountain and bleached it out. Being in the watch tower at daybreak had been her favorite thing to do when her father was alive; she had felt as if the entire park had been their kingdom. After he was gone, Leigh found that she hated the morning, so she hadn't risen this early in years.

Having had a restless night, with barely any sleep, she had made the decision to get up and head out early. As painful as it had been for her to climb the stairs, with memories hovering everywhere she looked, there came a sense of relief that she was finally facing them.

Jared's truck swung into the parking lot below and she watched as he looked up and saw her before he headed for the tower stairs. There was purpose in his stride; obviously he had been looking for her. Damn it. She sighed out loud. Though she enjoyed his company and their verbal sparring, she had been avoiding him. Her nightmares had convinced her that she had made a mistake in letting anyone get close.

But should she confide in Jared? His footsteps were getting louder, closer. Would he understand that she needed to find this man and his band of poachers, and bring them to justice, or would he try to deter her from her quest? Could she handle the pain if something happened to him? The guilt of drawing him into her nightmare? It would be taking a dangerous risk, one that she had already put Shari and her children in, and in the moments it took him to reach her, she agonized over it.

Leigh focused on the vague dark outlines of the distant mountains. Opening up and letting herself trust Jared would be risking everything. It would be tempting fate, again. Closing her eyes and bowing her head, she gripped the edge of the railing and fought down the urge to flee.

• • •

The sun rose above the tree line, tossing out rays that soon would punish an already dry and brittle land.

"Looks like it's going to be another hot one," Jared announced, stepping onto the observation platform, his camera in hand, to stand beside her.

Leigh straightened but couldn't turn to look at him, afraid that he would see the conflict in her eyes.

Jared's presence was all male and the woodsy scent of his aftershave, though faint, teased her senses, and then seemed to surround her. Turning slowly to face him, she noticed that he was dressed in his usual jeans and T-shirt, and well-worn hiking boots. He looked like a model straight from the pages of a magazine with his tanned face, strong chin and eyelashes that most women would kill for. Her pulse jumped at the sight of him. She tried to mentally slow it down.

Putting binoculars to her eyes, she scanned the horizon. "Weather reports don't see a break anytime soon," she replied.

"Well, let's hope that there aren't any fires in the meantime." Turning to lean back against the rail, with all his weight on his elbows, he looked at her face. "So, how did your date with Cole go last week?" He could have still been talking about the weather for all the inflection he put into his voice.

"It wasn't a date. I went over to check out his ranch. End of story." Leigh held the binoculars firmly in place.

"Come on, I need more details than that. Gertie is expecting a full report when I go for breakfast tomorrow. What are Cole's long-term plans? What did the two of you talk about? Did you meet anyone else while you were out there? Are you planning on going out with him again? Inquiring minds want to know!"

Annoyance surged up in her as she lowered the glasses to glare at him. "If Gertie wants to know about my "date" with Cole then she can ask me herself, or are you just being nosy and obnoxious?"

Jared gave her an infuriating grin. "I'm a journalist. I can find out anything that I want to know about you, including the color of the underwear you're wearing right now." His eyes roamed up and down her body. "Of course, it wouldn't be as much fun if you just told me."

Wasn't she just thinking that she enjoyed his company? Smiling sweetly, she leaned in closer to him and whispered, "That would be kind of hard to do, since I'm not wearing any."

Turning, she stalked over to the other side of the platform, leaving him in stunned silence for a moment before he gave a shout of laughter.

"Jerk," she scowled, scanning the northern section of the park for smoke. Just when she thought that he was someone she could confide in, he'd shown his true colors.

Jared crossed the platform and stood next to her again. "I'll look forward to confirming that piece of information." He put up his hands in a defensive motion when she turned to glare him.

"Hey, I just wanted to hear about Cole's ranch. You're the one that got all defensive. This is just a normal conversation between two friends."

He looked out over the landscape before he continued.

"I'd like to know more about you, Leigh. What were you like growing up? What were your parents like? Are they still living? Why do you get so defensive when anyone asks a personal question? What are you hiding from?"

Leigh sucked in her breath. Damn. She should have known that the reporter in him would consider her a mystery. She should have followed her instincts and kept her distance from him.

With a shrug, she made herself meet his eyes. "I don't know what you're talking about. I told you where I grew up. My parents died in a car crash when I was a teenager so I had to live with my aunt and uncle. I don't really like to talk about it. Too painful." Shaking her head, she added, "Sorry to disappoint you, but I'm just a private person. No mystery here."

Peering through the binoculars again, pretending a calmness she didn't feel, Leigh scanned the horizon as Jared studied her.

He didn't reply right away, giving the impression that he was thinking, but Leigh wasn't fooled. He was digging for information, trying to find the right thread to pull. She'd need to be very careful about what she said from now on. He'd pick up on any deviation from the smallest detail of her story.

Somehow, she needed to put space between them and keep it there. But how? He was always around, and until he finished his story, their paths would continue to cross. Swinging the binoculars to the right, she almost missed the thin plume of smoke that came from the direction of the gorge.

Sucking in her breath, she thought for a moment that she was mistaken, but as she focused in on the area, the smoke became thicker and the red glow of flames became visible. Swearing, she grabbed her cell phone from her pocket and speed dialed her supervisor, Gus. She tried not to look at Jared as she waited for Gus to answer.

"Speak," Gus' voice boomed over the airways.

"It's Leigh. I'm at the main watch tower. Just spotted smoke and flames in Area Four. Are you guys doing a controlled burn?"

Leigh had witnessed controlled burns with her father, always keeping well back from the flames, so she understood the importance of burning areas of dense undergrowth and vegetation, which were at a high risk of catching fire, in order to reduce the brush that would fuel a forest fire. She was sure that all the rangers in the park would have been notified if a controlled burn had been planned for that day.

Gus wasn't one to waste words. "No. Meet at the Area Six overflow parking. I'll send out the call." He hung up.

Jared kept pace as Leigh descended the tower stairs at record speed.

His eyes dared her to protest as he got into the passenger's side of her truck. She threw the truck into gear; sending stones and dirt flying as she sped out of the driveway.

. . .

The fire was in an area that had no real access roads. Primitive fire roads crisscrossed the region but they were not well maintained, due to budget cuts. To try and get a fire truck and heavy equipment into the area would be nearly impossible. This fire would have to be fought by hand with every available ranger, fire fighter and volunteer called in to help knock it down. Each hour that passed would make it more difficult to contain and therefore more dangerous.

There was a light, hot wind and Leigh knew that if it became any windier, it would fuel the flames and cause the dry grass and timber to become an inferno. Praying that the wind would die down, she pulled into the crowded grassy parking lot. Finding a small space to squeeze her jeep into, she and Jared jumped out and headed to where the men and women were congregating.

Her stomach did a slow roll as she got closer and saw that Gus was busy looking at a map draped over the hood of his truck. Several men were gathered around him as he marked off where the fire lines needed to be dug and where controlled fires needed to be set in hopes that they could contain the fire before it got ahead of them.

Gus Connors was a veteran ranger who had battled many fires over his career. He and Peter had been friends and coworkers for as long as Leigh could recall. At six-foot-four, Gus was an imposing figure. His hair, buzzed cut as usual, had a few more patches of grey and there were more lines on his weathered face, but otherwise, he looked the same as she remembered him. She had taken great care to avoid him during the past month, afraid that he might recognize her, or that somehow she would give herself away. Now there was no way to avoid him, hopefully he would be too preoccupied to look at her too closely.

• • •

Leigh was very much aware that Jared had followed her from the truck and was just inches behind her.

The next group took a step forward.

"Fan out from the gorge and clear out any campers who might be downwind of the fire. I want at least a two-mile perimeter, in case the wind decides to switch direction. If someone refuses to leave, use force. I have no intention of having to save someone due to their stupidity." Gus's commands were delivered in calm, efficient detail, even though his voice boomed and could probably be heard in the next county.

The rangers took off in several directions.

Having received their orders, the line of rangers and few volunteers who'd promptly responded to the fire alert, quickly dwindled until it was only Leigh and Jared left standing in front of Gus. He narrowed his eyes at them. It was obvious from the pursing of his lips that he didn't like putting a new recruit and an untrained reporter into the fire lines.

"You two," he said pointing at them. "Get to fire tower number five and be my eyes. I need to know where this fire is heading and if there are any more flare ups. Stop at the station and pick up some equipment. Lenny will know what you need."

Fire tower number five was on the other side of the gorge. It would give them a bird's eye view of the fire while also keeping them well out of its path.

Leigh nodded.

"Is the old logging road still passable or do we take the ancient Indian trail?" she asked.

Gus was silent for a moment, his face unreadable, before he replied, "Take the trail. The road was lost in a mudslide several years ago."

Too late, Leigh realized what she had revealed.

Avoiding Gus's eyes, she nodded before turning to head for the jeep, silently berating herself all the way. She paused to let a battered green Dodge back up, and then join the convoy of vehicles that were quickly leaving the lot. A green baseball cap matching the faded color of the vehicle was pulled low over the driver's face. He gave a quick wave of his hand in thanks, but Leigh was too preoccupied to notice.

*Would Gus wonder how she knew about the old trails?* Getting into the vehicle, she put her forehead against the steering wheel and tried to slow her racing heart.

Hearing footsteps, she straightened and started the engine. Her mind was busy trying to come up with some sort of explanation, but Jared was already hopping into the passenger seat. He gave her a quizzical look but thankfully didn't say anything. Maybe he hadn't noticed her slip up. *Yeah right, the man is an investigative journalist! He gets paid to notice the slightest detail.* Leigh had to assume that he caught the glaring fact that she knew much more about this park then a newcomer to town should know.

• • •

With no vehicles in sight, Leigh pulled out onto the road. She and Jared had made the trip to the ranger's station in silence, each busy with their own thoughts. Lenny must have been alerted that they were on their way because he had everything for them packaged and ready to go. Within a half an hour, they were back on the road and crossing over the bridge that spanned the gorge. The air was tinged with the smell of smoke even though the fire was well over two miles away.

Pulling into the small dirt parking lot of Area Five, Leigh noticed a green truck was already parked there. Making sure that she had her cell phone and snatching up her backpack off the rear seat, she got out and walked over to the truck. It had seen better days. The cab was empty and there was no sign of its driver.

"Hello?" she shouted, scanning the surrounding area.

There was nothing but an unnatural silence. Grabbing her cell, she called Gus.

"Central," came his reply.

"I've got an unattended vehicle in the number five rest stop. No sign of anyone around. We'll keep an eye out as we head to the tower, but you might want to send someone over here to check it out."

She walked around to the back of the vehicle to check out the license plate and was surprised to see that there wasn't one. "It may be abandoned. No plates."

"Copy that. I'll send someone down later to take a look, after we get this fire under control."

Glancing at Jared, who was waiting near her truck, Leigh headed to the far end of the lot to locate the opening to the trail.

The path, which ran parallel to the edge of the gorge, was an ancient route that Indians had created hundreds of years ago. Low bushes and small trees lined the trail near the gorge, where rocks kept their roots shallow. Farther up the slope, larger trees grew in thicker stands, in some places growing into the trail as it climbed the side of the mountain to where the park service had placed a fire tower. Perched two miles up, on the steep summit, the structure had a clear view of the east side of the park.

Leigh was hot, sweaty and winded when she and Jared finally reached a fork in the trail. Taking the right trail would lead them straight to the tower; the left trail stayed parallel with the gorge. The trail up to that point had been a steady uphill slope but this last leg would be much steeper, forcing them to climb over large boulders that helped make up the mountainside.

Stopping to catch her breath, Leigh turned to survey the fire on the other side of the gorge. Smoke poured into the sky as the blaze seemed to be gaining in momentum.

The heat from the sun was becoming unbearable; the heat from the fire had to be stifling. Leigh felt guilty about not being on the front lines, fighting the flames with her coworkers, but she also knew that being in the tower and reporting to Gus was just as important.

"Looks as if they have their work cut out for them," Jared broke the silence, reading her mind. He had been clicking pictures on the trek up.

"Hopefully it won't take long." Turning, she headed up the path on the right.

Leigh hadn't gone more than fifty feet when a strong odor assailed her nose. Before she could place the smell, there was a loud, sharp crack in front of them and then a small explosion behind them. A plume of smoke shot up from the trees.

Jared reacted by tackling Leigh to the ground and covering her with his body. Rolling to the side of the trail, he shoved her behind him and pulled out a gun.

"Stay down," he commanded as he searched the trail.

There was a hissing sound followed by a loud whoosh. Within seconds, a wall of flames swept through the forest and encircled them on three sides. The unmistakable smell of gunpowder and gasoline filled the air as thick black smoke disoriented Leigh for a moment. As the flames ignited the dry underbrush, she realized that someone had shot at them, setting off an explosion and creating a second fire. With flames behind and on both sides of them, the only way out was to go forward, up the slope and toward the tower. It was also the direction that the shot had come from.

Leigh eyes were burning and she couldn't get a breath without coughing. Jared was still surveying the surrounding forest for any movement, the pistol gripped tightly in his hand.

The heat of the flames made turning back down the trail impossible. The fire was starting to close the trail in front of them so, by silent agreement; they ran through the small opening before the flames closed it in. Slowing down as soon as they were through, Leigh took her cell phone from her pocket and was surprised to see the screen was cracked. It wouldn't turn on. It must have broken when Jared slammed her to the rocky ground.

"Damn it!" she cried. "Do you have your cell on you?" She watched as he reached into his pocket.

Looking stunned, he patted and checked his other pockets. "It's gone. It must have fallen out."

Great, she thought. Someone was shooting at them and starting forest fires, and here they were, trapped on the other side of the gorge with no means of communication.

"We need to get back to the car," Leigh said.

As they turned to go around the flames and run back down the trail, towards the parking lot, a projectile hit the ground in front of them, causing a spurt of earth to fly up, followed by the unmistakable sound of a rifle shot. Spinning around, they raced along the trail, trying not to go upwards. As they turned a slight bend in the path, another explosion sounded and the dry underbrush below them went up in flames.

Leigh ran blindly as the old panic welled up inside her. Once again, she was running through the forest as someone who wanted to kill her gave chase. Jared grabbed her around the waist to prevent her from falling as she tripped over a tree root. That was enough to snap her out of her panic. Stopping for a moment, she drew in big gulps of air to help to clear her mind.

*Who the hell was shooting at them?* Most arsonists didn't shoot at people. Leigh knew they got their perverted kicks out of setting fires and watching things burn. Whoever it was, they were in for a surprise because she wasn't a scared teenager trying to deal with the murders of her relatives, and she wasn't alone. Pulling Jared forward, they crouched down behind an outcropping of rocks.

"We need to make our way back to the gorge," she told him.

He looked at her as if she had lost her mind.

"We can't, we'll be trapped. There's no place to take cover. We'll be sitting ducks for him to pick off," he protested.

She shook her head. "Listen to me. We can backtrack a little, and then get over to the gorge. I know of a trail that leads down to a spot where we can take cover. He'll never see us."

Jared didn't look convinced, but he wasn't coming up with any other alternatives.

"What's your plan?" he asked.

"I don't think he'll be expecting us to go back to the gorge. He'll expect us to try to get above the fire. What we need to do is find out where he is. Most likely, he wants to keep us trapped by the fire so he'll try to get ahead of us anyway. By the time he figures out that we aren't going his way, we'll already be halfway down the side of the gorge."

Jared thought it over for a second. The fire was gaining in intensity; if they were going to make a plan work then it would be now or never. "All right, how far do we have to backtrack?"

Looking around to get her bearings she replied, "Go back about a quarter mile until we reach a copse of trees on the edge. There's a small trail on the left that leads down the side to a cave. If we can get to the cave, it will bring us down to the floor of the gorge. We could be miles down the river before he figures out that we're gone."

Leigh could see that he wanted to argue with her but he didn't have a better plan. Embers were falling all around them. They needed to move quickly, before the whole mountainside became one massive inferno. The smoke was getting thicker and the heat was becoming unbearable.

Jared looked into her eyes. She knew that he was debating whether to trust her or not. After a moment, he nodded and a sense of relief washed over her that she couldn't explain. Using the smoke as a screen, they started making their way toward the gorge.

. . .

The wind was pushing the smoke and flames toward the edge of the gorge when Leigh finally found the copse of trees she had been looking for. Holding onto a tree trunk, she stepped down and onto a narrow ledge that was only a little wider than her foot. Small trees and roots growing from the creviced rock wall helped to provide some handholds as they followed what was loosely called a path. Inching, with their backs against the rocks, they climbed down ledge to ledge. Leigh's fingers ached as they grasped at any small protrusion in the slippery walls, searching for anything to help her keep her balance. She slipped several times on the steep slope but Jared was quick to grab her arm, stopping her from sliding too far.

Smoke billowed over the rim above and embers started raining down on them, causing them to pick up their pace. The ledges became wider as they got closer to a huge gap in the gorge's wall.

Leigh leapt the small distance to the entrance of the crevice then slid through the narrow opening. Having reached the safety of the cave, she leaned up against the cold wall, closed her eyes and tried to slow down her breathing as sweat rolled down her back. She hadn't realized how scared she was until she saw Jared leaning against the opposite wall, his eyes wide as he looked around the cave. It was dark, with only a faint light coming through the small opening, so it took a few minutes for her eyes to adjust.

The entire cave had been carved out of water, millions of years ago, and was no bigger than twelve by twelve feet. A tunnel sloped at the far end and wound its way down the inside of the wall before exiting into a smaller cave at the bottom. That opened into the now present riverbed.

The only sound above their breathing was the dripping of water from some underground source. Leigh had explored the cave years ago, with her father, but they had rappelled down the side of the gorge in order to access the cave.

"How did you find out about this place?" Jared wanted to know. "I grew up in this town and I had no idea that this was even here."

Leigh tried to think up a lie quickly. It would have to be something believable, but her mind was blank. Instead, she changed the subject. "Do you think he was planning on starting another fire and we surprised him? There would have been no way that he could have known we were heading for that tower."

"Who knows what goes on in a psycho's mind?" Looking around again, he asked, "So this leads down to the river? Is there another way to get back up to the top of the gorge? As far as I know, the only way to get back up is in Guilford, about 20 miles downstream from here. That's a hell of a lot of walking."

Leigh rummaged through her backpack. Using a flashlight, she peered further into the bag. Pulling out some flares she set them aside and then grabbed some rope and climbing equipment. Her mind was already developing a plan.

"Hope you ate your Wheaties this morning," she told him with a grin. "You're gonna need your strength."

• • •

The man in the green cap looked down the slope but couldn't see any movement through the heat and smoke. *Damn it. Where were they?* They should have headed this way; there had been no other options. He had

| 84 |

spent weeks planning how to make her death look like an accident. Killing her straight out would bring too much attention at a time when he didn't need it. The weather conditions gave the perfect avenue to have her caught in the middle of a forest fire. Having the journalist with her was unfortunate, but it couldn't be helped.

He glanced at his watch; they had been trapped for over two hours now and it seemed highly unlikely that they could have escaped. It was time to cover some tracks and get back to business. Whistling to himself, he climbed up past the tower to the other side, where he had a four-wheeler parked. He had important clients arriving soon and he didn't want any more distractions.

• • •

The trip down was slow, since the tunnel wasn't very big, and in some places Leigh and Jared had to slide down on their backs, but they finally reached the river bottom.

With no recent rain, the water was running low. Climbing out onto the rocks, Leigh looked up at the rim. Smoke still billowed over the opening and filled the sky. Ashes were falling around them as the fire raced toward the edge.

"I think we should wait until dusk before we head out. We can use the flares to light our way once we get further downstream."

It had been over three hours since they had made their way down the side of the gorge. Jared was ready to head downstream immediately but Leigh was worried that the arsonist was still around, waiting.

"I disagree," Jared continued their argument. "If we head out now, we can have a better chance that he's still in the area. I'll bet that was his truck at the rest stop. We can get to a phone, put out an APB and have roadblocks put up to catch this guy."

"What's an APB?" she wanted to know.

"An all-points bulletin. Every law enforcement agency in the state will be on the lookout," was his answer.

He sounded like a cop causing Leigh to remember something. "Do all photojournalists carry guns?"

Jared gave her a quick glance and then looked away. "You'd be surprised how many people you meet in my line of work who can be threatened by someone with a camera. I delve into some of the most undesirable situations and places. Drug traffickers, coyotes, sex slave traders, pimps, you name it I've covered it." Running a hand through his hair, he gave her a crooked grin. "This isn't the first attempt on my life. In fact, I was starting to get worried that things around here were a little too quiet."

There was a brief silence before Leigh asked, "What's so bad about coyotes?'

"I'm not talking about the animal coyotes. I'm talking about the human kind. Coyotes smuggle people illegally over borders."

"So, they're human traffickers?"

He shook his head, "No, human traffickers kidnap or take people against their will. Coyotes take money from people who want to get out of their country and go somewhere else in the hopes of finding a better life. Unfortunately, these desperate people put their trust in criminals who often dispose of them if they think the authorities are closing in on their operation. Coyotes are the assholes who sell people to traffickers."

There was a haunted look in his eye that testified to the truth that he had seen things she couldn't even begin to imagine. Leigh decided to change the subject.

"You think that this was an attempt on your life?" Leigh hadn't looked at it from that angle.

Jared got up and stretched. "It wouldn't surprise me. My last assignment had been about the connection of the drug lords between Mexico and the US. It's about to be on the front pages of worldwide newspapers and magazines. These cartels have a lot to lose once my piece hits the newsstand."

There was no arrogance in the statement, only fact. Jared looked over the slow-moving water, appearing calm for a man who had almost died in a forest fire.

Sitting on boulders at the edge of the river, hidden under a low overhang in case anyone looked over the side, they both became lost in their thoughts as they waited for darkness.

* * *

Jared stared out onto the rocky riverbed and slowed his breathing. God, he hoped that Leigh couldn't see his fear. It was one thing taking risks and dealing with the consequences when it was just him, but quite another when there was someone else's life on the line. Now that they were safe, for the moment anyway, the adrenaline was wearing off and he was beginning to realize just how close they had come.

Jared had never feared anything before. It had always been a game, a rush to get these assignments to flush out the bad guys. But now he was afraid that he was vulnerable. What was the saying his grandmother used to say? 'You have to care about something, or someone, to fear losing it.' The stakes had suddenly become unbearably high. Life and death, and not just his. Instinct was telling him that this wasn't the work of a random arsonist. The gunpowder and gasoline had been placed so that whoever had been walking up the trail had no choice but to head up the slope or be trapped by the flames.

If this had something to do with the drug cartel that he had just exposed, then he had put Leigh in grave danger. Grinding his back molars, Jared wondered how the hell they could have tracked him here. He'd only used burner phones and his alias had been rock solid. The only way they could have possibly tracked him to Ramsey was if someone on the inside had sold him out. That thought didn't sit well with him. He needed to do something. He wasn't used to feeling helpless.

Although Jared didn't glance Leigh's way, he was acutely aware of her. She appeared remarkably calm for someone who escaped a brush with death too. God, she had guts and brains, and it was lucky for them that she knew this park so well. If she hadn't known about that tunnel leading down the side of the gorge, well, they wouldn't have had a chance. The thought furrowed his brow. Leigh seemed to have an uncanny knowledge of the park: more knowledge than someone who had just arrived a few weeks ago. His reporter instincts told him that there was much more going on than she was letting on. He did like a mystery, if only he could keep them alive long enough to figure her out. Jared smirked to himself. He'd find out who was trying to kill them and why. He'd stop them and then get the girl. All in a day's work.

Turning back to Leigh, he said out loud, "Okay, I'll wait one more hour, then we're heading out. In the meantime, why don't you fill me in on your date with Cole?" He crossed his arms and waited for the protest to start.

It had been a long day at the café and Gertie was exhausted. It seemed as if everyone in town had stopped by to find out how the firefighting was going. Her café had always been the informal headquarters for any communal event. Feeding the rangers and fire fighters had become a community effort. Volunteers kept the food plentiful and coffee flowing to the crews. It was small town unity at its best.

Now it was past midnight and the majority of people were home, resting up to start over again tomorrow. Word from the frontlines was that most of the fire was controlled and that they would work on the hot spots through the night. Now, with a handful of diehard volunteers holding down the fort, Gertie decided to head home to get some sleep. Saying goodnight, she walked through the kitchen and out the back door into the alleyway, heading for the stairs that led to her apartment over the café.

A figure separated from the shadows.

Gertie jumped a little, although he hadn't really startled her. She had been waiting for this visit for a while now and she would have recognized him anywhere. Sighing, she slowly climbed the stairs, knowing that he would follow her.

Turning on the living room light and sitting on the worn couch, Gertie watched as he shut the door, and then sat down opposite her.

"Hello Dean."

Dean Langford looked out of place in her cozy apartment. He was wearing a short-sleeved green cotton shirt and creaseless tan khakis. His Italian leather shoes were equally spotless. He looked exactly like who he was; a tanned, rich politician, thought Gertie. The watch alone cost more than she could make in a year of slinging hash.

Dean appeared to be without any rancor, almost relaxed, but she had known him too long. His eyes darted around the apartment as his fingers tapped against the arm of his chair. She remembered those strong, capable fingers. Not liking where her thoughts were taking her, she looked back at his face and waited, knowing what he was going to say, had known it for years.

He came right to the point.

"We have a problem. It appears that that Whittier girl is back and looking for answers." He ran his hand through his hair and leaned forward. "If she finds out the truth, then you know what will happen."

Gertie cursed, silently. She supposed that she shouldn't have been surprised that Dean had found out about Amanda. He had a large network of informants at his disposal. It was only a matter of time before he found out who she really was.

"I would think that you had covered the trail well enough not to be worried," she replied, getting up to look out the window.

He also got up, but he started to walk back and forth. His long strides easily eating up the small space, like a lion pacing in his cage, frustrated with the confinement.

"I did everything I could think of at the time. I can't control what people are going to do or say. You know how unpredictable he is." He paused for a moment. "He knows that she's back."

Those words sent a shiver down Gertie's spine. She had hoped, foolishly, that he wouldn't have found out who Leigh really was. There would be no stopping him from hunting her down now. Damn it, why couldn't Amanda have stayed where she was safe and left it alone?

"So, what are you going to do now?"

Looking back, it seemed Gertie had always run to Dean to fix her problems. It was just that he had been so strong and engaging back then, but he had needed her, and she had been more than willing to be needed. Lord, she had been a blind fool. Had fallen hard for him, certain that he would marry her, once he graduated college. Certain that they were meant to be together, but she hadn't understood the dynamics of politics. Hadn't understood that she was a nobody, a commoner, that her humble background was not one that would help him get to the White House someday. She hadn't understood any of this until Dean came home with a debutante as a wife and he'd pretended that Gertie didn't exist.

She had left town shrouded in shame, in the middle of the night, unable to watch the man she loved creating a family with someone else. Worst of all was having to call him, months later, with the news of her pregnancy.

At first, Dean had denied that the child was his and Gertie had wanted to crawl up and die, but then anger had taken hold. Only with the threat of a scandal, how an illegitimate child wouldn't look so good for his presidential bid, was she able to get Dean's attention and help. He'd made all the arrangements. Their baby, a boy, had been taken away before Gertie could even hold him. Closing her eyes now, the long-suppressed pain resurfaced, just for a moment, before she willed it back down again.

It had taken years, but she had finally come home and been at peace with the past. Until ten years ago, that is, when all hell had broken loose. Hanging her head, Gertie knew that she would have to answer Saint Peter at the Pearly Gates, someday, and she wasn't looking forward to trying to explain how a mother could surrender her child.

Dean's next statement shook her out of her maudlin thoughts.

"He may have already taken care of things for us."

Gertie whipped her head up to stare at him. Her heart was in her throat and she could swear that it wasn't beating. "What are you saying? He's already killed her?"

"The girl and the photographer are missing. They were sent to tower five, across the gorge. There was another fire over there. No one has seen them since."

"Good Lord!" Gertie was stunned. She had been dreading this moment since Jessie had called to warn her that Amanda was back. *Damn!* Why were they destined to keep paying for their past mistakes?

Dean hurried over to her and led her back to the couch. It seemed that time had stopped moving. *So it had all ended with Amanda's death after all.*

"Why haven't I heard anything about this? No one mentioned it when they came in with reports. How can we be sure that this is…" she faltered over the words, "him?"

"I had Gus keep it quiet. I want to make absolutely sure before news gets out. They have people over there fighting the fire and searching for the bodies. They found the photographer's cell phone, smashed, in the burn area. There's no doubt in Gus' mind that this fire was intentionally set. I'll bet he tried to make it look like an accident but I'm not holding out any hope of finding them alive. Even if they somehow didn't burn to death, he would have shot her and thrown her off the side of the gorge."

He suddenly looked old. "Look, Gertrude, I'm not sure that I can fix this one. People were angry and upset about Joan. If they find out who this girl was, well, I think they will talk. We need to be prepared."

Gertie got up and made her way to the kitchen. She had to do something, anything. Her mind was a jumble of incoherent thoughts as she made coffee by instinct. Guilt was trying to thrust its way through, but she pushed it back down; there would be time for that later. Right now, she needed to think and to make a plan.

It scared her that Dean was so unsure of himself. He'd always had full control over any situation, arrogant even when the situation looked hopeless. There was no arrogance in his posture tonight.

Turning, Gertie walked back into the living room, placed two cups of coffee on the table and sat down on the couch, across from him. She had loved this man once, with her whole being. Now, there was only a fondness for all that they had shared. Quietly, she told him her plan, knowing that no matter what, the truth was finally going to come out. It was time. They should have stopped what was going on ten years ago; should have never let it get to this point.

There was no question that she had taken the coward's way out, and in an odd way, Gertie was relieved that it would soon be over.

• • •

"It's late and I have to go," Dean announced.

Gertie gave him a hug and looked into his eyes. "It will all work out for the best," she told him. She just wished that she could believe it.

After he left, Gertie picked up the phone and called Jessie, who answered on the first ring. "We need to make some plans" Gertie told her. "Leigh and Jared are missing and possibly dead. It's time to end this once and for all."

# CHAPTER NINE

*Damn, but she was out of shape.* Leigh and Jared had navigated the rocky riverbed downstream, not an easy task on the slippery rocks, and they had made it to the trestle bridge that spanned the gorge. There was an old goat trail on the side of the bridge that novice rock climbers had used to practice on, before they tackled the steeper gorge walls. Pins had been set in the wall at intervals and Leigh was relieved to see that they were still there. Reaching up, she tugged on the lowest pin and smiled when it didn't move. Crouching down, she opened her backpack and took out a coil of nylon rope.

"Now only if he put one in here," she muttered plunging her hand back into the pack.

"Yes!" She exclaimed as she pulled out a carabiner clip. "Thank you, Lenny!"

She turned to Jared and was pleasantly surprised to see him already twisting his rope to make a harness. "I take it you've done some rock climbing before," she said, getting busy with her own harness.

"Some. In fact, I think I learned on this very course while I was in high school. I'd forgotten that it was here." He paused and gave her a searching look. "Funny how you knew about it when you haven't been at the park that long."

Keeping her eyes down, the lie came easily to her lips. "Not really, Gus showed it to me. We were going to do it together so that he could check on my skill level."

Clipping the carabiner to the highest anchor that she could reach, Leigh stepped onto the first pin and inched her way up the steep incline. Jared waited until she was a good distance before he started up behind her. Several times scree, loose pebbles and dirt shook loose from her hand or toe holds and showered down onto Jared's head. They used small trees and roots as extra leverage, but the pins and anchors were still solid and held their weight.

It was slow going and every muscle in Leigh's body screamed at the unaccustomed exercise. Reaching the top, she pulled at anything within her grasp to haul herself up over the ledge. Turning onto her back she lay still, trying to catch her breath as she waited for Jared. It was several minutes before he reached the edge and heaved himself over. Moving into a sitting position, she let him take a moment to regain his breath.

"I gotta think about retiring," he said between gulps of air. "I'm getting too old to do this crap anymore."

Leigh snorted at that. He was the adrenaline junkie type. Somehow, she couldn't picture him as the sit-behind-the-desk type of man. He'd be pulling out his hair in a week. The image of him bald made her smile.

Turning away, so he wouldn't ask what was so funny, she started to remove her harness.

Sighing, he followed suit.

Once the gear was stowed in their packs, they moved to the edge of the road, where the long dry grass hid them from view.

A heavy smell of smoke hung in the air and Leigh's eyes began to burn. She had no way of knowing how far and fast the fire had spread, and they had no idea who had wanted them dead.

Agreeing on a plan to keep hidden for a day or two, until they could reach someone who they could trust, Jared and Leigh couldn't agree where to hide out. Leigh was worried about Shadoe and she wanted to go to her cabin. Jared figured that someone would notice them missing and go get the dog, so he wanted to hide out somewhere else. Now that they were out of the gorge, they had to make a decision.

"I'll compromise," Jared told her. "Let's head for my place. We can load up a few days of supplies and some camping stuff, and then we can check to see if Shadoe is still at your place. If he is, then we'll decide what to do. Okay?"

Not having a better plan, Leigh agreed.

• • •

After two hours, they reached the woods at the side of Jared's house. It was dark out, the sun having set in a fiery red ball several hours earlier. They had followed the main road, hiding anytime a vehicle passed, some of which containing fellow rangers.

Crouching behind trees, they scanned the area for any movement. If anyone was watching the house, they had hidden themselves well. Jared skirted the woods and came up behind the woodpile. Leigh had gone the other way and was up against the side of the house, crouched down by a bush. There were no signs of life other than the sound of ducks quacking down at the dock. Jared moved silently to the back door and entered the house, his gun drawn.

It seemed like hours before he reappeared and gave Leigh the signal to join him.

While Jared grabbed the camping gear, Leigh filled their backpacks with canned goods, a can opener, a small cooking pot, two lighters and some plastic dishes. It was slow going in the muted glow of a nightlight, but they didn't want to attract attention by turning on any lights.

Raiding the kitchen cupboards, she noticed that Jared ate like a typical bachelor. The cabinets were filled with boxes of macaroni and cheese, ramen noodles and peanut butter. His refrigerator held leftover cartons of takeout food, several bottles of beer and a bottle of ketchup.

She shook her head. Talk about depressing. The man was a processed food garbage dump.

Jared had just returned to the kitchen, carrying two rolled up sleeping bags and a bigger hiking backpack, when headlights illuminated the room. They heard the sound of a truck's engine approaching. Ducking down, Leigh thought for a moment that the arsonist had found them until she realized that the headlights had moved on. Peering through the window, she watched as Jessie's truck drove past Jared's house and continued toward her cabin.

A few minutes later, she heard the truck door slam shut, then Shadoe barking. Several more minutes elapsed before another door slammed. When Jessie's truck came back down the road Leigh ducked away from the high beams, but not before she saw the silhouette of Shadoe in the passenger's seat.

"Well, that answers the problem of the dog." Jared said, in the shadows behind her, tying the sleeping bags onto his pack.

Leigh was relieved that Jessie had come to get her dog, yet she felt a deep sadness too. Shadoe had been her constant companion for a lot of years and she had wanted the dog with her now. Being alone with Jared was not an ideal situation.

"So where to?" she asked.

"I've been thinking on that. I think the best place to hold up is the old Whittier house. No one has been there for years."

Leigh felt the blood drain from her face.

"You're kidding, right?" Panic began to well up in her chest. "That place is infested with…with all sorts of things. No telling what's living in there!"

Jared looked at her strangely. "We have sleeping bags and it will be a roof over our heads." He started for the back door. "Being a ranger, I thought you'd be a lot braver about roughing it. Didn't take you for a prima donna."

The words were said jokingly but the unintentional criticism still hurt. How was Leigh supposed to explain that she had grown up in that house? That all her dreams had died on the same day that the house had been abandoned? That memories would whisper from every corner, reminding her of what she had lost? How was she supposed to explain that the Whittier house had been her home and now, the decaying shell would mimic the landscape of her soul until she could find the man who had murdered her family?

She couldn't. Leigh would just have to close her mind to the memories and focus on the present. Taking a deep breath, she eased herself out the back door and followed Jared into the shadows.

• • •

They made their way through the dark to the abandoned house. It was a surprise to see light seeping through an uncovered window in the back room that had once been Mark's office. Peering through filthy, broken windowpanes, they could see into the room.

Leigh and Jared watched in silence as Cole pried up several floorboards with a crowbar. Ripped jeans and a dirty T-shirt now replaced his usual immaculate appearance. His hair was mussed, as if he had run his fingers through it in frustration a thousand times. His pace was frantic as the light from his lantern threw shadows throughout the room, making the scene appear even more surreal.

Leigh exchanged a glance with Jared, and by silent agreement, they crept away from the house to a vantage point where they could still see Cole but they wouldn't be overheard.

"What do you think he's looking for?" Leigh whispered.

"I'm not sure, but it must be very important for him to find it."

Leigh thought back to her conversation with Cole at the ranch. "He told me that this property had been in land court and that it was coming up for sale any day. He was pretty sure that he'd be able to buy it. So why tear this house apart now? Why not wait until it becomes his and just raze the place?"

She focused on Cole for a second. "This land has nothing special to add to his beside acreage. There's no spring or water source that he would need and the old silver mine was played out years ago. So, what the hell is he looking for?"

She hadn't realized that she had spoken out loud until she saw that Jared was looking at her with his eyes narrowed.

"What?" she asked.

"You seem to have an extraordinary knowledge of this area. I can understand you knowing the park's secrets, but how is it that you know what's on this property? About the mine? Just who are you?"

His gaze bore into hers. Who was she? That was the question that Leigh had been asking herself for the last decade. She had been living under an alias for so long that she sometimes forgot who she truly was. There had been lots of times when she had wanted to tell people the truth, but fear had always stopped her. She was Amanda, Mark and Tracy Whittier's only daughter, but she couldn't tell anyone. Afraid because she was the only witness to the murders that had changed the course of her life. She would never be the same again. The question was, who had she become?

Now looking at Jared, she met his gaze squarely. "Cole took me by the mine the other day. Said it was deserted in 1888 after a partial collapse. Apparently local legend claims there's more silver to be found, but there was some sort of scandal that resulted in the mine's sudden closing. Cole said that just before the collapse, the miners found another vein of silver but the owners refused to reopen it. From what I understand, no one has ever found anymore silver, or knows what the scandal was about. Cole says it's haunted."

How easily the lies came from her lips. She wasn't sure that Jared believed her. He looked like he was weighing her words before he turned his attention back to the house. Cole was punching numbers into his cell phone. His voice carried through the broken windows.

"It's not here," he told the person on the other end, frustration evident in his clipped words. "It must have been moved with all his personal things unless there's a safety deposit box that you don't know about." He listened for a moment, pacing back and forth. "I've torn up all the damn floorboards… I don't care what you were told… I've ripped this place apart. Go back to your source and find me the goddamn map."

Ending the call, Cole appeared to stare at the destruction he had caused, but Leigh didn't think that he actually saw it. There was something maniacal in his posture. After several minutes, he grabbed the lantern and stormed out of the study. A few seconds later, they heard the front door slam and the sound of a horse trotting away.

Leigh and Jared sat in the dark, listening to the hoof beats recede into the night.

"Well, I guess we can't stay here," Jared broke the silence a few minutes after Cole's departure. "He's pulled up all the floorboards and we'd probably break our necks. Besides, he might be back."

"Where do you suggest we go now?"

Jared looked thoughtful for a moment, "How about the mine? As you said, it's been abandoned for years. Of course, as you also pointed out, it's supposed to be haunted. You weren't thrilled about bugs and creepy crawlies here, but how do you feel about ghosts?"

Leigh opened her mouth in surprise, and then quickly snapped it shut again. "Lead on McDuff," she smiled sweetly.

• • •

It had been a long, exhausting day and by the time they reached the entrance to the mine Leigh was sore, tired and hungry. She had been up before dawn, trapped in a fire, shot at, climbed the side of a gorge and spent the better part of the night traipsing through the forest.

A steel gate blocked the opening to the mine shaft and the padlock was still solid, but Leigh ignored both. Pushing through the thick bushes that flanked the entryway, she followed an overgrown path around the side, Jared following close behind her. The beam from her flashlight lit a wooden door that had been built into the hillside, hidden from view. This door had a combination lock attached to it and without hesitation Leigh dialed a sequence of numbers. With a click, it opened.

Glancing at Jared, she opened the door and stepped inside a small room, no bigger than ten feet by ten feet. The floor was hard-packed dirt and Leigh could see some wooden boxes stacked along one wall.

Turning on his flashlight, Jared glanced up before straightening his tall frame, confirming that he wouldn't hit his head. The ceiling was supported with large beams and the walls were framed with log posts. He gave a low whistle. "I never knew this room existed. It's not on any of the plans of the mine."

Leigh turned to look at him. "That's because it was added in the twenties to hide liquor during the Prohibition. If you check at the library, you'll find it referenced in several books on the history of the town."

She walked over to a natural ledge and pulled down an ancient candle that had been attached to a plate. Jared produced a lighter and lit the wick, but the weak light didn't quite reach the darkened corners.

"Does the book also reference the combination to the lock?" he asked.

Leigh had anticipated that question. It was the lock her father had put on the door, years ago. He had made her birthday the combination.

"No, Cole told me the combo the other day. I guess it never occurred to him that I might actually use it."

Untying her sleeping bag from the pack she had set down inside the door, she glanced over at Jared, but was unable to read his expression in the flickering light. She relaxed a little when he spoke.

"There's no place to make a fire in here so I guess we'll have to rough it and eat our meal cold."

She had moved to the far side of the small space and began unrolling her sleeping bag. Dipping into his backpack, Jared pulled out several cans, which he put to the side, before producing some granola bars, crackers and bottled water.

"Not much of a meal but it's better than nothing," he said as he rolled out his bedding. Leaning forward, Leigh chose a granola bar and bottled water, then sat cross-legged on her makeshift bed. The room felt small and intimate with Jared sitting across from her, their sleeping bags touching. *How was she going to fall asleep next to him?*

Opening a can of peaches, he speared one with a fork and offered it to her.

*Didn't Eve use an apple to entice Adam? Stop thinking like a teenager,* she scolded herself silently as she shook her head and looked away. "Let's just get a good night's sleep and figure out what we need to do in the morning."

Jared was grinning at her, which made her nervous. "What?"

"I'm beginning to figure you out. Just gave yourself a little pep talk about us sleeping side by side, didn't you?" He leaned in closer. "Well? What did you decide? Are you going to be able to keep your hands off me tonight?"

Looking into his deep blue eyes, for a second, Leigh could think of nothing better than curling up next to him. What would it be like to lose herself in this man's embrace; to forget the past and have someone else help her look toward to the future? He was strong, smart and sexy as hell, but unfortunately he was a player. He was just looking for a diversion while he finished his article and then he'd move on. Leigh was afraid that she was falling for him and she knew that she couldn't give herself to him, or anyone, knowing that she would just be another proverbial notch on the bedpost. Besides, he thought she was someone else. Until he knew her as Amanda Whittier, it was best if she just kept her distance. Tears burned behind her eyes but she was able to keep his gaze. "Yea, I think I can manage it."

With that, she slipped into her sleeping bag and turned away from him.

● ● ●

Leigh awoke to find that her head was on Jared's chest and his arms were wrapped around her. He had pulled her tight against him as they slept. She could hear his heartbeat; it was strong and steady.

*Funny, it doesn't sound like the heartbeat of a heartbreaker.*

She felt content in his embrace, protected even, which didn't make any sense because she suspected that this man could hurt her more emotionally than any other man she had ever met. Her sleeping bag had slipped down her hips until it only covered her legs but she wasn't cold against his warm body.

Jared's arm tightened around her, warning her that he was awake. He shifted so that they were face to face, but she kept her eyes closed. Maybe if she pretended to be asleep, he would get up and act as if nothing had happened. His hand brushed back the hair that had fallen into her face and lingered under her chin.

"I know you're awake," he said. "It doesn't matter if you keep your eyes closed or not. I'm going to kiss you either way."

With that warning, he rolled backwards and pulled her on top of him. His hand cradled the back of her head and pulled her down to his lips.

She was lost in an instant. All her senses became consumed by the sensations that his lips and hands were creating. Leigh had been burying her emotions for so long that they now boiled to the surface in the length of a heartbeat. For too many years, there had been nothing but anger fueling her thoughts and decisions. It was almost a celebration to let go, even for a brief time. For once, she didn't think about the consequences of her actions, or those of someone else's. It was enough just to be.

Jared turned her so that she was under him without breaking contact. Her breath came in small bursts as he started to kiss her neck while working the buttons of her shirt.

"God Leigh, you're beautiful," he rasped.

Time that had seemed to stop before came crashing back into her brain. *How could she have been so stupid?* He wasn't making love to Amanda; he was making love to Leigh. She pushed him off her and rolled to the side. Gasping for air, she stumbled to her feet, fumbling with her buttons. The sense of loss was numbing. She could still feel the heat of his lips on her skin. Wrapping her arms around her middle, she put some distance between them before she turned around.

Jared was lying on his back with his arm flung over his head. She expected him to be angry. Sure, she had led him on and now the guilt made it hard for her to look at him. "I'm sorry," she managed. "I told you before that you don't know me. I'm not looking for an…to get involved with any-one. I'm sorry that I led you to believe otherwise."

She waited for him to say something, anything. He turned onto his side and propped his head on his hand. He studied her for a moment and then, in one fluid motion, he jumped to his feet and crossed the distance between them. She wasn't sure if she should be afraid, he had never given her a reason to be, until now. Walking past her, he grabbed the backpack and sat down.

"What are you in the mood for this morning? I'm starving," he asked.

Leigh felt the heat rush to her face at the double entendre.

Of course it meant nothing to him, she told herself, mentally smacking her forehead. It was just an opportunity, another conquest. He must have women throwing themselves at him all the time. *He could at least pretend to be disappointed*, she thought. Clenching and grinding her teeth together, she didn't trust herself to speak.

Jared regarded her for a moment and dammit if there wasn't a knowing look in his gaze. "Not hungry?"

Stabbing him with her eyes, she headed for the door. His chuckle followed her as she tried to slam the old wooden door behind her. Stalking away, Leigh found an oak tree with a low thick branch that she settled herself onto. It was uphill from the mine so she could catch glimpses of Jared through the leaves. Once he had looked up from the bottom of the hill, located her and then wisely turned away to disappear from her view.

* * *

It took several hours away from Jared, and a lot of telling herself that she was a damn fool, to settle down and come up with a plan.

They had to get to someone whom they could trust. Thoughts of Jessie, Gertie and Shari came to mind, but Leigh immediately dismissed them. She wouldn't put them in danger and all the other rangers were suspect at this time. The arsonist must have been at the meeting spot yesterday morning to know where Gus had sent them, if she and Jared had indeed been the true targets. The gunpowder and gasoline had been placed along the path effectively cutting off any escape. That couldn't have been a coincidence. The more she thought about it, the more Leigh was sure that it had to have been the man in the green truck that had pulled out as she was walking to her jeep. She hadn't really looked at the vehicle, but she'd bet anything that it was the same one they'd found in the parking turnout.

Her mind refused to dwell on the possibility of which ranger it could have been. They were old friends; a betrayal from one of them would cut deep. It would be like losing another part of her family. Unfortunately, she was going to have to face the facts. The arsonist had known that she was sent to tower number five and they had set things up so there should have been no escape. It had been such a close call. Too close.

Leigh jumped down from the low branch that she had been brooding on. There was only one person whom she knew she could trust and who knew who she really was. He'd helped her that fateful night, had made all the arrangements to get her to Celeste and Roy's place. He'd made sure that her identity had been well hidden and that her inheritance had been protected. He wasn't going to be happy to know that she was back, and was obviously looking for the poachers, but she had no one else that she could turn to right now. Besides, she had no intentions of spending another night alone with Jared.

Feeling better at having made her decision, Leigh retraced her steps to where Jared waited for her back at the makeshift camp.

. . .

Jared wasn't sure about this plan, but he had to admit that he was intrigued. Leigh wanted to go and meet up with a man who had barely been seen in over twenty years. Also, he had to admit that no one would think of looking for them in the mountains. He just wasn't sure why she thought hiding out with a hermit was the safest choice. For all he knew, Old Billy could have been the one taking potshots at them.

As Leigh marched up the ancient path ahead of him, Jared kept coming back to the question of how she knew so much about the area. He wasn't buying the "I read about it at the library" or "Cole gave me the information" crap. The Cole he knew didn't give out any information that didn't benefit Cole.

It was a crazy thought, but it was almost as if she had grown up in the area. That didn't seem likely though, because Jared would have recognized her, or at least heard of her if she had been a local girl. Ramsey wasn't a big town so people knew everyone, if not generations of their family, whether you wanted them to or not.

Jared definitely would have remembered such a beautiful girl. Especially one so smart and resourceful. Leigh had kept her cool and had saved their hides back there. She wasn't anything like Debbie, his ex-fiancé, who had told him she loved him, but that she wasn't going to wait around for him when he got sent away on assignments for weeks and months at a time. Debbie had wanted him to get a nice safe job, like taking pictures of babies or weddings; wanted him to be home every night so that they could socialize with her friends. Shaking his head at the memories, he barely noticed that the air was becoming slightly cooler and the trail more difficult.

To be fair, Debbie hadn't known the importance of what he did or how his real work helped to make the world a safer place. She hadn't appreciated the risks that he was taking nor the danger that staying with him could have put her in.

Jared wasn't all that surprised when Debbie had packed her bags and left while he was away on assignment. Now she was married to a dentist and had two kids, with another one on the way. He was happy for her. He had thought that he had loved her back then but now he knew that he hadn't. If he had loved her, he would have gone after her and done anything to get her back. Even give up his job.

Dragging his attention back to the present, Jared wondered if Leigh would do the same thing in Debbie's place. Would she be able to deal with his job? Not knowing where he was because he was undercover and in so deep that no one could get a hold of him? Would she try to make him quit and settle him down too?

Well, he would never know, because he couldn't afford to get close to anyone. Today had proved that someone might have found out about his cover and he had inadvertently put Leigh in danger. Even if they hadn't discovered his location, it just went to show that any aspect of his work could be dangerous. Hell, he could fall off the side of a mountain.

• • •

When they came to a rocky incline of the almost nonexistent path, Leigh stopped to take a swig from her water bottle. Jared drew up beside her and pulled out his own bottle. As he took a sip, he noticed that she refused to look at him, causing him to bite back a grin.

Jared was secretly pleased that she had gotten so mad with him earlier. It was obvious that she was attracted to him and he had almost lost control. She was totally pissed at him now, thinking that he didn't care and that her anger was feeding his ego. If she hadn't pulled away from him when she did then they would still be in that cave, enjoying each other. He didn't dare let his thoughts take that turn in his imagination.

Thinking back to when she had pulled away, he realized that it was when he had used her name. He'd bet anything that Leigh wasn't her real name at all. His investigative instincts told him that she was hiding from something, or someone. He just couldn't figure out why she would come here, to nowhere USA. Big cities were better to lose yourself in. Here, newcomers stood out like sore thumbs. That's why he believed that the poachers had to have some local connection, otherwise people would have talked about seeing strangers around.

Leigh was a small distance ahead of him when the thought hit him. Could Leigh have something to do with the poachers? Had she made his cover? The notion almost stopped him in his tracks. Damn, why hadn't he put that together earlier? It could explain why she knew things about the park and the mine that even a seasoned ranger might not know.

He watched as she stumbled on a root in the path and had to grab onto a small tree to stop herself from falling. Had he been the only target of the arsonist today and she had saved him because she had inadvertently been trapped too? Or had she set it up to throw him off track?

Now she was leading him into the mountains, miles from any civilization to meet with whom? A hermit? Or the poachers? How would she explain his disappearance? Damn it! If it was true then he had bought her charade hook, line and sinker.

Out of habit, Jared checked for his revolver and felt relieved when he felt the weight of it next to his hip. He had the advantage right at that moment. If she was part of the poaching operation, then he would be ready. If it turned out that he was wrong, he'd see where she led him. One way or the other, he was going to figure out what was going on and what secret she was hiding.

# CHAPTER TEN

Jessie had been up all night making plans with Gertie. There was only one way to stop what was going on and it wasn't going to be easy, but they had both known that this day would come, eventually. There had been some hard phone calls to make, but once the sun had started to rise, things that should have been done ten years before had been set into motion. The worst part was thinking that they had saved Amanda all those years ago just to have her become a victim anyway.

There was still one more call that she needed to make but Jessie was holding out, praying that Amanda and Jared would be found alive. Now, as she paced her small living room, the phone rang. Shadoe was curled up on the rug keeping track of her with his eyes. He had raised his head at the sound, and she could have sworn that she saw encouragement in those big brown eyes.

"Hello?" she grabbed the receiver before it had a chance to ring again, putting a hand over her racing heart as it slammed into her chest. Her knees gave out and she sank down to sit on the worn couch when she heard Gus's voice.

"There were no bodies," he told her without preamble. "Second fire was set with gunpowder and gasoline, just like the first. Son-of-a-bitch knew exactly where I was going to send her." A brief pause. "He ambushed them and must have fired off a couple of shots to keep them in the burn area. There were some bullet holes in a few trees. If they got out alive, the only way out was to take the flume down the side of the gorge, but it would have been a long shot."

Jessie could hear the resignation in his voice and she knew that he was afraid to hope. She could hear the guilt that they had allowed this to happen, again.

"If there are no bodies then it must mean that they got away, or he took them hostage, but either way it means that they could still be alive."

"He doesn't take hostages," Gus told her bluntly. "He takes trophies. Think about it, why go to all that trouble and then take them alive? No, I'm betting Amanda backtracked on him and took the flume down. I'm guessing that she and Jared are hiding out somewhere. He'll be hunting them if he finds out they ain't dead. This is sure goin' to piss him off. If they did make it out then we need to find them, before he does."

Jessie closed her eyes and took a deep breath. At least there was some hope. Amanda had escaped from him once before. She was a smart girl. Surely she could have escaped him again.

At least this time Amanda wasn't alone. Jared would protect her. Glancing down at Shadoe, who was back to dozing on her braided rug, she told Gus, "Gertie and I have made some phone calls. This has got to stop, right now. We should have never let it get to this point. Gertie talked to Dean and he agreed."

"Have you called …?"

It was the one call that she had been putting off, not sure what to say.

"Not yet, but I can't postpone it any longer. He'll be devastated if she's dead."

"He needs to be told," Gus said, the resignation back in his voice. "I'll let you know if we find them."

With that he hung up.

Jessie rubbed the back of her neck as she replaced the receiver onto the cradle. Suddenly she felt very old. Knowing that she couldn't procrastinate forever, she stood and walked slowly to the small secretary desk in the corner. Pulling out a drawer, she turned it over and looked at the piece of paper that had been taped to the underside. It had yellowed with age. Carefully peeling it free, she returned to the couch and sat back down. Shadoe didn't stir as Jessie slowly unfolded the paper and stared at the number that was written on it.

Quickly, before she lost the nerve, she picked up the receiver and punched in the numbers. Her heart pounded as she heard it ring on the other end. *"God help us,"* she thought as a voice from the past answered her call.

# CHAPTER ELEVEN

Strategically placed in such a way that the occupant would have a clear view of anyone approaching, the hermit's cabin was tucked against the side of the mountain. Located just outside the western boundary of the park, it blended so well with its surroundings that they were almost upon it before Jared realized it was there.

The modest structure was made from logs and had a stone chimney. A small wisp of smoke curled upward from the flue but was dispersed by the trees, making it almost undetectable. A rustic log fence protected the vegetable garden that had been planted in the front of the house. Chickens scratched in the dirt and a cow mooed in the distance. Everything had an appearance of being well taken care of.

It made Jared nervous that no one had questioned their approach. It was far too quiet. The cabin didn't appear to be a place where poachers would hide out but was more of a carefully maintained homestead. Feeling like a fool for letting Leigh talk him into following her, Jared grabbed Leigh's arm and pulled her to the side of the trail, about five hundred feet from the cabin.

"What are you doing?" she gasped.

"Being careful. How do I know this isn't a trap?" He kept his voice low and his eyes on the cabin.

"What the hell are you talking about?"

"A trap," he repeated. "How do I know that you haven't been lying about more than what your name is, because we both know that Leigh isn't your real name? You've been lying since the day you drove into town. I want to know who is in that cabin and what is going on."

She stared at him like Jared had lost his mind. When she realized that he still had her arm in a vise-like grip, she wrenched it free and gave him a withering look. "I am tired and not in the mood for riddles. I want to sit down and have a large, cold glass of water and possibly sleep for a week. We talked about this. Billy, who was a friend of my father's, is in that cabin with maybe a dog or two. Other than that you'll have to just trust me."

Trusting her was the last thing he wanted to do but he had agreed to come this far so he saw no option of backing out now.

"Fine," he huffed, "but if this is an ambush, you'll be the first one I shoot."

Rolling her eyes, Leigh stepped back out onto the trail and started for the cabin. Reaching the gate, she fumbled for the latch as the cabin door opened a crack and a shotgun barrel appeared in the space.

"That's about far enough," a voice growled from inside the dwelling.

Jared moved to grab Leigh but she stopped him with a withering glare.

"Billy!" she called out. "It's okay; it's me, Morning Star."

"Morning Star?" the gruff voice repeated.

The door opened wider, revealing a Native American man dressed in a camouflage jacket, buckskin pants and tall moccasins that reached his knees. It was impossible to guess his age despite the shoulder length black hair, streaked with gray, that was pulled off his face with a leather tie. His lined face could have been carved from stone, for all the emotion it showed, but his eyes became alive as they fixed on Leigh. He didn't lower the shotgun as his gaze moved quickly to Jared.

"Jared is an acquaintance of mine," she said, answering his unasked question.

Billy stared at Jared before lowering the rifle and holding out his arms towards Leigh.

She was already pushing open the gate and stepped into his embrace with a strong air of familiarity.

"I've missed this place," she whispered. "I've missed you, Billy." It felt wonderful to be held by someone who knew her. She had been away for far too long

"What have you done, coming back here, little one?" Billy asked softly.

The name brought back a flood of memories: Leigh and her father bringing supplies up to the cabin when the weather got too cold for Billy to make his trek down the mountain; hours spent listening to stories of the old days and Indian legends, the most memorable being the night she earned her Indian name, the year that she had turned twelve.

The rite of passage was usually reserved to prepare Indian boys for manhood, but Leigh had nagged Billy until he'd agreed to blindfold her and lead her deep into the forest. Billy had performed a ceremony, asking the spirits of the woods to help to protect her, and to give her a vision for her future. He had sat her on a tree stump, told her not to move from the stump or remove the blindfold, no matter what, until the next morning, when he would come back for her. He had warned her that she needed to be brave and trust that the ancient spirits would protect her. Removing the blindfold prematurely would dishonor herself and her family.

Wolves and mountain lions had roamed the forest all around where she'd sat that night. Leigh could hear them calling to each other in the distance as they hunted in the dark. She had been terrified by the sense of bugs crawling on her skin, but she had not removed the blindfold, not until Billy came back.

She had been so proud of herself the next morning. Billy had asked her what vision the spirits had shown her. Confused, at first, about what had occupied her mind while blindfolded, Leigh shared her vision of an avalanche that had wiped out everything in its path, but when she had gotten closer to the bottom of the mountain, she had found that roses were growing in the snow. Billy had nodded, thoughtfully, before he conducted a small ceremony that thanked the spirits for the vision. He then gave her a Shoshone name, Morning Star, because that was the first thing she had seen when she'd removed the blindfold. It was several months later when she found out that her father and Billy had been camped out within sight of her the whole night. She had not been alone after all.

It was that same courage that had seen Leigh through the death of her mother, then losing her uncle and father, two years later. She understood now that the vision had been showing her the death of her family, but Leigh still couldn't figure out what the roses were meant to represent.

• • •

Leigh caught Billy's questioning look and shook her head slightly as she glanced at Jared. Billy's eyes brightened as he, too, glanced at Jared. He stepped forward and held out his hand.

"Any friend of Morning Star is welcome in my home," he said.

Nodding, Jared took the offered hand.

"Come in," Billy invited them up the steps and into the cabin.

As soon as she entered, it was obvious to Leigh that nothing had changed in the ten years that she had been gone.

A large stone fireplace sat in the center of the one-room cabin and a low banked fire glowed in the hearth. A Dutch oven was nestled in the hot ashes, giving off an appetizing aroma.

To the left of the door were several tables, each one covered with fresh herbs and produce. Canning jars sat on a counter nearby. Dried herbs, onions and plants hung from the rafters. To the right of the door was a kitchen area containing an old-fashioned wood cooking stove that dominated one wall. Leigh smiled to see the patch of worn floorboards in front of the soapstone sink, which had a pump handle on one end. She'd seen Billy stand in front of that sink many times as he looked out the small window, watching anyone who made their way up the mountain side.

Bright colored enamel cups and bowls had been neatly arranged on shelves that were nailed to the log walls. The uneven, smooth wood floor was decorated with colorful woven rugs. Billy's bed, a pallet with bright quilts, was pushed against the back wall.

It looked like every usable space in the cabin was functional. Unlit kerosene lanterns hung from rustic iron brackets, and even though it was a bright day, the room was dark because the small windows didn't let in a lot of light. Billy mostly used candles to see by, saving the lanterns for special occasions, to ration the oil.

Billy mainly lived off the land, but there were a few things, other than the kerosene, that he would have to buy. He had a sweet tooth, so a large crock of jellybeans was set on the floor next to his armchair.

Relief washed over Leigh at the sight of the familiar, yet out of place, lounger. It gave her peace knowing that it, too, was still there.

Looking around, she realized that this was the one place where she had always felt safe. She knew that Billy had alarms set all around the cabin, and halfway down the mountainside, to warn him of anyone approaching. She had never understood his paranoia and aversion to strangers, but right now she was grateful for it.

Pulling out a chair at the table, she sat down. Jared was at the sink and she watched as he ran his hand over the shelves before grabbing two glasses. He pumped some water into them from the old-fashioned handle and brought one over to her. She smiled at him. Billy had taken the seat across from her.

"So, how have you been Billy?" She didn't know where to begin.

"Good," was his reply.

Leigh had forgotten that Billy wasn't one to waste two words when one would suffice; he was like Gus in that way. Without revealing a lot of information that she didn't want Jared to hear, she was at a loss as to what to say next.

Jared inadvertently came to the rescue by asking, "Do you mind if I take some pictures of your place, Billy? Basic shots of a mountain cabin, the gardens and your canned goods? Stuff like that."

Billy looked confused for a moment, until Jared explained about his photo assignment.

"Nothing to identify where I am," was Billy's answer.

With Billy's approval, Jared started snapping photographs. A few minutes later, he headed out the door and left the two friends alone.

Again, Leigh was at a loss as where to start; she had so much that she wanted to say.

"I'm so happy to see you," she said quietly.

Billy had been like a grandfather to her. He had never spoken about his real family and had always lived in this cabin for as long as she could remember. There was the rare occasion when he had come to her house and had dinner or celebrated a holiday or birthday. That all seemed like a lifetime ago.

"I have missed you, too, little one. I have thought of you many times over the years. Celeste kept me up to date, whenever she could, but it's not the same as seeing you."

He closed his eyes as a rare smile crossed his face. "You have grown into the beautiful woman that I had foreseen in my dreams." The smile faded. "You are looking for justice, but you should not have come back. Things have been quiet. I'm afraid that is about to change. The poachers have come and gone through the years. The signs show that they have returned to the park for something big. You should not be here. Go back to Celeste's and find the destiny that was written for you."

It was the longest speech she had ever heard from Billy. Tears pricked her eyes. "I can't go back. They murdered my family. They may as well have murdered me too. I know I didn't get tossed over the side of the Gorge, but I have felt the pain of loss every day since."

Standing up and walking over to the window, Leigh could see Jared across the yard. He was staring intently off into the distance but as she watched, he turned and looked back at the house, staring straight at her. It was impossible, but she felt as if he could hear her. She turned and looked back at Billy. "I'm not trying to be a hero here. I just want to find out who they are and bring them to justice. I owe my father and uncle at least that much."

"Your father would want you to stay far away from here. To be safe." Billy was adamant.

Again, Leigh looked out the window but this time she was looking at the past. She couldn't see the future. She leaned her forehead against the smooth glass. "I guess we'll never know what my father wanted." She turned to Billy again. "I need to do this, Billy. I need to finish what they started. Besides, they know I'm alive. I'll never be able to live in peace until they are caught."

Billy let out a sigh and met her gaze. Then he nodded.

• • •

Outside, Jared removed the earphone from his right ear and swept his eyes over the landscape. Neither Billy nor Leigh had noticed him place the electronic bug on one of the pantry shelves, behind some mugs. He knew that Leigh wouldn't have talked openly to Billy with him in the room. Instinct had warned him that there was much more going on here, but he had never expected to overhear that Leigh was in fact Amanda Whittier.

Of course, she hadn't come straight out and said her real name, but she had said enough. Jared couldn't believe how stupid he'd been. It hadn't occurred to him that Amanda was still alive. All the signs were there, as to whom she really was, yet he had never connected the dots, distracted by a beautiful face. No wonder she had known all about the park. She had been raised in it. Some investigative reporter he was – it was surprising that he could find his own ass to wipe it!

Lifting his camera, Jared took some random shots of the distant mountain range but his mind was focused on Leigh. She was a complication that he didn't need, and his bosses certainly weren't going to be happy about this development. He felt a flash of anger at the thought that she had willingly come back to the park and put herself in danger. How was he going to get her out of his investigation? Leigh, or should he call her Amanda, wouldn't leave without a fight.

Continuing down the slope, Jared slipped into the cover of trees, out of sight of the cabin. Leaning up against a tree trunk, he thought back to the day of the Whittier funerals. According to news reports, officials had only found one body, Leigh's father; no, Jared corrected himself, Amanda's father. Most of the county had attended the service, since it was the most sensational thing that had happened in decades. He had been working an internship at the local newspaper and had been assigned to cover the story, along with another reporter. It had made a lasting impression on him, shaking him to his core to realize that violence could happen to anyone, anywhere, even a young girl from his hometown. If he was honest with himself, Jared would have to admit that it was the reason he'd become a photojournalist and investigative reporter. Maybe, deep down, it was the reason that he had accepted this mission when it had been offered to him.

Jared was surprised to find out that it had all been a cover-up. It would have taken some serious strings to pull off the suicide/murder angle and then wipe out all traces of poachers. The only person with that kind of money in the area was Dean Langford, but Jared hadn't been able to tie the good ole Senator to anything more than a parking ticket. It was just a gut feeling that somehow Langford was involved. What he couldn't figure out was how? Why would someone cover for a bunch of poachers? It made no sense.

Finding out that Amanda was alive changed everything. Was she right, did the poachers know that she was alive? Was the recent attempt on their lives related to her past and not his? The thought unnerved him. He hoped that Leigh wasn't the target.

"Damn," he muttered out loud. Pushing himself away from the tree, he made his way back out to the open slope and started back up toward the cabin.

How was he supposed to keep her safe and continue on his mission? Sitting down on a makeshift bench outside of the barn, Jared leaned back against the rough wood and closed his eyes to contemplate the question. The blazing sun's rays were blocked by the leaves of the trees, creating a dappled shade. Chickens scratched in the dirt at his feet and he could hear the cow moving around in the wooded area behind him. At least Billy had sounded like he shared Jared's opinion. Maybe the two of them could talk Amanda into some semblance of reason. *And maybe the poachers will just turn themselves in and we can all go home happy*, he thought with a snort. Well, he'd better come up with a plan soon, because if the poachers were aware that Amanda had returned, there was no telling when they would strike. Glancing at the cabin, he pushed himself away from the wall and strode purposely toward it.

. . .

Leigh watched as Jared crossed the distance from the barn to the cabin. His stride was that of a man on a mission. Somehow that didn't seem to bode well for her but she wasn't sure why.

Deliberately keeping her back to the door, she did her best to ignore Jared even though every fiber of her being was aware of him. What was it about the man that made her so attracted to him? Maybe the high altitude was to blame, not enough oxygen to her brain cells. She heard him greet Billy, who was working at a table in the corner.

Jared seemed to suck up all the air in the room, and for a brief moment, all she could think of was that she needed CPR.

Taking a deep breath, she turned to grab the two glasses from the table then walked over to the sink. It only took her a couple of minutes to wash them. With that done, she had no choice but to turn and look at the two men.

Billy was still seated at the table, his back to her. Jared was sitting next to Billy, astride a chair, facing her. There was an odd expression on his face as he nodded his head in acknowledgement of her presence but she couldn't tell what Jared was thinking. Was it her imagination, or did she detect a subtle difference in his attitude? Gone was the cocky, egotistical jerk that she had become used to and in its place was a quiet, reserved stranger. It was surprising to realize that she had become accustomed to his teasing and devil-may-care attitude.

Moving to the other side of the table, she pulled out a chair and sat down. The silence was unbearable. She had to speak. "Do you still have extra cell phones Billy? Mine was broken in the fire."

She had filled Billy in, regarding the attempt on her and Jared's lives, while Jared had been out of the cabin. It had only made Billy more adamant about her going back to Celeste's.

Billy nodded. "Why would you need a phone? Once I put your number in it, they will be able to trace you."

"Good question," Jared chimed in.

Leigh glared at him before turning back to Billy.

"I'll need to get in touch with Celeste. If she somehow hears that I'm missing, then she's going to assume the worst. I can also monitor online the progress of the fire and how the investigation is going. You know how to set it up so they can't trace my number. I'm assuming that you still have untraceable Wi-Fi still hooked up?"

Billy gave a boyish grin. "It's the only way I can catch my baseball games," he admitted.

Jared looked stunned. "I thought you lived simply, off the land and all that?"

Leigh laughed. "Billy has a few modern conveniences that he can't do without. Like a small solar generator out back so we can flush the toilet and take a hot shower."

The look on Jared's face was priceless. "Thank god. I thought we were going to have to use an outhouse and bathe in a copper tub after heating our water on the stove."

Billy chuckled as he stood. "I may be old-fashioned, but I'm too old to be freezing my ass off using some damn outhouse and lugging water for baths. I'm entitled to a few modern comforts!"

With that, he walked to a desk that was tucked into the far corner of the cabin. Opening a drawer, he pulled out a phone and a small machine with a cord, returning to the table he put them in front of Leigh. Pulling his laptop across the table, he flipped up the cover and turned it on.

There was silence as they all waited for it to boot up. Extracting an ancient set of glasses from his shirt pocket, Billy set them on his nose and started to type. Once he got to the screen he needed, he looked at Leigh. "Number?"

She told him her cell phone number and watched as he typed it in. Then he attached the small machine's cord to the laptop and typed some more.

"What exactly are you doing?" Jared asked.

Billy gave him a sideways glance over the top of his glasses. "Hacking into the phone company."

Jared's eyebrows shot up in surprise. "Hacking into the phone company? Just like that?"

Billy unplugged the machine from his computer and plugged it into the phone before he looked over at the younger man. "I'm a man of many talents. I haven't always lived my life on the side of a mountain." His eyes shifted to the kitchen area for a second. "Don't make the mistake of thinking I'm some old fool."

Leigh was mystified at the message that he was sending to Jared. It seemed that Jared got the message because he narrowed his eyes before giving a small nod of acknowledgement to Billy.

• • •

Billy had set up a pallet in the cabin for Leigh to sleep on and Jared had decided to sleep in the loft of the barn. The cow was lying in her stall and the chickens were roosted around the small space. Once in a while, one of them would squawk in its sleep and Jared had to wonder if chickens actually had dreams. How the hell would you know and why the hell was he up at some god forsaken hour thinking about it? He had retired to the barn right after dinner, hoping that Billy and Leigh would talk some more, but they must have been tired because there had been no chit chat before both had gone to bed.

Propping his head with his hands, Jared stared up at the ceiling. He had tried logging onto Billy's illegal Wi-Fi, as Leigh had called it, to do a search on Billy, but it had been secure, and he hadn't wanted to ask Billy for the password. The old coot was definitely computer savvy and Jared didn't need him to know that he was investigating him. Billy had hacked into the phone company like it was the easiest thing in the world. Jared knew several hackers who were some of the best in the world, but he'd bet money that none of them could have just done what Billy did. Which left the question, who the hell was this guy and why was he living the life of a hermit?

• • •

Rough hay poked through the thin blankets that Jared had laid down to create his bed, causing him to sit up. Judging by the lack of light coming in through the window, it was still several hours before dawn. It didn't seem likely that he was going to get to sleep anytime soon. He could usually fall asleep just about anywhere, especially after the kind of exhausting day he'd had with Leigh. "Amanda," he corrected himself out loud.

Pulling on his boots, Jared climbed down from the small loft and walked silently to the door. He stood still in the barnyard and listened. The moon hadn't risen above the trees yet, so it was as dark as a tomb, causing the outline of the cabin to be nothing more than a mere suggestion. Tree frogs and crickets competed in an unbridled competition of noise that appeared to be coming from all around him. An owl hooted in the distance. Farther away, a coyote or fox yipped, probably looking for its mate Jared thought, as he started to walk.

Several feet from the cabin, he became aware of another sound. Flattening himself to the ground, Jared heard the click of a door closing quietly. The silhouette of Billy came into view and Jared watched as he headed down the open slope, without looking left or right. Billy was wearing dark clothing that blended into the night. He made no noise as he walked. After giving Billy a few minutes head start, Jared started to follow.

Jared had always prided himself on his sleuthing prowess, but as he followed the silent older man, he cringed. It seemed that tonight he was stepping on every blade of dry grass and brittle stick, which made fireworks sound quiet by comparison. Surely the older man had heard him stumbling through the woods not far behind him. Jared could see Billy's outline a couple of hundred feet ahead of him but Billy didn't slow down nor turn around to confront him.

They had been walking this way for about ten minutes when Billy stopped at the edge of a clearing. Jared moved to the right and crouched down by the stump of a rotting tree. From its earthy smell and spongy bark, he guessed it had fallen several years before.

Billy stood stock still, as if he was listening for something, or someone. The moon was cresting the trees to Jared's left, creating a little more play of shadows, yet nothing moved.

Was this some sort of Indian ceremony for the rising moon? Jared wondered. He didn't think so. His knew to stay put. Minutes passed, and Jared's muscles began to cramp, but he stayed crouched and motionless; his gut instincts had never failed him. Something important was about go down and he wanted to be there, to see what Billy was waiting for. Over fifteen minutes had elapsed and the cramp in his right leg had become excruciating. When he suddenly saw Billy stiffen, Jared wasn't even sure he could stand up.

Pushing back the pain in his leg, Jared watched the older man step behind a tree, then raise a pair of binoculars. Even from this distance, Jared was able to make out that they were night binoculars, military if he was to take a guess.

*What the hell is he doing with government issued night gear?* Jared knew binoculars like that would be invaluable to someone who wanted to hunt animals at night. They would give them an advantage of tracking an animal without the warning of flashlights. Or tracking rangers, for that matter. Which begged the question, was Billy part of the poaching operation?

Leigh couldn't have known, he surmised. She had said that Billy was an old friend of her father's, and it was obvious from his greeting that the old man had been genuinely concerned to see her.

As Jared sat debating about Billy, he became aware of the unmistakable sound of a helicopter approaching. Looking toward the clearing, he scanned the darkened sky. The sound of the chopper's engine was low, and the blades made a rhythmical whooshing sound that broke the silence. Jared couldn't see anything, but when he looked over at Billy, the older man was following something in the sky with his binoculars. Concentrating on the direction Billy was looking, Jared could just make out a small helicopter as it crossed the star-studded sky in front of him. The copter's running lights were off and the aircraft seemed to be flying low, as if to stay under radar level. As it got closer, he saw a soft glow in the cockpit from the instrument panel. The next moment, the craft was gone, the sound of it dissolving back into the night.

Jared watched Billy pull something from his vest pocket before checking the time by the glow of his watch. In the dim light, it looked like he was writing something down before stuffing the objects back into his shirt pocket.

The older man turned and started to walk directly toward Jared's hiding spot. Without trying to move too much, Jared pressed himself closer to the oak's trunk. Billy stopped abreast of the tree and stood still for a moment.

Jared could just make out the faint outline of his body against the dark shadows of undergrowth. He closed his eyes and waited for the older man to speak. Billy didn't turn, nor say anything, he just started walking again, whistling under his breath.

Jared allowed a few minutes to pass and then he raised himself up enough to turn and sit on the soft bark. The balls of his feet were numb and his left calf muscle felt as if it was being stabbed. Gritting his teeth, he began the painful process of massaging the knot of muscles, trying to loosen them.

Jared realized that Billy must have heard him following, and had known all along that he was crouched behind the fallen tree, but why hadn't he called him out? Why had Billy let him see the helicopter and then leave without saying a word about it?

Billy must have known the helicopter was going to show up at exactly the time it did. It wasn't even dawn yet, so it was no coincidence that Billy had been at the edge of the clearing when the helicopter passed over. Only drug runners and other criminals flew choppers without running lights. Why else would they want to fly under the radar? Jared assumed they had to be flying by instruments alone, so as not to hit any trees. It was a calculated risk, considering a down draft could pull the chopper into the trees, causing it to crash.

Standing carefully, Jared felt his leg muscle relax enough to take a few tentative steps to the spot where Billy had stood to peer through his binoculars. The chopper had come out of the east. The nearest city or town in that direction was at least fifty miles away. There were no airstrips in the area that Jared knew about. That didn't mean that there weren't places to land a helicopter though.

Jared swore as he ran his fingers through his hair. He wanted to get back to civilization and to his computer. There were a lot of things going on, and he needed to find some answers, but it didn't look like he was going to get them anytime soon. If only he could acquire the password to Billy's computer. He felt certain that Billy wasn't about to give it to him. That left Leigh.

An owl hooted off to his right. Jared realized that the sky was starting to lighten as shapes that had been walls of darkness began to separate, becoming more recognizable by the second. As his eyes adjusted to the mute, predawn light, his mind locked onto a way to coax Leigh to give him the password. Whistling softly to himself, he turned to make his way back to Billy's cabin.

•  •  •

The moment Leigh opened the cabin door she was hit by a wall of heat.

It was a little before seven in the morning, but the temperature was already climbing into the low eighties. It was usually ten to twenty degrees cooler in the higher elevations, so if it was this hot here, Leigh knew it must be stifling down in the valley. Looking up at the cloudless blue sky, she longed for rain. Even though the cabin was in the shade, it was still muggy and sticky inside. Billy had kept a low fire burning in the stove and also in the fireplace all night, which just added to the oppressiveness of the small space. She had tossed and turned on her makeshift bed on the floor all night.

Wiping away a bead of sweat from her forehead, Leigh watched Jared walk confidently out of the barn. His blond hair glowed in the sun's rays and he was looking curiously well rested, even sporting a change of clothes. She glared at him, assuming that he had obviously grabbed some clothes when they had gone back to his house to get supplies. Leigh felt positively grubby after two days of sweating in her ranger uniform. She was about to duck back into the cabin when she stopped in response to Jared calling her name. Placing a bright smile on her face, she waited for him to reach the fence.

"I've been waiting for you to wake up," he announced. As always, his grin had a rakish air about it. "We've lost half the day already."

Irritation coursed through her, but she tamped it down. "Didn't realize you were such an early riser," she told him stiffly. "I'm more of a night person."

Not sure why she was even defending herself, Leigh closed the cabin door behind her, stepped through the gate and headed for the barn.

Jared fell in step with her. A quick glance at his face showed that he was still grinning.

The barn door was left open so Leigh walked hastily over to the stall that held the cow. Opening the lid to the metal trash can that was stored in front of the stall, she bent over to scoop up a coffee can of sweet oats. Straightening, she turned around in time to see Jared staring at her rear end with a gleam in his eyes that she didn't appreciate. "Just what do you think you're doing?" she demanded, feeling her face flush.

Blushing so easily was one of the things she hated about being fair-skinned. His grin, if it was even possible, grew even more lethal.

"Just admiring the view," was the outrageous reply.

Leigh's mouth dropped open at his audacity but before she could form a reply, he was advancing toward her, making her heart leap into her throat as adrenaline coursed through her body. Her fight or flight mechanism was temporarily frozen, but her mind cataloged the danger that he represented. Some of her thoughts must have shown on her face because his eyes narrowed as he regarded her.

All she could manage was a small squeak as Jared gently pinned her with his body up against the solid oak stall door. She dropped the can, spilling oats at their feet. The cool stall door against her lower back was in direct contrast with the warm, hard-muscled body that now pressed against her stomach, pelvis and legs.

Jared's hands began to lightly rub up and down her forearms. Leigh couldn't think straight as her nose filled with the scent of his aftershave, causing her skin to tingle where his fingers had been. His closeness made her want to get closer, to be held, cherished, protected. *Stop it! You're acting like a romance novel character. This man is dangerous and not your type!* She silently scolded.

No man had ever touched her like this before. There had been several dates in high school, with the awkward, obligatory kissing, but she had never let things go any further. She couldn't remember the last time any-one had shown her affection, since her dad had died, with the exception of an occasional hug from Celeste. Closing her eyes, Leigh willed herself to speak. "Please stop." *Was that whisper from her? In her mind she had shouted the words.*

From above her head came a chuckle and then a nibble at her right ear that almost made her knees buckle.

"I need to check my emails, but I don't have the password to the Wi-Fi," Jared whispered between nibbles of her ear lobe. "So, I've decided to find some other pursuit to occupy myself with."

Leigh's head fell back, allowing him to nibble his way down to her neck. He smelled like mountain air. Her breath kept catching in her throat as she struggled to comprehend what he was saying.

"You need the password?" she finally asked, trying to keep up with the conversation.

Another chuckle. "Is that what I need? A password?"

He pressed against her some more, then gasped as their chests collided, which gave him the opportunity to raise her chin and plunder her mouth. Leigh was lost. Wrapping her arms around his neck, she kissed him back.

Jared pulled her shirttails out of her shorts and laid his hands on the skin of her back just as the cow, clearly tired of waiting for her oats, put her head over the stall door and mooed loudly in their ears.

Leigh shot forward in surprise, pushing Jared into a backwards trip. He fell to the floor, taking Leigh with him.

Scrambling to her feet with as much grace as she could muster, Leigh put some distance between the two of them.

"So, what is it?" Jared asked, grinning up at her.

Hugging herself, she turned to look at him. "What is what?"

"The password to Billy's network? I have a few things I have to work on. I can't be playing around all day. Not that it's not tempting, mind you."

*Playing? Was that what she was to him? Some sort of game?*

Jared stopped grinning and jumped to his feet. "Look Leigh, I didn't mean that the way it came out." He stepped closer. "You know you're a beautiful wom..."

She put out a hand to stop him. "Please, don't say anything more. I have chores that need to be done."

Leigh would have fled if he hadn't grabbed her by the shoulders.

"Now hold on a minute, we have some things to discuss."

Shaking her head, she broke free from his grasp. Her emotions bubbled to the surface then exploded. "No, we don't. You think that you're a hot shot world photographer who can just crook his little finger and women come running...."

"That's award-winning world photojournalist," he corrected her quietly.

"Whatever!"

"You seemed willing enough just then," he replied, smoothing out his hair.

"You're mistaken; I'm not interested in having a casual affair with you, or anyone else!"

"Okay then, we'll have an un-casual affair. I'm not that picky."

The grin on his face infuriated her and she took a swing at him, which he ducked easily. He grabbed her arm and held it but there was no pain.

Angrily she wrenched free. "You think you are god's gift to women but you are a chauvinistic, shallow jerk and I wouldn't sleep with you for a million dollars. You have no idea who I am or any interest in knowing the real me. You are impossible." She had run out of steam, but his last comment caught her attention. "Wait, did you just say that you're not that picky?" Her voice rose in octaves and strength. "Am I supposed to be flattered or insulted?"

"Since you say you're not interested in me, what does it matter? I might not know who you are, or what games you're playing, but I definitely know who you aren't." Jared leaned forward to look her in the eye. "You aren't who you say you are, and neither is Billy. My guess is that you aren't even sure what the truth is anymore."

Leigh flinched at the closeness of his breath on her face.

"I know you say that you don't want me but your body is telling me a whole different story. You never know, you might just change your mind."

Her eyes widened as he leaned in even closer.

"I'm very good at my job and I will find out who you are and what you're hiding. When I'm through, there won't be one freckle on your body that I won't know about."

There came that grin again! Leigh felt her defenses crumbling as Jared took a few steps backward before he strolled out of the barn, leaving Leigh alone to sweep the oats back into the can.

# CHAPTER TWELVE

Shari paced around her house. Dread circled her like an invisible web, teasing her with the feeling that something bad was about to happen.

She'd been having premonitions, like a sixth sense, since she was eight years old. One night, she had woken up at three in the morning to run to her mother's bed in tears. Although she didn't understand how, she just knew that something awful had happened to her older brother. Her mother had shushed her as she tucked her back into bed. The next morning, a policeman had arrived at the door to notify them that her brother had been in a serious car accident just after 3a.m. It had taken him months to recover.

Shari had experienced other instances of foresight over the years. Now she had that same feeling again and it was making her very jumpy.

Her husband, Ben, had been helping to fight the forest fire, coming home after midnight to sleep for a few hours, and then leaving again before dawn. Firefighters had been battling the blaze for three days. Ben had called Shari at around eight o'clock that morning to tell her that the fire had been mostly contained and they were now monitoring some hot spots. It always worried her sick whenever he went out on a call so she had been relieved to hear his voice. Forest fires were some of the worst fires to fight and also the most unpredictable, which made them extremely dangerous. Her deep sense of dread had gone away after she hung up from his call so Shari had called everyone that she could think of to make sure they were all fine. Only Leigh hadn't returned her call, but that was to be expected. Like Ben, Leigh was probably out fighting the fire and catching sleep whenever she could.

Shari's daughters were playing outside on the swings and she smiled at Olivia's constant chatter, which filtered through the open windows. Poor

Sam, Shari thought, her youngest twin could never get a word in edgewise, no matter how hard she tried. The twins shared a close bond but they were definitely two very different personalities. They reminded Shari of her friendship with Amanda. She had been quiet and scared of everything, but Amanda had been outgoing and brave. Shari silently reminded herself to call her old friend Leigh.

Taking a sip of her coffee, Shari walked over to the window to watch the girls for a moment. Maybe she was just being silly. Ben was fine, the fire was just about out, and her girls were safe in their own backyard. It was time to shake off the heebie-jeebies and get to all that laundry that had been piling up for the last hectic week. Sometimes she thought she'd go mad if she saw one more blasted dirty sock!

Sighing, she was about to turn away when a movement down the driveway caught her eye. A man was walking away at a fast clip. Putting down her cup, Shari bolted out the door and headed for the driveway. In the distance, she heard a car door slam and then a car engine start. Frowning, she broke into a run, her sneakers gaining purchase on the gravel surface.

The car was gone by the time she made it to the road.

*Why would someone park on the road and walk up to the house but not come in?* she wondered.

Retracing her steps, Shari was almost back to the front yard when she smelled the unmistakable odor of a cigarette. Following the scent, she noticed ashes flecked the mulch she had put around the bushes and shrubs that edged the driveway. Looking around, she realized that this could have been where the man was standing. He would have been hidden from view from the house but could have had a clear view of her girls playing in the front yard. If the amount of ashes on the mulch and the indentations from his shoes were any indication of how long he'd been watching, then he had been there a while. Shari did not see any cigarette butts.

Panic seized her at the implication. Someone had been watching her babies! But why? Shari knew everyone in the area; had even been in most of their houses, for one occasion or another. Her head was spinning. Gulping for air, she fought against the urge to rush to her girls and scoop them up, but she didn't want to frighten them. Pasting a smile on her face, she stepped back onto the gravel driveway and walked calmly toward them.

"Mommy!" they cried in unison when they spotted her.

Kneeling down on one knee, Shari held out her arms as they both rushed at her, almost knocking her over. She held them closely for a moment. They were warm from playing and smelled like fresh air and sunshine. Closing her eyes, she hugged them even tighter before they started to squirm.

"What's wrong Mommy?" Sam wanted to know. She had always been quick to pick up on people's feelings.

"Nothing's wrong, sweetie. I just wanted a hug. I was thinking about going into town and checking in with your daddy. Maybe doing a little shopping."

Amid cheers of delight, Shari herded the twins back toward the house.

Shari snatched up her purse and car keys from the table next to the door. In her haste, she didn't notice Sam pick up her cell phone off the kitchen counter and put it in her jeans pocket. Shari wanted to get to the relative safety of town and talk to Ben about the strange man in their driveway. Her sense of foreboding was growing as she buckled the girls into the car and drove quickly down the driveway.

. . .

He'd watched Amanda's friend's house for over an hour this morning but hadn't seen any sign of Amanda. *Damn, that bitch has nine lives*, he thought as he crushed out another cigarette. Picking up the burned filter, he stuffed it in his pants pocket.

The man was parked outside the abandoned mine, having tracked Amanda and the photographer to it. Anger seethed from every pore in his body as he struggled to hold it in check. He didn't have time for this. There would be a multi-millionaire flying in for a hunt in less than a week. He didn't need this girl messing up the deal.

She had already cost him a lot of money over the past ten years. He'd been forced to go underground, change locations every few months, before anyone had caught on that he was operating in the area again. The black market was demanding more of his product and would look elsewhere if he couldn't deliver. It had taken him years to build up his clientele and network. Bears, lions and other exotics were hard to find and even harder to smuggle. Zoos were keeping better track of their inventory and bribing an employee to hand over the animals was getting expensive.

He marveled at what the rich could get away with and the amount of money they would spend to get what they wanted. Of course, they all aspired to being trophy hunters, yet they didn't want to have to go in to the wild to actually hunt down the animal. God forbid they get their lily-white hands dirty. No, these clients liked to be driven out to a site where the prize would already be drugged. An easy target, just sitting there waiting to be shot. And man would these guys pay handsomely for the thrill of it. They usually just took the head, to be mounted on a wall in one of their houses, after having had their triumphant photographs taken with the prize. This left the poacher free to sell the rest of the body parts for a nice little profit, in addition to his sport fee.

But this deal was different. This job meant more than the six-figure price tag that he usually charged. This client could open up doors to all the right people. All he had to do was deliver a rare black panther for the trophy case and he was in. Top traders would seek him out for their product. He could name his price.

Unfortunately, he still had the problem of the girl to deal with. It was just his crap luck that they hadn't found two bodies in the burn area. *How the hell had she made it out of there?*

Lighting another cigarette, the man stared at the opening to the mine. Amanda had escaped from him again and he knew that she could wait him out. If he didn't have so much riding on this next client, he would relish hunting her down. He needed to lure her out quickly, but how? What bait would persuade her to come to him alone? His mind locked on the image of the girls playing in the friend's front yard.

Rolling the cigarette between his fingers to force the hot ashes to drop to the ground, he put the unlit filter into his pants' pocket, then inhaled deeply. *Of course, what female could resist sacrificing herself to save a child?* He climbed into his car and drove away.

• • •

Shari had to park a block away from Gertie's café since it seemed that half the town was there. Olivia kept up a constant chatter as they made their way along the sidewalk.

The bell tinkled above the café door when they entered but the place was so noisy that no one heard it. Every available seat had been taken and people were lined up against the wall. Gertie and several other waitresses were rushing around filling coffee cups and serving up plates of hot food. Shari craned her neck to look through the crowd and found her husband having lunch at a table on the far side of the restaurant. Breathing a sigh of relief, she made her way over to him.

Just as she reached his table, Shari felt a tug on her sleeve. Looking down she looked into Olivia's eager face.

"Can we sit at the counter and order a hot chocolate?" the little girl asked.

Feeling the safety in numbers, Shari agreed, then turned her attention to telling Ben about the events of the morning.

• • •

Samantha felt very grown up after she'd climbed onto the newly vacated stool. She and Olivia ordered hot chocolates and sipped at their treat in silence. They really didn't talk much to each other. They got bored quickly, after all, most of the time they knew what the other was thinking. Samantha watched as Olivia started talking to the customer sitting next to her. She was always so bossy! Sometimes Samantha felt jealous of her sister because Olivia was so quick to make friends. She wasn't afraid to go anywhere or do anything. Samantha wanted to be brave, too, but she always had to think things over before she did them. Olivia teased her for being slow because by the time she'd made up her mind to do something, the fun was usually over.

Samantha looked around the café as her sister's voice chattered loudly. Out the window, she noticed a boy across the street that was holding a puppy. There was a cage next to him. Samantha's heart raced when she saw several other puppies were looking out the wired door, their tails wagging.

"Goldens!" she exclaimed excitedly.

She wanted a dog very badly and the golden retriever was high on her list of favorite dogs. She turned to get Olivia's attention but then thought better of it. Olivia was always hogging the limelight. If she had Olivia go with her to see the puppies, then Olivia would be the one to pick out the puppy, and that wouldn't be fair because Samantha had seen them first.

A quick glance over at their parents showed that they were deep into a serious-looking conversation. *Should I tell them where I'm going?* Samantha wondered. No, they would only make Olivia go with her, or tell her that she couldn't have a puppy, which would be awful. Maybe if she went and picked a puppy out, then brought it in to the café, they wouldn't be so quick to say no.

Feeling brave, Samantha slipped off the stool and headed for the front of the cafe. No one noticed her open the door and slip outside. As she made her way to the edge of the sidewalk, she suddenly remembered that she was not supposed to cross the street, except at a cross walk. Samantha walked quickly to the corner traffic lights and pushed the button to stop the traffic.

The 'walk' symbol soon started its countdown from ten to one, signaling that it was safe to cross the street. As Samantha stepped onto the pavement, an arm clamped around her waist and yanked her backwards. Before she had a chance to cry out, a hand covered her mouth. Seconds later, she was being roughly carried away from the edge of the street towards the alley behind Gertie's Cafe.

Samantha could see a car was parked at the entrance of the alley. Its trunk was already open and she was dropped inside. Before she had a chance to catch her breath, as the wind had been knocked out of her lungs, the trunk was slammed shut, enveloping Samantha in darkness.

# CHAPTER THIRTEEN

Leigh set the bowl of salad in the middle of the table with a thump. Billy was grilling chicken outside on his homemade barbeque. Thankfully, he had butchered and dressed the chickens before she had arrived back at the cabin.

Glancing over at Jared, who was sitting in Billy's armchair and staring off into space, she wondered where he had gone after leaving her at the barn. She had finished the chores, and then walked to the meadow that overlooked the park, where she had spent hours berating herself for being a fool. Against all logic and just plain common sense, she was falling in love with Jared. That was not to say that he still wasn't the most egotistical, infuriating, obnoxious man that she had ever had to deal with. Why was she so attracted to him? He was totally wrong for her on so many levels. She knew the type of man she wanted. The man of her dreams would be sensitive, gentle and not think he was god's gift to women. Her future husband would help with the chores and be home every night instead of jet setting around the world on assignments. And they would agree on everything. Throw in lots of kids and dogs running around and life would be perfect.

*Sounds boring except for the kids and dogs*, her mind argued. *He also likes dogs so maybe he likes kids too. You're just afraid to take a chance.*

Yes, she silently admitted. She was afraid of taking chances. No one knew better than she did that life could change in an instant. She was terrified of finding someone, only to lose them and be left alone again. A million times over, she had wished she'd had a brother, sisters or even a cousin. Some relative her own age to confide in, someone who knew who she was, deep down. Someone who could understand her loss and share her sorrow.

Jared was acting as if Leigh wasn't even in the room. She was surprised to find that his indifference unsettled her. She could smell his aftershave again. It made her think of him waking up, his eyes half-closed with sleep, his chest bare, sheets slipping. *Get a grip!* She was about to say something, anything to make him notice her, when Billy came in with dinner.

He set the platter next to the salad and glanced from Leigh to Jared. His eyes were thoughtful. "Come, eat."

Jared ambled over to the table and waited until Leigh and Billy were seated before he took a seat across from Leigh. Glancing up briefly, he gave her a small smile. He seemed genuinely surprised when she glowered at him.

"Are you still mad at me from this morning or have I done something new to offend you?" he asked with an arched eyebrow.

"Since you haven't even spoken to me in the last nine hours, I guess it must just be your presence."

He seemed to ponder this for a moment. Taking the salad bowl from a watchful Billy, he served himself. "I was under the impression that you weren't particularly fond of my company, so why would my silence bother you so much?" He gave her another quick grin. "Besides, I thought we um, ...communicated perfectly this morning."

He spoke these last words in a low, seductive voice that made no mistaking of his meaning. Leigh felt her cheeks get flush as his eyes roamed over her, conveying knowledge that he didn't possess. She heard Billy choke on his food and embarrassment made her react. "Seriously, Jared? You are the most conceited man I have ever met!"

His smile broadened.

"So, this morning was just a game to you?" Rising too fast from her seat sent the chair skittering backwards across the wooden floor. "Unlike you, I don't play games. If and when I 'communicate' with someone, it will be because he wants me. Not because I'm the only available female for miles. Excuse me, Billy, I've lost my appetite."

Leigh strode out of the cabin, slamming the door behind her, anger coursing through her body. *The gall of that man! What would Billy think?* Jared had made it sound as if she had spent the morning rolling around with him in the hayloft. Billy was the closest thing she had to a father and his opinion of her mattered.

As Leigh walked away from the cabin, she realized that she shouldn't have given Jared the satisfaction of a reaction; she should have just smiled sweetly and then ignored his innuendo. She kicked a small stone that was lying in the path. Leigh had spent years creating a cool, calm exterior that he could make crumble in seconds. *It's because you're falling for him. Isn't* it time to let the past go?

"No, I can't," she scolded the voice in her head.

Yes, you can. You need to move on, Amanda.

Shaking her head, she hurried down the mountain until she found an outcropping of large rocks. She sat down to take in the 180-degree view of the valley.

Leigh had spent the last ten years planning her return to Ramsey so that she could find out who the poachers were and have them arrested. Only then could she reveal to everyone who she really was and claim her old life back. But that life had involved her father and her uncle. Could she stay here without them?

She glanced up at the sky. She wasn't a religious person, but she had to believe that things happened for a reason. The notion that the events of a decade ago had no meaning made her family's deaths useless. Something good had to come from all of this.

The cell phone in her pocket suddenly came to life, its ringtone echoing across the valley below. Brushing away a stray tear that was trailing slowly down her cheek, Leigh took out her phone and stared at Shari's number but before she could make up her mind to answer it, the ringing stopped.

It immediately rang again. Shari was probably wondering where she was and getting worried. Leigh hesitated to answer it. Would her friend keep quiet if Leigh told her that she and Jared were alright? She decided to at least put Shari's mind at ease. Besides, Leigh wanted to make sure that someone was taking care of Shadoe.

"Hey, Shari."

There was a brief silence on the other end then a small, quivering voice asked, "Leigh?"

Leigh's lungs stopped for a moment as she realized it was the voice of a child. The familiar tentacles of fear rose from her chest and wrapped themselves around her throat. Leigh mentally fought them off. "Who is this?"

"Sam." The voice cracked and rose a little. "The bad man took me and I'm scared. I want my mommy."

*What bad man? Where was Shari?* Leigh's head reeled with questions. Shari would never have left her daughter without a fight. *Was Olivia taken too?* She had to calm Sam down. The little girl was only six, she reminded herself.

Taking a few shaky breaths, Leigh asked, "Alright Sam, tell me what happened and where you are?"

The words came out in a rush. "I wanted to see the puppies and didn't want Olivia to come 'cause she would have hogged the puppy. So I went to the crosswalk, just like mommy always says to. The bad man grabbed me and put me in the car trunk."

"Are you still in the trunk?"

"No. I'm in the cellar."

"Which cellar?"

"At a house."

"Your house?"

"No. He locked the door. I can't get out."

"Where is the house? Is there a window?"

"I can't see," came the sniffled response. "It's dark down here. I'm scared."

"Use the light from the phone." It was a long shot, but Leigh was desperate. "What do you see, Sam? Tell me everything you see"

The silence dragged on until Sam finally returned to the phone.

"Some old chairs. A big pink box."

Leigh sucked in her breath. "Sam, open the box and look inside for me."

"Okay."

Leigh could hear Sam put down the phone. She closed her eyes and prayed that this was the trunk she was thought it was.

"It's open."

"Alright. Do you see stickers stuck to the lid?"

Another moment of silence.

"Yes. It says Princess. There's another one. Girl's Rule."

Leigh closed her eyes. It was her trunk! It had belonged to her uncle and he had given it to her when she was four years old. She had kept toys and other things in it for whenever she visited him. Whoever took Sam was using her uncle's house.

"Leigh?" Sam sounded nervous at her silence.

"I'm still here. Did you try to call your dad?"

"He's at Gertie's with Olivia and Mommy. I called but he didn't answer the phone. Can you come get me? Please!!! The bad man will be back soon. He said you, me and him have a date."

Leigh's heart skipped a few beats. "What else did the man say?"

A small hiccup then a light sigh. "He knows you. From a long time ago. He said you and mommy are friends. That's why he took me."

"Does he know that you have your mom's phone?"

"No. Mommy forgot it on the kitchen counter when we left for Gertie's. So I picked it up." Her voice rose again. "I'm scared Leigh! Come get me, please!"

"I'll come get you. But right now, I need you to be very brave."

"Okay."

"Sam, turn the ringer on your phone off so the man doesn't know you have it. You'll see the phone light up if someone calls it. If you see the light, I want you to answer it. Tell the person on the other end that you're at Peter Whittier's house." Another deep breath. "If the bad man comes back, I want you to do everything he tells you to do. Okay?"

"Uh-huh."

"I'll get someone to you as fast as I can."

Looking back at the valley that had been so peaceful, Leigh shuddered as a cloud dimmed the sunshine.

"Leigh?" Sam's voice sounded tearful now.

"I'm right here, sweetheart."

"The man's got a gun. He was talking on his phone and he sounded really mad. He said…." There was a muffled sob.

Before Leigh could reply, the phone went dead.

*Breathe*, she told herself. Panicking won't help Sam.

Scrolling through her contacts, Leigh hit Send when she came to Jessie's number. The line was busy. She felt sick at the thought of Sam, alone in a dark cellar, with her kidnapper.

Googling Gertie's Café, she tried to call but that line was also busy. 911 produced no result either.

Dropping her head to her knees, Leigh willed herself to breathe slowly. She needed a plan; now was not the time to rush in unprepared. Obviously, the kidnapper knew exactly who she was and that she and Jared had survived the fire. There was no doubt in her mind that this was the man who had hunted her, ten years ago, and he was now using Sam as bait to get to her.

She had put Sam right into his hands.

He must have been watching her for a while, trying to get the advantage, but not this time. She lifted her head. He didn't know that Sam had given her the ultimate weapon by taking away his element of surprise. This time, the hunter was about to become the target.

Resolve rising in her chest, Leigh began to pace back and forth. She'd have to leave tonight, without Jared and Billy knowing where she was going. She couldn't risk them trying to stop her. Going with her could get them killed.

Adrenaline replaced fear. It coursed through her, filling her with determination to finally confront the man who had destroyed her family. She would stare right into his eyes. The potential scene in the courtroom, after he was captured and locked up, had replayed in her head thousands of times. Turning back to look over the valley one more time, she finalized her plans.

Gertie's dogs were barking, as her mother used to say, whenever her own feet were aching. Gertie had been serving food since dawn and couldn't remember the last time she'd sat down. What she wouldn't give to put her feet up and relax for a few minutes. She was sure most of the rangers and firefighters were packed into her café. In fact, it felt as if most of the town was crowded into her small restaurant. It would probably be quicker for her to name the people who weren't there.

Shari and the twins had arrived a little while ago. Those girls were sure getting big. It seemed like only yesterday when Shari had brought them in for the first time. They had yawned in sync, their tiny fists waving in the air, looking like porcelain china dolls. Now they were old enough to sit at the counter all by themselves. They had acted so grown up when she'd served their hot chocolate but they had both giggled when she had squirted some whipped cream on their drinks.

Gertie glanced over to where the twins were sitting and was surprised to see Olivia was alone, talking to Maggie, the librarian. It was unusual to see one girl without the other. One of the Clark girls had taken the stool that Samantha had been sitting on. Craning her head to look through the crowd, Gertie located Shari talking to her husband in a booth. Samantha wasn't with them. Further searching of the crowded dining room didn't reveal the missing twin. Making her way through the mass of bodies, Gertie looked in the ladies' room but Samantha wasn't there either.

A shiver curved its way down her spine. She shook it off. She must just be getting fanciful in her old age. Her parents didn't look concerned. Sam couldn't have gone far, besides, she had been in a room full of people. Maybe Samantha had left with a friend. This was Ramsey, Idaho, small town

USA, after all.

"Hey, Gertie!" One of the waitresses yelled from behind the counter. "Phone's out again."

"Great," huffed Gertie as she made her way to the phone. Just what she *didn't* need today. Damn phone was always going out. Most likely everyone in the county was on the lines, getting updates about the fire. They'd probably overloaded the circuits, again. She'd have to call the phone company on her cell phone, which was in her purse in the storeroom, because she hated carrying it around. Wouldn't even have the darn thing, if she had the choice, but the modern world made having one a necessity. Cell service in the area was spotty, at best, with all the surrounding mountains in the way.

"We're almost out of bacon," the cook yelled to her as she was heading through the kitchen. "And the toaster is on the blitz again."

Gertie stopped to rub her eyes. She was getting too old to run a business like this. She had been toying with the idea of selling the cafe and heading south to one of those warm beach resorts they were always advertising on TV. On days like these, she was actually tempted to do it, too. Taking in a deep breath, she turned to examine the broken toaster.

* * *

Cole lay in bed and stared at the ceiling. He had been out late last night and was in no rush to get up. He'd been through Mark Whittier's old house from top to bottom; his muscles groaning at the memory. If Mark had hidden anything there, then it wasn't in the house. Cole didn't have the time or the resources to dig up the entire property.

He'd also checked every courthouse and land office in the county, never mind half the state. If there had been a map showing another vein of silver in the mine then he should have been able to find it. Cole considered that the source of his information had just as much to gain as he did. It didn't make sense that he would lie to him. That map had to be somewhere.

Being the son of a senator had its perks but it also had lots of downfalls. His father liked to dictate every move that his youngest son made. His older brother, Kyle, had been lucky to get out when he did, Cole thought. He still didn't know what the falling out between his father and Kyle entailed, but sometimes he was envious. It had been years since he had seen his older brother. Last he knew, Kyle was in Australia, or was it Africa? It was always some place far from dear old dad.

Putting his arms behind his head, Cole thought about his next move. Maybe he should check out the brother's house. Peter was younger than Mark, but it still seemed possible that he might have kept any important family documents. If only there had been some way to find out where all of the Whittier possessions had gone after the funerals. There had been no surviving relative to inherit anything. He'd heard that everything had been placed in a trust and had basically disappeared. If it had gone to some distant relative, then he might have been able to persuade them into giving him the document. Without it, he wouldn't be able to get the bankroll he needed to finance his endeavor.

Cole stifled a yawn. Turning over, he decided that he needed some more sleep before he tackled another demolition job. Closing his eyes, he smiled. Yes, Peter Whittier's house wasn't going anywhere; it could wait a few more hours. He was soon sound asleep and never heard his cell phone ringing in the other room.

. . .

Leigh jabbed at the End Call button on her cell phone. She had tried every number she knew, yet she couldn't reach anyone. Even the State Police line wasn't working.

Frustration coursed through Leigh's body. Poor little Sam was being held by a psycho murderer. How could Leigh get help to her? She could only imagine how scared the little girl must feel right now.

Closing her eyes, Leigh tamped down the urge to run back to the cabin, grab an ATV then head straight down the mountain. Jared and Billy would certainly want to know what she was doing and there was no way they would let her go alone. She had already inadvertently put Sam in jeopardy. She wasn't going to put anyone else in harm's way. If she didn't come up with a plan soon then Sam was as good as dead.

There was no doubt that she needed to take advantage of the element of surprise that she had been given. This bastard was keeping Sam alive to use her as bait. For now, as much as this terrified Leigh, Sam was relatively safe.

*Think,* she coached herself. *How are you going to save Sam and nail that son of a bitch?*

Running her fingers through her hair, Leigh's mind started to clear. Another deep breath brought focus. First thing she'd need is one of Billy's guns. That was going to be tricky since Billy was very observant and not easily fooled. Getting to the ammunition was also going to be tough. Second, she must borrow one of the four-wheelers. Billy always kept the gas tanks full so that they were ready to go at a moment's notice. Lastly, she would have to gather up some odds and ends.

God, she hoped that Billy hadn't changed up where he usually stored things. Looking at the sun, Leigh knew that time was running out. A glance at her phone told her that she only had several hours before dark. Depending on how much time it would take her to gather everything together and then sneak out, she planned to get to her uncle's house before dawn.

Taking a slow, deep breath, she headed back to the cabin.

Cobwebs hung from the ceiling and brushed against Samantha's face whenever she moved. Her breathing came in fast, shallow bursts. Sniffling, she wiped away tears, smudging the dirt on her face. She could hear rustling sounds moving across the expanse of cellar so she sat very quietly in the corner, as far away from the noises as possible. Dirty windows barely let in any light. Aiming the cell phone flashlight toward the main part of the cellar didn't help because the light wasn't as bright as it had been earlier. Samantha peered into the darkness and saw a chair was lying on its side. It started to look like a goblin in the gloom. Samantha gasped, then shut her eyes. She had felt better while talking to Leigh. She wanted the lights on. Now!

Samantha groped her way to the bottom of the basement stairs, to her left, and then she carefully climbed to the top step. She flipped on the light switch but it didn't work. The door she had been carried through earlier, which led from the kitchen, was now bolted shut. Turning, she kept her back against the cold concrete of the foundation wall as she slowly descended the swaying wooden structure then ran back to the relative safety of the far corner.

Wrapping her arms around her bent legs and hugging them to herself, Sam put her head down on her knees. In the distance, she heard the faint sound of a car engine. She had heard the sound earlier, but no one had come into the house.

A few seconds later, she heard footsteps approaching the house. Raising her head, Samantha turned on the phone's light and peered into the shadows for a place to hide. Her eyes landed on the old trunk a few feet away. Lifting the lid, she recoiled as the smell of mothballs assailed her nose. Samantha paused. This was too obvious a place to hide. Olivia was always hiding in the trunk at home, whenever they played hide and seek, so Samantha always found her. Spinning around, her heart began to race.

A door slammed.

Samantha noticed some boards had been nailed up against the lowest steps, creating a space below the stairs that she could hide behind.

She dashed over to the small space and squeezed into it without disturbing the boards. She silently turned off the light on the phone.

Someone was walking across the floorboards overhead and then she heard the bolt on the basement door slide open. Samantha stared upward as the cellar door creaked and a shaft of sunlight poured through it, creating a shadow of a man on the far wall as he slowly descended the stairs. His boots made a thudding noise, causing the stairs to shake directly above Samantha's head. She pressed her body tight against the wall as the man reached the bottom step.

"Okay kid, where are you?" he asked softly. "I know you're down here 'cause there's no way out."

Samantha closed her eyes as she listened to him walk around the basement. He stopped to lift up the lid of the trunk. Samantha jumped when he let it slam shut.

"Come out now, if you don't want to make me mad."

His footsteps were heading toward her. Samantha slid deeper under the stairs, as close to the boards as she could get. She winced when he ripped away some of the panels and flung them behind him. Curling up to make herself as small as she possibly could, she covered her head with her arms and squeezed her eyes tight. She waited for him to grab her and pull her out.

Silence.

Opening one eye, Samantha slightly raised her head. The two boards she was leaning against were still nailed to the stairs. She saw the man peering into the hole but he didn't turn his head in her direction. Catching her breath, she tried to stay as still as she could.

The little girl almost screamed when a cell phone rang out, startling them both. The man jerked backwards and hit his head on the bottom of the stairs. Cursing loudly, he stepped back and straightened up.

"What?" he snapped into the phone.

Samantha couldn't see him as he walked away but she could hear the irritation in his voice.

"I told you I had some loose ends to tie up. I'll be ready when the client gets here." There was a pause.

"Don't threaten me. You work for me, remember? I said I'd be ready." His words were clipped, his voice rising. "You make sure that animal is there on time. I got over half a million dollars tied up in this deal. I don't intend to lose it." Another pause. "Fine, I'll be at the drop site in time."

He listened for a moment.

"I said I'll be there." He ended the call.

With another glance around the cellar, the man swore, then thudded back up the stairs.

Samantha could hear him going from room to room, slamming doors. After a few minutes, the searching sounds stopped. She didn't hear the car start up. Quietly readjusting her position, to make herself more comfortable on the cold concrete, she decided to remain hidden beneath the stairs.

. . .

Samantha had no idea how long she had been hiding, but it looked like it was nighttime outside because there was no light showing through the dirty windows. Taking out her phone, she pushed the on button but the phone remained dark. She tried the button again. Nothing. Straining her ears, she listened for any noise coming from upstairs. It was getting hard for her to keep her eyes open. A long yawn escaped her. Pressing deeper into her hiding space, Samantha rested her head on her outstretched arm. The cell phone remained clutched in her hand.

Less than five minutes later, she was asleep.

# CHAPTER SIXTEEN

Leigh eased the cabin door shut behind her, and then listened for any unusual sounds. It was pitch dark as she quickly crossed the yard. The moon, which wasn't due to rise until just before dawn, wouldn't be any help tonight.

Reaching the side of the barn, she grabbed the backpack that she had hidden there several hours before. A flashlight stuck out from one of the side pockets. Shifting the pack to a comfortable position on her back, Leigh headed down the path. She waited until she reached a bend, putting the cabin out of sight, before turning the flashlight on.

Leigh had returned to the cabin to eat the dinner she had so abruptly left on the table. Billy, or so she assumed, had covered her plate and set it aside. It wasn't as if she was hungry, but it would take all the strength she had to carry out her plan. She had no idea when she would have time to eat again.

Thankfully, Billy had been occupied with weeding and watering his garden and didn't notice her gathering the items on her mental list. She was relieved that Jared had left the cabin and she hoped that he wouldn't return before she could leave. Billy still stored his guns and ammo in the same place so grabbing a handgun was relatively easier than Leigh had expected. Working as fast as she could, she had found all the supplies, then carried them out behind the barn, where she'd loaded them onto the back of a four-wheeler. The hardest part of this phase of her plan had been to hide the vehicle on the trail, far enough away from the cabin, so that it wouldn't be accidentally discovered.

Now, guided by the small beam of the flashlight, Leigh picked her way carefully down the old path. Billy had set up devices that warned him when someone was coming. She smiled as she located and avoided each one. It brought back some happy childhood memories of her trying to sneak up to the cabin without setting an alarm off. Billy had always known that she was coming, however, no matter how hard she had tried to surprise him. Her smile faded as she thought of all the things that had passed since those carefree days.

The path got steeper, so Leigh had to slow her pace. The irony that she was trying to sneak away from a place that had always been a safe haven was not lost on her. She hadn't meant to put anyone else in harm's way, especially Samantha.

The ATV was where Leigh had left it. Sighing with relief, she pushed it further down the path until she felt that she was a safe distance from the cabin. Confident that she had found all of Billy's devices, Leigh started the engine and cut across a small stream, heading for an old logging road.

The wheels of the ATV snagged a string that had recently been placed along the side of the stream, sending a signal back to the cabin, betraying Leigh's passing.

• • •

Jared had decided to sleep in the cabin, figuring he could keep a better track of Billy's coming and goings. A makeshift bed, next to the stove, had been made out of an old sleeping bag and some blankets. He had intended to stay awake but had fallen into a restless sleep. Jared was soon lost in a dream where Leigh was pointing a gun at him and telling him that she knew who he was. Blaming him for the loss of her family. He tried to explain but she wouldn't listen. Tears coursed down her face and she sobbed as she listed his supposed crimes.

Out of nowhere, black helicopters appeared, swirling around them and making a loud beeping noise that wouldn't stop. The beeping continued to get louder until Jared couldn't hear her anymore. All he could do was watch her eyes, like an oldgunslinger, waiting to see what she was going to do. Then he saw her gaze waver for a fraction of a second and he knew that she had made her decision, he had been found guilty. He jerked awake as she pulled the trigger.

Sitting up, Jared ran a hand through his hair and let out a shaky breath. Even though he knew that it had been just a dream, he was tempted to run his hands over his chest and check for the bullet that had been heading for his heart. Adrenaline was still pounding through his veins so it took him a few minutes to realize that he could still hear the beeping.

Looking around the dark cabin, he could tell that it was coming from a cabinet in the corner of the kitchen area. Flipping back the covers, he made his way toward the noise. Opening the door carefully, so as not to awake Billy and Leigh, he found a large electronic box with rows of red bulbs inside. It looked like an old circuit breaker box or something out of a sci-fi movie. One of the bulbs was blinking in time to the beeping. Looking closely, Jared read the label underneath: South Path, half mile.

"It's the motion detector at the stream," Billy's voice came from the darkness behind him. "Someone tripped the wire."

Billy lit a kerosene lamp and set it in the middle of the kitchen table. Jared turned and wasn't surprised to see that the older man was fully dressed.

*Didn't the man ever sleep? What was Billy so paranoid about that he had motion sensors set up all over the place? Just who was this guy?*

"How do you know it isn't an animal? Seems to me that those things would be going off all the time."

Billy moved past him and switched off the alarm. The older man then headed over to grab a couple of glasses out of another cabinet before crossing to the well pump to fill them with cold water. Making his way over to the table, Billy sat down and indicated the chair across from him. Jared glanced over to Leigh's pallet but she didn't stir. He figured that she must be exhausted, to sleep through all the noise they were making.

Joining Billy at the table, Jared pulled out a chair and sat down.

"I've lived on this mountain for over twenty-five years, but I lived another lifetime before that," Billy said as he shook his head. "Yet it still amazes me how stupid people think I am. All they see is an old man. They assume I must be senile to want to be up here alone. They think I have no eyes to see, or ears to hear, or a brain to think with."

Taking a sip of his water, he stared directly at Jared and waited.

Jared met his gaze. He wasn't sure what Billy had on his mind but he needed to tread lightly, so as to not give himself away. Maybe the older man was talking about the morning he'd followed him. He knew that Billy had known he was there, but Billy could have put that down to Jared's being an investigative reporter. The thought made him relax a little.

"I don't think you're stupid Billy, maybe a bit paranoid." Billy leaned back in his chair. "I just wondered how you were sure that it wasn't an animal that set off your alarm."

"Animals don't drag their feet. Only humans do that. Animals are used to picking their way through underbrush. The sensors are set up to be dragged a certain way by humans, or by vehicles."

Leaning in toward Jared, Billy pinned him with his eyes. The lantern flickered and created shadows across the older man's face, making it hard for Jared to read.

"I've been watching you. I'd wager that you aren't what you say you are." A small smile played around Billy's mouth.

Damn it, Jared thought, but he showed no emotion. How had Billy suspected him? He had spent years perfecting his acting abilities. Even those who were closest to him had no idea about his real activities. Feigning surprise, Jared asked, "And what part don't you believe?" He leaned his seat back on two legs as nonchalantly as possible but his nerves were on edge.

Billy's smile widened. "Your name's real enough, and I bet you started out as a photo-journalist, but you're too good to be an amateur. There are parts missing in your story and they tell me a hell of a lot about you."

"And what am I not telling?"

Billy took another sip, then crossed his arms over his stomach. He leaned back in his chair and studied the younger man, taking his time in answering.

"My guess is Fed, most likely undercover, looking for the men who murdered Peter and Mark Whittier ten years ago? Handpicked, since you grew up in the area."

It was the first time Jared's cover had ever been challenged. He was at a loss for words. Grabbing his glass, to give himself some extra time to think, he tipped it back to take a sip and noticed something move in the bottom of it. It was his bugging device. He set the glass down, carefully avoiding Billy's gaze. While he silently debated what he should say, Billy slammed his hand down on the table. Once again, Jared looked behind him and wondered how Leigh could possibly sleep through all of this.

"She's gone," Billy told him. "That's who set off the alarm. She's halfway down the mountain by now. I don't have a lot of time to play games with you. I need to know if you're who I think you are, and what the Feds know about this poaching operation."

Jared stared at the older man for a moment letting the words sink in. "What the hell do you mean, she's gone?"

Crossing the room, he grabbed the blankets off Leigh's pallet and stared at the empty space.

"Why would she sneak off in the middle of the night? We need to bring her back before they find her." Jared started for the door but Billy stepped in front of him. "Look, I know she's Amanda. Something must have happened if she took off. We're wasting time."

"Again, I need to know what the Feds know about the poaching operation."

Jared wanted to fling Billy across the room and go after Leigh but he restrained himself, just barely. Taking a step back, he ran his hand through his hair and started to pace. *What the hell was she thinking? Someone had tried to kill them not more than forty-eight hours before and now she pulls a stupid stunt like going back there on her own?*

Billy silently watched Jared pace back and forth.

"Fine," Jared finally said, "I'll tell you who I am but only if you tell me who you are. Deal?'

Billy just shrugged and gestured for Jared to sit down again. Once they were both seated, they stared at each other in silence. Billy was the first to speak.

"I served my time in Special OPS. That's all you need to know. You're turn. Why did the Feds send you in now, after all these years? Is there something new?"

Jared shook his head. "That's not telling me anything. You obviously have more information than we do, if you know what time their helicopters are passing by, or was that just luck?"

Billy leaned forward, his eyes narrowed to slits.

"I don't have time to get into a pissing match with you. I've been watching these sons-of-bitches for years, yet I can't seem to pin them down enough to actually catch them in the act. They're smart, sophisticated and they keep coming back to this park. Why? My guess is that they have some unfinished business here; they're looking for something, or someone." He paused, leaning in even closer. "I don't need to tell you that Amanda being here is the game changer. What hunter can resist going after the one that got away? They killed my best friend and almost killed the closest thing that I'll ever have to a daughter. So give me something so that I can catch them with and know that Amanda will be safe again."

There was pain in Billy's voice and eyes as he spoke.

Jared relented.

"I don't have much to go on. Several months ago, there was a memo asking for a volunteer to go undercover. Seems as if there was some chatter of these guys coming back here for a major deal. Word is that the client is on the FBI's most wanted list. You can bet if it's illegal, he has his hands in it; drugs, human trafficking, black market and trading weapons all over the world."

Billy had leaned back in his chair but he was frowning. "Why only one agent if such a bigwig is coming to town?"

"As you said before," Jared answered, "these guys are sophisticated and smart. Too many strangers showing up, just when their biggest deal is about to go down, would be too obvious." He spread his hands wide. "Yet who is going to question a local man coming back to do a magazine article on the dwindling attendance at state parks? One who wants to help his hometown in such troubling economic times? Since I'm from the area, it just seemed like a perfect cover. Once I found something, I could have the team here within hours."

He couldn't tell if Billy believed him or not, but he was aware that for every second that they sat staring each other down, Leigh was getting farther away.

Billy must have decided to trust him because he nodded.

"All right. That all makes sense. But Amanda coming back must have changed something. He's changed his game plan."

"What do you mean he's changed the game plan? Who the hell is he?" Jared didn't like the sound of that.

Billy rubbed a hand over his face.

"A little girl disappeared yesterday. The mother and Amanda were best friends growing up. My guess is that she's been taken to lure Amanda out. He must have contacted her somehow because I'm pretty sure that Amanda has gone to get the girl back. Several of my guns and ammo are missing and I'll bet you so is one of the ATV's."

Jared swore.

# CHAPTER SEVENTEEN

Samantha rubbed her eyes as she listened to the birds singing outside. Sitting up, it took her several moments to realize that she wasn't in her own bed, surrounded by her stuffed animals and toys. She was underneath a staircase in an abandoned house. The dampness of the concrete had seeped into her clothes and she felt cold, stiff and hungry. Weak rays of light from the windows created shadows that clung to the corners. Moving slowly, she crawled out from her hiding space and noticed a faint light coming from the top of the stairs. Looking up, she saw the kitchen door was ajar.

Placing her foot carefully on the bottom step, she held her breath as the wood popped and groaned beneath her sneakers. There was no sound from above. Taking each step slowly, she was careful to hug the wall, creating less noise where the steps were nailed to the risers. Still, every creak sounded extremely loud in the quiet house.

She had once read in a book that a young girl had been stolen but had outsmarted her captors and was able to escape. The girl had saved several other children who had also been taken. Samantha wished that she felt as brave as the girl in the story, but her heart was beating fast and her breaths were coming in short gasps. With every step, she expected the bad man to open the door and grab her. She wished for the thousandth time that her mommy or daddy were here. She'd even be glad to see Olivia.

Reaching the top of the stairs, she peered silently through the small gap.

Seeing nothing, Samantha slowly eased the door open and stepped into the kitchen. She saw that the opening for the living room was on the far side wall. She kept her eyes on it as she backed up to the door that led outside. The old linoleum tiles snapped and popped underfoot as she crossed over them.

Reaching the outside door, Samantha felt for the door handle behind her back, never taking her eyes from the living room. Yanking open the door before turning on her heels, she bolted out onto the dilapidated wooden porch. When she rounded the corner, she crashed into a man. His strong hands grabbed her shoulders, cutting off her bid for freedom.

• • •

Gertie was at the café bright and early, as usual. The place was empty, her wait staff due to arrive at any moment, so she set about her morning routine of filling napkin holders, salt and pepper shakers. She hadn't slept at all the night before and the routine of the restaurant helped to calm her nerves.

Ever since Shari had sounded the alarm that Samantha had gone missing, the town was in an uproar. Searchers had been out all night looking for the little girl but Gertie knew that they weren't going to find her, not yet anyways.

Gertie had no doubt as to who had taken Samantha. He must have found out about Amanda and he was going to finish off what he had started years ago. Gertie bowed her head as regret washed over her. Things should have never gotten to this point. If anything happened to either one of those girls, she wasn't sure that she could live with herself. The problem now was that she had no idea where he would have taken Samantha. He knew every square inch of the surrounding area; they could be anywhere.

The little bell over the door jingled and Gertie wasn't surprised to see Billy stroll in, followed by Jessie and Gus. In fact, she had been expecting them. One by one, they weaved their way around the tables and up to the counter. None of them sat down.

It reminded Gertie of another time that they had all banded together, ten years ago, when all hell had let loose. They had moved quickly to get Amanda to safety, and they did as much damage control that they could, at the time. If only they could have stopped things before Mark, Peter and even Joan Kent had been involved. They all felt responsible and now Amanda and Samantha were in grave danger.

Billy was the first to speak. "Checked the fire towers. Nothing on the east or south sides. North reported a low-flying helicopter, about an hour ago, headed south. West is still crowded with firefighters. If he's still in the park, then he's laying pretty low."

Gertie looked at them in alarm. "If? You don't think he would go somewhere else, do you?" It hadn't occurred to her that he would leave the park. If that happened, then the chances of saving the girls were very slim. It didn't bear thinking about.

Jessie came around from behind the counter and put her arm around Gertie's waist. They had been friends for over forty years. Gertie had always counted her blessings to have such a good friend.

"I don't think he'll go far. He has too much money tied up in his ventures to get sidetracked now."

"One of my informants said a rare animal is being flown in for this particular client. We can only hope that that's what's on the chopper." Gus poured himself a cup of coffee. "We should concentrate on the North side. That's where his operation was planned to go down. I think he'll stick around that area.

Several of the staff could be heard arriving in the back, so the friends kept their voices low.

"When does the client arrive?" asked Gertie.

Gus and Billy exchanged a look. Gus busied himself taking a sip of his coffee.

It was Billy who finally answered, avoiding Gertie's eyes. "Two days. That only gives us today to find them."

Gertie felt as if she had been sucker-punched. All of her breath came out in a great whoosh. The park spanned over three thousand acres. A day to find the girls was like trying to dig the Panama Canal with a spoon.

"Anyway," Billy continued. "I don't think he's met up with Amanda yet. I checked her phone records. The only incoming call was from Shari's phone. That must have been from Samantha. After that, Amanda placed some outgoing calls to the State Police and each of us. If she had talked with him, then I don't think she would have involved the cops. He's on a tight schedule. He'll be contacting her soon."

Jessie gave Gertie another hug. "We'll find them. Amanda is a smart girl. A survivor. She'll get that little girl and herself to safety or find a way to let us know where they are. I'm trusting in the Lord to protect them."

Gertie wasn't so sure that the good Lord was paying attention this time. She had lost her faith in him years ago. For Jessie's sake, she gave a ghost of a smile and nodded her head.

Several of the waitresses wandered out of the kitchen. One waitress brewed more coffee while the other went to turn the sign on the door to OPEN. Both gave curious glances at the four people huddled at the end of the counter before they headed back into the kitchen.

They only had a few minutes left before some of the early customers started to file in, looking for their regular breakfast.

Gus finished his coffee and placed the mug down on the counter with a thunk, making Gertie jump. "I promised Mark, years ago, that I'd keep his daughter safe if anything ever happened to him. I'm not about to break that promise now. I intend to catch that son-of-a-bitch and finish this thing once and for all. My guess is that with Amanda showing up, he's going to make a show out of this. He had lost her in the north quadrant, where we were clear cutting. Most likely that spot has some meaning to him considering that's where he lost her trail. The only other place would be the clearing at the gorge, where Peter and Mark were gunned down. He's egotistical enough to return there."

Billy nodded. "Makes sense. I'll get on the horn and have both places covered."

Jessie stood shoulder-to-shoulder with Gertie. "What do you want us to do?" she asked.

"Pray," was the answer as both men headed for the door.

# CHAPTER EIGHTEEN

It was an hour past dawn when Leigh finally reached her uncle's house. The trek had been slow on foot, but she hadn't wanted to be heard so she'd hidden the ATV well off the road, a half mile back. Once the house was in sight, she had settled behind a copse of trees to watch.

This house hadn't fared any better than her father's house had. Trees and weeds popped up throughout the once-meticulous lawn and there were even a few plants growing out of the rotting gutters. Shrubs were in desperate need of pruning. Roof tiles were missing in spots and the porch tilted at an unnatural angle away from the main structure. Despite the evident neglect, there were several signs of recent activity at the house. Styrofoam food containers were strewn about the once-pristine lawn along with several paper coffee cups.

The place was eerily quiet so Leigh was startled when her phone beeped from inside her pocket. Pulling it out, she saw a low battery alert. Not having the option to recharge it right at the moment, she shoved the device back into her pocket.

Working her way around the wooded perimeter of the house, she noticed that there were car tracks in the long grass that had filled in the driveway. Making her way cautiously to the porch, she pulled the revolver from her pocket and unlocked the safety. Peering through the gaps in the plywood wasn't much help as the windows were too filthy to see anything. The dead bolt on the back door was open and the door was not latched.

Easing through the door, Leigh crept into the kitchen then paused to listen to the house. In a fanciful moment, she wondered if the house knew who she was. It seemed as if a lifetime had passed since the happy hours she'd spent here. She'd had so much fun having the run of the house, since her uncle never had children. If only it could talk and tell her its secrets.

The kitchen was in as bad shape as the outside. The whole place smelled like rodents had nested in the walls. Water must have leaked through the ceiling and run down the sheetrock, causing the drywall to disintegrate into moldy heaps. The interior of the kitchen was dim but the living room beyond was in complete darkness.

Leigh noticed that the cellar door was ajar and the brand new deadbolt unfastened. Turning on the flashlight that she had purloined from Billy, she kept her gun trained toward the top of the stairs as she made her way down the rotting steps. Her heart stopped with every creak and she expected to see a figure in the doorway at any moment. Trying to even out her breathing, which escaped her lips in small gasps, it was impossible.

She had figured that Samantha was no longer in the basement when she found the unbolted doors, but she wanted to search the cellar anyways. Waves of relief fought with panic at not finding the little girl.

Taking the steps back up to the kitchen two at a time, Leigh hurried back outside to resume her hiding spot once more. *Think, dammit, think.* Her words fell like a prayer from her lips.

There were so many places he could have taken the child. Gnawing on her fingernail, she closed her eyes and considered the surrounding area. This was the only abandoned house that she knew of, other than her father's. Cole had ripped up most of the floorboards so she doubted that her father's place would have any use to the kidnapper. That left the park. He wouldn't run the risk of being caught by the fire crews or anyone searching for Samantha, but she would scour the entire park if she had too.

Leigh jumped when her phone rang. The caller ID was unlisted. "This is Leigh," she answered breathlessly, standing up.

The voice on the other end gave a short laugh. "Really? I remember your name being Amanda. I also remember that you were a very smart girl so I'm going to assume that you already know who I am and what I want."

It's amazing what memory can do to the senses. The voice brought back the rush of terror that Leigh had felt that day at the gorge, and the enormous pain of her loss. It was so visceral that she almost dropped to her knees. It also made her spin around, suddenly afraid that he might be standing behind her. Feeling trapped, like a mouse in a never-ending maze, she closed her eyes and sucked in a deep breath. Rage flooded through her body as she pictured Samantha, alone with this monster. The adrenaline rush gave Leigh the courage to open her eyes and keep her voice steady. "Yea, I know who you are. You're the coward who killed my family. As for what you want? Go to hell. I intend to track you down and send you to the chair, so don't get comfortable."

His chuckle suggested that he wasn't intimidated. "I have to say that I admire your confidence, Amanda. You might have gotten away from me once, but I always get my trophy in the end. Always." He continued before she could reply. "Come alone to the clearing where I lost your tracks that day. And I mean alone. I've taken a little insurance policy by the name of Samantha. Adorable little girl. Shame to see something bad happen to her. If anyone else is within a mile of the place then, well, like I said, you're a smart girl. I'm sure you can figure it out. I'll expect you in one hour. And Amanda? Don't be la…"

With that the phone beeped and then went silent. Looking down at the screen, Leigh saw that the battery was dead. Sinking to the ground, she dropped her head into her hands and began to rock back and forth. It would take some doing to get to the clearing in an hour, but it was doable, especially since she had the ATV.

Leigh had to assume that he had no intentions of letting either one of them live. Samantha would be collateral damage. It would take her too long to get to town and find help, and the closest house with a phone was also too far away. For a brief second, Leigh wondered if he would end Samantha's life before she even got a chance to save it. He was a hunter. To have his prey on the run was what he liked more than the actual killing. Most likely, he'd give them a head start, and then hunt them down, together; knowing that Samantha would slow her down and that she would do anything to protect the child. He wouldn't want to just shoot them outright. He loved the hunt too much.

Rummaging through her backpack until her fingers wrapped around a lighter, a memory crossed Leigh's mind of a trick that Billy had taught her, years before. She felt a flash of hope. If she could get to the clearing early, then she just might have the upper hand.

Grabbing some of Billy's trail mix, she munched loudly as a plan took shape in her mind. Standing up, she wiped her hands on her shorts and headed out to the road. There was no sense in hiding now.

She had a meeting with unfinished business.

. . .

Jared had followed Billy down the mountain on one of the four-wheelers. They had split up just outside of town.

He felt bone-tired. Billy had grilled him for information most of the night. Jared saw no sense in lying after his cover had been blown. Billy had a lot of evidence. Once he knew who Jared was, he was willing to share it.

Jared headed to his cabin and sat down at the computer. He checked his emails first. Opening the one from his friend, Matt, he wasn't surprised to see a yearbook photograph of Leigh from her Cape high school. The picture was in color. Damn, but she was a blond and her eyes were so green. He knew that he had gone to middle high school with her, but he didn't remember her being such a knockout. He continued to scroll through the messages until saw the one that he was looking for. It had been sent the night before. He clicked to open it. As usual, it was brief and to the point. 'Will meet at arranged location and time.'

Jared swore under his breath. He had assumed the whole time that he was talking to Billy that Leigh was safely sleeping in the cabin. Now he had to find her, and quick. It pissed him off that she had been gone for several hours before Billy told him, never mind that he hadn't heard her leave. She'd had a hell of a head start. No telling where she was now.

Leigh had told Billy that she had just wanted to find out who the poachers were so that she could have them brought to justice, but they had upped the stakes. Of course, taking Samantha was a desperate move to flush Leigh out, but how had they found out she was back in town? Jared felt sure in his gut that Leigh was going to sacrifice herself to save Samantha. She had no idea that she'd be walking into a no-win situation.

With the information that Billy had given him, Jared fired off an email to his commander with an update. Even though he marked it 'Urgent', he knew it would most likely be several hours before it was read. This was fine with him, because it left no time to argue. What he planned was definitely going to be against orders.

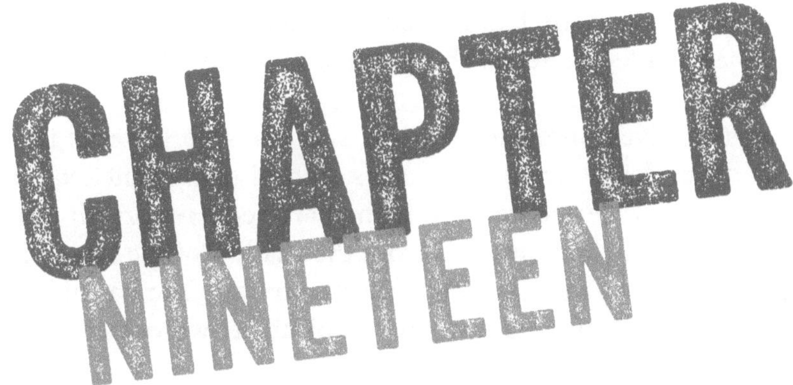


Leigh took one detour on her way to the clearing but she still made good time. Less than a quarter mile back, she had gathered together a large pile of dry leaves, small sticks and anything else that was combustible. Using moss, she'd lined the indent she had made on the top of the pile before filling the cavity with more kindling. Pulling Billy's lighter from her pocket, she'd closed her eyes and taken a deep breath.

Billy had shown Leigh how his ancestors had carried fire from place to place. The moss had kept the ashes smoldering long enough for the tribe members to reach a new location and start a new fire. Her hope was to create hot embers that would smolder for a while, then eventually burn through the moss to start a fire. The resulting smoke would be her signal for help; an insurance policy in case things didn't go as she planned.

Opening her eyes, she flicked the lighter and touched the flame to the dried leaves. It took several tries, but a few twigs caught and created a small fire. Slowly, she added bigger pieces of branches. Only after she felt sure that there was enough hot ash in the moss, did she head out. With the moss?

• • •

The clearing had changed in the last ten years. This wasn't a surprise, but Leigh had dreamed about the place so much that she had almost expected it to look the same. The fallen trees had been cleared out and new saplings had taken their place.

She surveyed the area from the safety of the tree line, one of Billy's cowboy hats shielding her eyes. As she had expected, the clearing was empty. He would never have given her an open target. He had most likely followed her to make sure that she came alone. She wondered if Samantha was still alive. He seemed sadistic enough to dangle the child as bait by placing her in the center.

Taking a deep breath, Leigh closed her eyes and said a small prayer. She felt hypocritical, since she had turned her back on religion the day that her world had shattered. Yet, at this point, she would take all the help she could get.

Stepping tentatively into the clearing, she was several yards in before she stopped, suddenly aware of the sensation of being watched. He was close. A movement alerted her that he had arrived. Her breath caught in her throat as she watched him step from the shadow of the forest. He was wearing the same hat that she remembered so well. The hat hid his features, just like it did in her nightmares. It took all her willpower not to turn and run.

Leigh felt sick to her stomach when she saw no sign of Samantha. Taking a calming deep breath, she blew it out slowly, easing some of the panic in her chest. Glancing up at the sun, she figured that she had just about an hour to find Samantha before all hell broke loose. Her plan relied on having Samantha here, if they were both going to get out of this alive. With her heart pounding, Leigh walked forward before halting in the middle of the clearing. Each step had brought her closer to becoming her real self again; Amanda Whittier, daughter of Mark Whittier.

Amanda waited for the poacher to come to her.

* * *

Shari paced back and forth in her kitchen, alternating between looking at her cell phone or out the kitchen window. Her baby had been gone for twenty-four hours now. One minute, Samantha had been in the crowded café, the next she had vanished into thin air. Guilt tore at Shari. She should never have let the girls out of her sight, not even for a second. It just seemed incomprehensible that no one had seen a thing. How could a six-year-old disappear in a crowded room?

Damn, she hated feeling helpless. She wanted to get out there, like her husband, and beat every bush until she found her daughter. Olivia had been beside herself when they noticed Samantha was missing. Shari had brought her home and rocked her to sleep with the promise that they would find Samantha no matter how long it took. Olivia had been inconsolable. The news was filled with missing children that were never found. No, Shari told herself furiously, she wasn't going to go there!

* * *

Pouring herself another cup of coffee, even though the last cup had sat untouched on the counter, Shari sat down at the kitchen table and tried not to let her mind think of all the terrible things that could happen to a lost six-year-old. She bowed her head. "Lord," she prayed, "Please bring my baby home safe. She's probably scared to death."

The house was quiet. Too quiet. Ben was out with a search party and a friend had taken Olivia for the morning. Shari had been hesitant to let Olivia out of her sight, but in the end, she'd figured that it did her daughter no good to watch her mother wait helplessly for news.

The sound of a car's engine came from the driveway. Shooting out of the chair, Shari ran through the house and out onto the front porch. She recognized Cole's car instantly and bit back her disappointment.

Grabbing the railing of the porch, she watched as he got out of the car. It took her a moment to register the movement in the back seat, so when Cole opened the back door of the car and Samantha climbed out, Shari didn't react immediately.

"Mommy!" Samantha yelled as she ran to her.

Relief rushed through Shari's body at the sight of her daughter. Leaping off the porch steps, she dropped down on one knee and held out her arms. Samantha rushed into them and Shari hugged her close. Tears ran unchecked down her face. She must have been holding on extremely tight because Samantha started to squirm. With some reluctance, Shari relaxed her hold.

Looking up at Cole, she asked, "Where did you find her?"

"Peter Whittier's old place."

"What were you doing there?"

Samantha saved Cole from answering. "That's where the bad man took me. I wanted to pick out a puppy so I tried to cross the street at the light but he grabbed me and threw me in the trunk of the car." Sam's voice rose as she grabbed at Shari's arm. Her face was flushed and tears started to form in her eyes. "He locked me in the cellar. I called Leigh. She said she'd try to get me as fast as she could but she never showed up. I hid from the bad man all night. The cellar door was open when I woke up this morning. He had told me that he had a date with Leigh. Who is he, Mommy?"

Shari was trying to take it all in as Samantha's monologue came out in a rush. As she looked at her daughter, the pieces started to fall into place. The bad man had to be the one who had murdered Amanda's father and uncle. He must have recognized Amanda and had set the fire to try to kill her, but she had obviously escaped. That's who had watched her daughters playing in the yard, waiting for the chance to grab one of them.

He was going to kill Amanda. If Samantha had escaped from him then she was in real danger. She had forgotten that Cole was there until he spoke.

"When did your daughter go missing?" he asked. "And what has Leigh got to do with all of this?"

Shari looked up at him suspiciously, but he appeared genuinely confused. She needed a few minutes to get her thoughts together, but first she had to call her husband and then the authorities. Scooping Samantha up, Shari turned to the house.

"Come in Cole," she said over her shoulder. "I'm sure the sheriff will want to know how you found Samantha. I'll explain everything while we wait for him to get here."

Cole hesitated for a moment, but his curiosity got the better of him so he followed her into the house.

• • •

Gertie almost fainted with relief when the call came in that Samantha had been found safe. Now, if they could only find out where Amanda was. Gertie had taken a much-needed break from the café and had been in her apartment when Jessie called her with the good news. After hanging up her phone and walking into her living room, Gertie was startled by a knock on the door.

She opened the door to find Dean standing there. Like his last visit, she had been expecting him. Stepping aside, she motioned for him to enter.

His usual tie and suit jacket were gone. The once-pressed shirt was wrinkled and the buttons misaligned. Deep circles below his eyes gave him a haunted look.

Gertie had never seen Dean this way. He had always seemed so in control and in charge of any situation. This was a man who had battled his way to the Senate and had a reputation for playing hardball. He had taken on corrupt corporations, organized crime and other ruthless criminals without batting an eyelash. Now it seemed as if his past could be catching up with him and the guilt was too heavy to bear. Gertie sat next to him on the couch and put her hand on his shoulder.

"You are a wonderful person, Gertrude. I was an arrogant ass not to have married you when I had the chance." He held up his hand to stop her from answering. "I was. I had lots of ambition and plans in those days. I listened to the people who told me that appearances were everything. You know, I even thought that someday I could become President of the United States, as long as I kept up the charade."

It broke Gertie's heart to hear the defeat and hopelessness in his voice.

He got up from the couch and walked over to the window that over-looked Main Street. As he stared through the glass, his back to her, his voice came out quiet, as if from a great distance.

"Marrying Catherine was a huge mistake. I should have known she couldn't take the pressure of being in the spotlight, having her every move analyzed in the tabloids. She was so fragile. Raising the boys was just too much of a strain on her. Of course she never warmed up to Kyle; she must have known what he was before we did. I don't think she ever wanted children of her own and she certainly wasn't thrilled about raising another woman's son."

Gertie shifted on the couch. She didn't want to play the blame game or rehash the past of what could have been. It had taken years for her to make peace with most of it, such as it was. Getting up, she crossed over to where Dean stood.

"Look, what's done is done. I don't know if things would have been different if we had married. The reality is that our son is a killer. We should have never let it get to this point. People are dead, and now there is an innocent girl out there who is paying for our mistakes, again. This must end, Dean. Now."

Dean made no comment. He looked as if he was staring into the past and didn't want to hear what she had to say in the present.

Well, damn it, he was going to hear what she had to say next. "If our son doesn't surrender, we have to kill him."

Slowly, as her words sank in, Dean turned toward Gertie, tears filling his eyes. "I guess I always knew that would be the way we'd have to stop him, in the end."

Defeat was evident in the slump of his shoulders. Gertie led him back to the couch and he collapsed hard against the cushions.

Life hadn't turned out the way either of them had planned it. Gertie had had such hopes for their child. Giving him up to Dean to raise, the day he was born, because he had the wife, the home and the money, had broken her heart. She had believed that she was giving their son everything a child needed to have a good life, full of opportunities. Yet Kyle had been a loner as a child. It was clear from the beginning that there was something very different about him. She could never have anticipated the hell he was going to put them all through. Dean had been too wrapped up in his political career to pay much attention to his son's unconventional behavior, leaving poor Catherine to shoulder all the responsibilities. By the time Gertie had returned to town, when Kyle was a teenager, her son had already had several brushes with the law. She couldn't blame Catherine for washing her hands of the whole situation. When she divorced Dean, Catherine had been forced to leave Cole behind because Dean had refused to give up either of his sons. *Catherine was probably sunning herself on a tropical island with the alimony checks*, Gertie thought bitterly, then immediately regretted it.

The situation wasn't Catherine's fault; it was hers and Dean's. They had no one to blame but themselves. They had failed to see that their son was a psychopath in the making. Gertie had lived with the guilt for over ten years. She would never forgive herself if Kyle succeeded in killing Amanda, too. Dean had been covering Kyle's tracks for too long

. . .

Amanda had thought she would be terrified, facing the man who had haunted her dreams for years, but she wasn't. It had been the unknown that had paralyzed her with fear all these years. A faceless murderer that lurked in every shadow or doorway. Now that she was facing an actual man, a feeling of calm came over her, giving her a feeling of power. This was it; the moment that fate had decreed ten years earlier.

They stood about ten feet apart.

*That damn hat is still pulled down too low over his eyes.* Amanda recalled the notion that the eyes were the windows to the soul. *Maybe that's why he hides them*, she thought, *because he's too evil to have a soul.*

He was wearing a black T-shirt, a camouflage vest, loose fitting camouflage pants and badly worn hiking boots. A semi-automatic rifle, complete with a scope, dangled from his right hand.

They studied each other for a moment. It was Amanda who broke the silence.

"Alright, I'm here. Where's Samantha? I want to see her."

His mouth quirked into a grin as he tipped the hat upward. Amanda gasped at his resemblance to Cole and Senator Langford. This had to be Cole's brother, Kyle, she reasoned. His eyes were strangely different, yet familiar. Amanda had seen those eyes before, but she couldn't place where. Did she remember them as being kind and reassuring? Perhaps. But this man's eyes were cold and unreadable as they wandered over her body in an assessing manner.

Revulsion fought its way to Amanda's throat but she tamped it down. Kyle had the Langford aristocratic good looks, but she had seen firsthand how evil this man was. No handsome face could hide the ugliness of his soul.

As Kyle strolled closer, it was all Amanda could do not to take a step backwards. She wasn't about to let him see that she was intimidated by him. He leaned in, as if he was going to tell her a secret. Before she could react, he backhanded her across the face.

The force of the blow threw Amanda off balance and she landed hard on her backside. Her hat rolled off to one side. Cradling her throbbing cheek, she glared up at Kyle with all the hatred that she had felt over the years.

"What?" he mocked, with a raised eyebrow. "Did you think that we would shake hands, like old friends?" His voice was low, his speech cultured.

Amanda fought down the impulse to scramble to her feet and attack him. He was a grown man; she would be no match for him physically. Besides, he still had Samantha. Getting out of this alive meant that she would have to outwit him. Again.

Taking several deep breaths, Amanda got to her feet and grabbed her hat, careful to keep a safe distance from Kyle.

He gestured to the clearing around them. "This is the place where I lost your tracks, remember? I circled this clearing for hours but there was no sign of you. Like you just disappeared. Poof!" He looked at her expectantly. "I have to say that I admired your cunning but, then I got to thinking, maybe it was just dumb luck. So, tell me, how did you elude me that day?"

Amanda knew that she had to keep him talking, but she'd be damned if she was going to answer his question. "You murdered my family and you tried to kill me." She circled around him, maybe fury making her reckless. "Answer my question, Kyle. Why'd you do it?"

Kyle just stood still as she circled him. Waiting until she was in front of him, he moved with lightning speed to close the distance between them. He grabbed her arm then pulled her tight against his body.

Amanda shivered at the contact.

"I don't need a reason to kill." His lips were inches from hers. "I enjoy killing. Enjoy the hunt. I like being in control of who lives and who dies. Guess you could say that I'm like a god. There isn't a species on this planet that I haven't hunted down and killed."

Amanda glared at his pupils, which were now dilated, and spit formed in the corner of his lips.

"What do you want to hear? That I spent my childhood in private schools and institutions? How teams of doctors tried to tell me how much my father and Catherine loved me?" He fairly spit the words out. "That I suffered from Reactive Detachment Disorder with manic tendencies." He snorted. "They all thought I didn't know who my mother was and that I wouldn't care that she threw me away. They thought I was stupid, but they were wrong. I outsmarted them all." He shoved Amanda backwards. "You were the only prey who ever got away from me. It's taken me ten years, but I'm going to finally win this hunt, too."

Amanda started circling him again. This time, she was careful to stay farther away. Her hand closed around Billy's pistol that was wedged into her hat. She caught a faint whiff of smoke. Help would be arriving soon, if she could just keep him talking a little longer. Amanda's eyes kept darting to the forest, hoping to catch a glimpse of Samantha. She prayed that he hadn't already killed the girl.

"How should we end our little game?" Kyle leaned against a small tree. Crossing his arms, he spoke as if he were discussing the weather with a friend.

"So that's what this is?" Amanda couldn't believe his ego. "A game to you? You kill people and ruin lives and it's all about you winning?"

Her life had been turned upside down by this maniac and now he acted as if she owed him something. She stepped closer to look him in the eye. "You have no power here. You are not a god. You're nothing but a psychopath. I got away from you because I'm better than you. I hope you rot in hell!"

Kyle's response was swift as he grabbed her by the throat and lifted her off the ground. "I have to say that you were a worthy adversary. But now I'm growing bored with you. I have an important client coming in tomorrow and you're wasting my time."

He flung Amanda away from him. There was a loud snap as she landed. Severe pain emitted from her right ankle as it buckled underneath her, causing her to fall flat on her back, knocking the wind out of her. Gasping for breath, she fought down the nausea that the pain brought.

Kyle took a few steps toward her, then stopped to look up at the smoke that was drifting into the clearing. Cocking an eyebrow at her, he asked, "I suppose that this is your doing?"

"An old Indian trick," she retorted. As she turned onto her side, she bit her lip against the pain radiating up her leg. "Every ranger in the park will see that smoke and be here any minute."

Kyle threw his head back and laughed. "Brilliant! I have to say that you just made this very interesting."

Then he paused for a moment before shaking his head and giving a slight laugh. "Thank you for making this worth the wait, Amanda. It would have been so disappointing if I had ended up killing you too easily. As it is, I would love to hunt you down, but it seems you've made it so that I don't have much time."

Amanda prayed that someone had spotted the smoke and had already called it in. She needed to buy some time. "Where is Samantha? Bring me to her and let us go. I'll even give you a day head start before I start hunting you down again."

Kyle's demeanor changed. His amusement gave way to a sinister stare that revealed his ruthless killer persona. He strode over to Amanda and kicked her in the ribs. Pain shot through her body and ankle as she rolled away from him. Rising on to one knee, she pulled the pistol from her hat and tried to aim it at him, but he was too fast and kicked her again. Colors spun in front of her eyes as she fought to stay conscious.

Kyle tossed her gun several feet away and glared down at her.

Every breath was a struggle. The pain in Amanda's chest was excruciating but she forced herself to meet his gaze.

"Defiant till the end. I admire your strength." Kyle slid a hunting knife from the sheath attached to his belt. "There's another old Indian custom that I particularly appreciate."

Amanda refused to let her gaze waver.

Straddling her now, Kyle pinned her arms to her sides so that she couldn't move. "Did you know that eating the heart of your greatest enemy will bring you their strength?" He caressed one of her cheeks with the blade.

Never would she let him see the fear that she was feeling, nor the pain that he was causing by sitting on her chest. She would not surrender to his madness.

A sharp bark in the distance echoed across the clearing. Shadoe? A lump rose in Amanda's throat.

Kyle slid the blade across her neck and down her breastbone, barely touching the tip to her skin. Tears quickly formed until one escaped her eye just as he shifted his weight. Waves of pain shot through her ribs.

"Tears?" he mocked. "Are you afraid of dying Amanda? Perhaps you will beg for your life, after all, like the others did?"

"Go to hell!" was all that she could manage.

Kyle applied pressure to the tip of the knife just above her left breast. She closed her eyes at the new pain as it broke the skin.

"Beg me to end your life quickly," he growled.

Amanda shook her head from side to side. She knew he had no plans to kill her quickly. He wanted to watch her suffer. She would pay for the insult of escaping from him.

She saw a sudden movement to her right. Through her tear-distorted vision, she saw a white blur charging towards her.

Kyle turned his head just as Shadoe jumped at him and knocked him off Amanda's body. Kyle tumbled to the ground but Shadoe recovered his footing first. Turned to Kyle with his teeth bared, his throat filled with a menacing snarl.

Dragging air into her burning lungs, Amanda pushed herself up into a half-sitting position.

Kyle struggled to his feet and as he turned, Amanda saw his gun, aiming directly at Shadoe.

"No!" she screamed.

Throwing herself at Kyle took every ounce of strength she had left. She grabbed Kyle around the knees and tried to pull him down.

Kyle turned and slammed the butt of the gun hard against the side of her face.

Spheres of light danced before Amanda's eyes as the darkness crept in, yet she clung to his legs.

His face contorted in rage as he aimed his rifle at her.

"It wasn't supposed to end this way," she thought as two shots rang out.

Amanda felt no pain as she surrendered to the blackness that engulfed her.

The beeping sounded like it was coming from a great distance. Amanda yearned for it to stop. It hurt her head and her heart persisted in taking up the rhythm. There wasn't a spot on her body that didn't ache. Trying to move produced no results and the beeping was getting louder. It would be so easy to let the blackness pull her down and take her.

Amanda struggled to open her eyes, but they felt too heavy. Someone spoke her name. The voice was familiar, but she couldn't connect it to a person she knew. With great effort, she willed her left eye to open. Unable to focus, it was several moments before she was able to see the face that now leaned into her line of vision.

A sob escaped her.

So, it was true. Kyle had won. That was the only explanation for her seeing this face again. But why was her uncle meeting her? She had expected her parents to be the ones waiting for her on the other side. She hadn't expected to see that people age in heaven. It seemed that heaven wasn't going to be what she had expected after all.

· · ·

The beeping came again, only this time it was louder and clearer. Recognizing it as the kind of heart monitor she'd heard on TV, Amanda lay still, absorbing the feel of her surroundings. There was a sense of peace and calm around her, but no one knew better than she did that this could all be an illusion.

Her right eye was swollen shut. Once again, she managed to pry open her left eye. She saw that she was lying in a hospital bed with tubes surrounding her. Voices were drifting on the air from somewhere to her right. They were low so she couldn't make out any words.

Moving her head to the side created a pain that pierced through her skull, making her cry out. The voices instantly stopped, then a man's face came into her line of vision. He was in his sixties, and he had streaks of grey running through his black hair.

"Amanda? I'm Doctor Davis. Can you understand what I'm saying?" He smiled and touched her gently on the shoulder when she nodded slightly. "Good, that's good. I'm going to raise the bed a little so that I can take a look at you. It's going to be painful. Are you ready?"

Giving permission with a faint nod of her chin, Amanda was not prepared for the intense pain that sliced through her chest as he raised the head of the bed and gently maneuvered her into more of a sitting position. Tears filled her eyes and she took light breaths.

Producing a small flashlight, Dr. Davis shone it in her open eye and then gently lifted the lid of her right eye to examine it. Her quick inhale of breath, at the pain, brought back the stabbing in her chest.

"You're doing great," the doctor reassured her. "You're in the ICU of Ramsey General. I'm afraid you suffered quite a lot of trauma. I know it hurts to breathe. That's because you have three cracked ribs. Try to take short, shallow breaths. You've also suffered a broken eye socket, a broken ankle and a major concussion which left you in a coma. I need to run some tests now that you're awake. Okay?"

With that, he turned and gave some orders to an unseen person before he left the room.

Amanda felt like her body had no substance; she was a piece of flotsam adrift, only going where the current pulled her.

True to his word, Doctor Davis soon returned with several nurses who spent the next hour poking and prodding her. Amanda answered questions with a thumb up or down motion because her voice was too weak to carry words. Finally, Dr. Davis and the nurses retreated from her room and she collapsed back against the pillow to tumble headfirst into the welcome abyss of sleep.

. . .

The next time Amanda awoke, the lights were dim in the hallway and her cubicle was encompassed in darkness. She could hear murmured voices and the distant beeping of machines, along with her own monitors. She recalled a vague memory of a kind doctor leaning over her, telling her that she was in a hospital and that she had been badly hurt. Her mouth was dry, and her head pounded as she struggled to lift her right hand to her temple. A movement to her left made her panic as she saw the faint outline of a man sitting in the shadows, watching her.

Fear flooded her veins. Had Kyle come back to finish the job he had started? If he was still alive, it could only mean that he had killed Samantha and somehow gotten away.

Flailing her arms, Amanda tried to scream but no sound came out. The monitor that measured her heartbeat accelerated its beeping and set off an alarm. Loud voices hurried towards her and suddenly she was surrounded by several doctors and nurses. They struggled to hold her down as she attempted to pull out the tubes that were attached to her. The glare from the overhead lights blinded her, only adding to her panic.

"Kyle, he's here! He's going to kill me!"

Her words didn't carry over the orders that were being shouted. A syringe was inserted into her IV line, against her protests.

*Why couldn't they see him?* she wondered.

A young nurse with brown hair pulled back in a bun grabbed her hands and leaned in.

"It's alright, Amanda. No one can hurt you in here," she said slowly and firmly. "You are safe. Can you understand that? You're safe now."

*Safe? When was the last time she had ever felt safe?*

Whatever was in the syringe began to work. Amanda slumped back on her pillow, unable to focus on the sea of faces that peered down on her with professional concern.

There was a whirring sound that she couldn't place, and then silence.

The sun was over an hour away from rising when Jared turned his jeep into a side road and killed the engine and lights. The darkness pressed against his eyes so he rested his forehead on the steering wheel and waited for them to adjust. It took a few minutes, but when he raised his head, he could see the outline of trees through the windshield. His shoulders felt as if they were attached to his ears so he took a big breath, then let it out slowly. The muscles in his shoulders and jaw relaxed a little, allowing his shoulders to lower to their normal level. It was always like this before a raid; the stress and mental anxiety at an all-time high. But this raid was different. This was personal.

It had been a long and sleepless three days and it was making him edgy. Every time Jared closed his eyes, he could still see that bastard standing over Amanda, smashing his gun into her face. Could still see her lying there, motionless. For a few terrifying minutes he had thought that she was dead. If Shadoe hadn't lunged at Kyle, deflecting his attention, then she probably would be.

He didn't remember stopping his four-wheeler or aiming his gun. His attention had been solely focused on Amanda's body crumbled on the ground. The reports about the incident say that he had fired two shots, hitting Kyle in the chest, causing him to fly backwards and lay sprawled on his back. Jared didn't recall pulling the trigger for the kill shot.

What he did remember was how he'd rushed to Amanda's side to cradle her head until the chopper arrived to transport her to the hospital. For a second, she had opened one eye at his urging, but she was unable to speak. He remembered that she had held his gaze before losing consciousness. The right side of her face had been discolored and started to swell. He remembered how a thin trickle of blood that was oozing from a cut on her cheekbone had soaked her shirt in a crimson red. Jared had never felt so terrified in his life. It was in that moment that he knew he had fallen in love with her.

Wiping a hand over his unshaven face, Jared let out another long breath. That moment had put a lot of things in perspective for him. He'd wanted to take away all of Amanda's pain and protect her. He'd wanted to pick up Kyle and shoot him all over again, this time so he could remember it. Not that it would have changed anything.

Reaching into the back seat, Jared grabbed a Kevlar vest. Large white letters spelled ATF across the front. Staring at the letters reminded him why he could never tell Amanda that he had fallen in love with her. His job was just too dangerous. Half the time he'd be deep undercover, spending months gaining some low life's trust, waiting for the split-second opportunity to act. There was no predictable timeline when your job was to get illegal guns off the streets and out of the hands of extremist cells. The rest of his time was spent working with other government agencies; his cases usually entwined with human trafficking, drugs, poaching and homeland security. Until now, he hadn't taken the prospect of falling in love seriously. Loving someone would mean putting them in the line of fire. It was just too damn risky.

A vehicle with only its running lights on pulled up behind him, closely followed by another vehicle pulling in behind them. Jared's fingers closed around the gun that was resting on the seat beside him, all the while he was watching in the rearview mirror. He let out his breath when he recognized the men belonged to the rest of his unit.

Getting out of the car, Jared shrugged into his Kevlar vest, then slid the gun into the holster that was tied to his waist and thigh. Heading to the back of the jeep, he opened the rear door and pulled out his backpack and rifle. Shutting the door quietly, he turned and acknowledged the driver of the first vehicle. "Any problems?"

Jed "Jedi" Abrams was one of the most competent agents that Jared had ever worked with. In his early thirties, he was tall, muscular and the most skilled sniper in the agency. He had earned his nickname because he could predict the best moment to use his skill. The rest of the team often teased Jedi for his GQ looks and about all the women who threw themselves at him. But the team had great respect for him, and more than one of them owed him their life. Jared was more than pleased to see that he joined this mission.

Jedi's blond hair appeared a dull grey in the dim light. He flashed his perfect white teeth and shook Jared's offered hand. "Negative," was the easy reply.

Jared nodded as they waited for the rest of the guys to grab their gear and gather at the back of his jeep. This was his team; the best of the best. They had all gone through basic training together, and then had been assigned to different areas. Several years ago, the director had decided to make an "elite" team and they had answered the summons.

Bruce Fitzpatrick was short and stocky, standing only about five-foot-seven, but he was pure muscle and a topnotch marksman. His brown hair was buzzed cut and he looked like he had just stepped out of a Marine unit. Next to him was Gary Iverson, whose specialty was explosives. Gary looked like he was twelve years old, with his sandy blond hair and freckles, but Jared knew that there wasn't an explosive device built that Gary couldn't deactivate.

The fifth member of the crew was Micah Connors. A former semi-pro football player, Micah had decided that he'd had enough of the sports life and signed up with the academy. At six-foot-four, two hundred and forty pounds, he was an imposing figure. Micah was also one of the best strategists the agency had.

Bringing up the rear was Tyrone Davis. From Louisiana, he was an accomplished cook who often hosted barbeques and dinner parties at his house. Tyrone liked to play jokes on the crew. Like Micah, Tyrone was tall, just topping six-foot-three but instead of the build of a football player, he was lean and had the physique of a runner. He was also a first-rate pilot.

Jared nodded to each man in turn and then pulled out a map of the surrounding area. Unfurling it, he pressed it against the jeep's rear window. Clicking on the pen light that he drew from his shirt pocket, he aimed it at the map.

"You all know what the plan is, right?" he started, looking at each of them. At their nods, he continued. "Good. Okay, so we're on this fire road, here." He pointed to a dotted line and then traced his finger about an inch to the right. "According to flight patterns of all the helicopters that have been recorded in the area recently, it's believed that the poaching operation will be in this meadow area here. It's got a large clearing so they safely can land a chopper and it's reachable by three different access roads. I've got wildlife services and local marshals covering those roads, so once a vehicle goes in, it will be stopped if it tries to leave. Whatever they're bringing in, they're going to have to transport it by one of those roads."

Jedi interrupted him. "Do we know what animal they have set up for this buyer? And do we know who the buyer is?"

Jared shook his head. "No, the cyber unit has been watching the on-line market but there haven't been any unusual animals advertised late-ly, although that could mean that they have an outside source. Rumor is that this buyer is someone real important. Ten-to-one this big shot wants something that no one else has in their trophy room." He exhaled a heavy sigh. "Something extremely endangered, no doubt. Our information has the buyer flying into the hunt by chopper. We're not sure how everyone else is arriving though."

Bruce snorted with disgust. "I can't understand how some jerk could shoot a rare animal just to display it in their trophy room. Some people really suck."

There were nods of agreement all around.

"How many subjects are we looking at?" Tyrone wanted to know.

Jared rolled the map back up and turned to face them. "We don't know. I took out a major player three days ago. I'm thinking Kyle was the leader, but I'm not sure. I've seen reports of anywhere from four to ten members of the ring, depending on the animal and buyer. We know there are defi-nitely a driver and a chopper pilot. I'm guessing a minimum of six players for this gig."

"With the leader dead, wouldn't they have packed up and moved this meeting somewhere else?" Micah asked. "It seems that they would have known they were compromised."

"They don't know Kyle's dead yet. No one in the area does," Jared told him bluntly. "I recovered Kyle's phone and have been answering text mes-sages on his behalf for the last couple of days. As far as they know, their boss has been detained with some other 'urgent' business, but he'll be at the meeting place in time. According to the texts, Kyle is the only one who can give the signal for the chopper to bring in the buyer. Without him, our plan is dead in the water. I intend for Kyle to make that meeting."

Jedi narrowed his eyes. "And how do you plan on doing that? They'll be on to us if you send the chopper, but they don't see this Kyle waiting for it."

Jared knew that they weren't going to like his plan, but he didn't have a better one right now. He was also pretty certain that Jedi knew what he was going to say before he said it. They had become fast friends at the academy, despite the fact that they were too much alike; bull-headed and stubborn, and neither afraid to speak their mind.

"I'm going to dress like Kyle and show myself at the edge of the clearing. By the time they figure out I'm not him, the chopper should be on the ground and you guys will be moving in."

Just as he suspected, there was no surprise on Jedi's face but the others looked startled and glanced among themselves.

"And what does headquarters have to say about this plan?" Jedi crossed his arms over his chest. "When we were briefed about this mission there was no mention of you dressing up and putting yourself in the line of fire."

Jared took a breath then looked directly at Jedi. "They don't know any-thing about it. This is something I've decided that I'm going to do. I want these sons-of-bitches locked up and I intend to get them. If we let this opportunity slip by, they'll be scattered and we won't have a snowball's chance of finding them again for months, or years, or ever."

This wasn't the first time that Jared and Jedi had disagreed over a plan and everyone pretty much knew the drill. Standing back, they looked as if they were watching a tennis match as they swiveled their heads back and forth between the two friends.

"Since when do you decide how a mission goes down? Last time I checked, we were a team. How the hell are we supposed to cover you if something goes wrong?" Jedi took a step closer to Jared. "You know as well as I do that once a plan is in place, there is no deviation. I, for one, don't feel like throwing away my career to go flip burgers for a living. But you don't care about that, do you? This wouldn't have something to do with a certain woman who was admitted to the hospital a few days ago, would it?" Jedi didn't even blink as Jared stepped forward so that they were nose to nose. The rest of the team glanced nervously at each other. "Oh yeah, I was briefed about her, too. Seems the chief is a little worried about your state of mind and personal involvement in this case, my friend. I've been given the authority to dismiss you if I feel that you will jeopardize this mission. It's my call."

Jared let the words sink in before taking a step back. Running a hand over his face, he wondered for a moment if he should walk away from this operation and let his team handle it. Get to the hospital and see if Amanda had awoken from her coma. No. He needed to see this through to the end.

"You can dismiss me, but I guarantee that I'll be there, whether you want me to be or not. Dressing like Kyle is the only way to get that chopper to deliver the buyer. You come up with a better plan and I'll be all for it. We are running out of time."

Jared could see that Jedi wasn't being convinced so he tried a different tactic. "Listen, I'm not talking about being a hero here, but I don't intend to lose this opportunity to get these sons of bitches." He looked at each of his team in turn. "I've seen this Kyle asshole; I'm pretty close to his height and weight. I know his brother, and I'm assuming that his mannerism will be similar. I'll only be standing at the edge of the clearing long enough to be seen. If anyone tries to get close, we'll take them out of the equation. I know this goes against orders but I'm asking you to trust me." He paused. So much was riding on this. He had to make them agree. "So, what's it going to be?"

All heads turned in Jedi's direction.

"We do not deviate from the plan." Jedi replied, accentuating each word.

Jared bit back what he wanted to say and made a visible effort to stay calm. "Okay, let's talk about the approved plan then. We don't even know if we're even in the right area. We have no idea who the buyer is or if he'll bring more muscle power of his own. No one knows how many members are actually in this organization and we don't have a clue as to what animal they're bringing in. So how the hell can we make a plan to take them down if we don't even know who the hell they are?"

Closing his eyes to take a calming breath, Jared waited a moment before he looked at Jedi again. "All I'm asking is that when I call in the buyer, I can be seen at the clearing just long enough for them to assume that everything is going according to their plan. Nothing else on our plan changes, guaranteed."

Jedi tried to stare Jared down but he must have seen something in Jared's face because he relaxed his stance and gave a shake of his head. "You know we better catch these bastards or headquarters is gonna have you singing soprano. Just for the record, I think it's a stupid ass plan. You have thirty seconds for them to see you and then you get yourself back in position, or I'll shoot you myself."

With that, he turned and walked away. The rest of the men gave a quick glance at Jared, and then turned to follow Jedi, talking amongst themselves.

Jared was grateful that Jedi had backed down as he wasn't sure that he had the extra energy to keep fighting him. Lack of sleep was making him desperate. Too much caffeine and anxiety for Amanda was all that was keeping him going. She deserved a life, she deserved justice and come hell or high water, he was going to get them for her.

• • •

Jared and his team were dressed in full camouflage as they walked through the dense forest until they were within a quarter of a mile of the supposed meeting place. Heavy dark paint smeared their faces, helping them blend in with the surrounding trees. It was promising to be another scorcher of a day and they were already sweating in their heavy gear. Knowing that they were close to the clearing, Jedi used hand signals to stop them instead of talking. Sound travelled in the forest and they didn't want to tip off anyone that they were there. They had worked together for so long that he didn't even need to gesture to Bruce to use his binoculars to check out the area. Bruce was already swinging onto a low branch of an oak tree. Within seconds, he was lost from sight among the thick leaves.

About ten minutes later, Bruce shimmied down the tree and made his way back to where they were building a makeshift camp behind a stand of evergreens. Kneeling down on one knee, he took a couple of swigs of water before speaking. "Definitely something ready to go down here. Two guys visible, each carrying some heavy fire power," he told them, keeping his voice low. "No sign of any cargo truck or animal enclosure, just a small jeep."

This wasn't surprising news since they had already suspected that the chopper wouldn't arrive until late afternoon to early evening. That way, any shots fired would be harder for the rangers to investigate due to encroaching darkness. This gang had used that tact before.

Now there was nothing to do, until the rest of the suspects arrived with the merchandise, and it was time for Kyle to make his appearance so the chopper could be summoned. The team would take turns climbing the oak to keep an eye on the activity.

Jared chose a spot a short distance from the others, and leaned back against the rough bark of a tree, closing his eyes. All he needed was a couple of hours of sleep and he would be good as new. Footsteps came closer. He opened one eye to see Jedi sit down and lean against a nearby rock.

Sighing inwardly, Jared closed his eye again and waited. There was no sense in trying to pretend that he didn't know what was on his comrade's mind. This moment had been inevitable since they had had their disagreement several hours earlier. "Forget talking me out of this." No sense in beating around the bush. Maybe if they had this out now, he could get some shut eye.

Jedi chuckled. "Now why would I do a damn foolish thing like that when you are so hell bent on getting yourself killed?"

That was one of the things that Jared liked most about Jedi. He certainly didn't sugarcoat anything. No sir, he just gave his unvarnished take on everything. Life according to Jedi. Sometimes Jared wondered if the nickname had gone to his friend's head and he actually did believe he was a Jedi Master.

"Don't be so melodramatic," Jared replied, turning his face to the side. "I have no intention of dying today. It's the only way to flush this buyer out and you know it. You're just pissed because you don't have a better plan." He could be blunt too.

Jedi snorted. "Tell me about this woman, Amanda, who's got you risking your life and my career."

Jared kept his eyes closed. "This has nothing to do with her. I'm done chasing these sons of bitches and coming up empty every time. I'm tired of the bad guys calling the shots and being three steps ahead of us." He sat up and wrapped his arms around his knees. "We have the upper hand on this one and I am willing to take the risk needed to draw this buyer in and maybe, just maybe, arrest these guys and get some leads that can take down the guys at the top that run these operations. The ones who use their money and power to ruin people's lives and kill those poor animals."

Jedi was silent for a moment. "I get it," he said quietly, "I would love to nail these guys as well but I'm not willing to put everyone's career and life on the line for one buyer. You know as well as I do that for every perp we arrest at least two more take their place. The only good news is that we have job security, I guess." Jedi stood up and waited until Jared looked up at him. "You know what I think?" Jedi didn't give him a chance to answer. "I think that this Amanda is the one and it's scaring the crap out of you. You'd rather take on a gang of poachers than face the fact that you could actually settle down and be happy." With that, Jedi turned and walked away.

. . .

The vibration in his shirt pocket woke Jared from a sound sleep. Fumbling for the phone, he yawned, and then a quick look at the screen made him jolt awake. The sender was just a phone number - no name. Snapping his fingers brought Jedi to his side. Kneeling down, Jedi looked at the screen and read the text.

"Where the hell r u? B arriving at eighteen hundred hours." 6pm.

The clock on the phone read 3:02pm. Jared looked up at the sky in disbelief. Damn, he had slept for over seven hours! Glancing around, he noticed that everyone else was awake and watching him and Jedi. Micah was missing, but Jared assumed that he was in the tree, keeping surveillance.

"Why did you let me sleep so long?" he growled as he rolled to his feet.

Jedi also stood up but wasn't fazed by Jared's temper. "Because you looked like hell when we got here. You obviously needed the rest. Besides, I didn't have to listen to your whining all day; just your damn snoring." He gave his famous grin. "Anyways, there's not a lot going on. I'd have woken you if there was."

Jared ran a hand over the stubble on his face and yawned again. He hated to admit it, but he had needed the sleep. "No sign of any more vehicles?"

Jedi shook his head and fell in step with him. "No, and that seems odd to me. I would've figured they'd have brought this animal in already. Get it set up in some type of outdoor enclosure so that it would be in plain sight when the chopper landed. Something doesn't feel right."

Jared stopped and turned to him. "You think they're spooked since Kyle hasn't made an appearance yet?"

Jedi thought for a moment. "I don't think they spook easily, or they would have been caught by now. Kyle not being around isn't stopping them from setting up this job. Kyle may be the leader, but they run like an outfit with a chain of command." Jedi called the other men over, Micah trailing in behind them. "We need to consider that we are dealing with a military trained unit."

"Guerillas or mercenaries?" Bruce asked.

"Doesn't matter." Jedi looked grim. "They aren't going to just give up once they know we're here."

The men stared at each other. This was not good news. A military trained unit meant that they would be heavily armed and, depending on how they'd been trained, were more likely to fight back as highly functioning soldiers. A random bunch of poachers were more likely to run and scatter.

Just then, a voice came through the earpiece that each of them wore. "Ranger McCoy for ATF unit."

Jared pushed the button on the wire that connected to his earpiece and leaned in closer to the mic attached to his shirt, under his vest. They were using a radio frequency that was tuned only for them. "McLean here."

"We got movement on the north fire road. Subjects are heading your way; three jeeps and a box truck. We counted five individuals but can't see what's in the truck. Looks like your guys, and from the sounds from the back, I'm guessing something big. It ain't happy."

"Roger that."

They had all heard the exchange.

Micah was the first to speak. "That makes it a minimum of seven players, a pilot and the client. We'll need to be in position as soon as that chopper hits the ground." He looked pointedly at Jared. "If they make you, before that chopper lands, then I guarantee we're going to have a hell of a fight on our hands. You'll need to convince them that you are Kyle and get back into position as soon as possible."

Jared nodded. The timing had to be just right to make his appearance. His cover would be blown if he showed too early and allowed one of them to get close enough to see that he wasn't Kyle. Appearing too late could cause them to abort the mission altogether, making things more unpredictable than they already were.

"Text them back and tell them you're on your way," Jedi instructed. "We need to get to our positions now!"

They disbanded and headed to where their backpacks were lying on the ground.

Jedi followed Jared. "I know this one's personal. Stick to the plan and we'll get these bastards. Okay?"

Jared turned. "You still think I'm gonna do something stupid?"

"Let's just say that I know you. "Jedi didn't grin like Jared thought he would. "I won't say that you'll do anything stupid, but I figure you have another plan in your back pocket and, given the opportunity, you'd be more than happy to run with it." He placed a hand on Jared's shoulder. "Like I said, I know this one's personal. If you care about Amanda at all, then you'll follow our plan. We'll catch these bastards and we'll all get out of this in one piece. I sure as hell don't want to bring you back to her in a body bag."

Without waiting for a reply, Jedi turned and strode away.

• • •

Crouching down and looking through the undergrowth at the edge of the clearing, Jared could see two men. They were also dressed in camo gear and carrying automatic rifles. With their backs to him, they leaned against the hood of their jeep, smoking cigarettes. Their voices were hushed and he was too far away to make out what they were saying.

Taking a few steps back, Jared joined Jedi and Micah. Bruce, Gary and Tyrone had separated about a hundred yards back and were headed for their positions. Bruce would cover the North road; Gary the South road and Tyrone would cover the East fire road. The goal was to keep all the players in the meadow until they could be apprehended. If, by chance, any of the vehicles made it past one of them, they would be stopped by agents and park rangers at the other end of the road.

The sun was filtering through the thick foliage in the western sky and the air was thick with humidity. Jared swiped at a stray bead of sweat that ran down the side of his face. A glance at his watch showed that they still had some time before he should make his appearance as Kyle.

His earpiece crackled with Bruce's voice. "Convoy has arrived boys."

Sure enough, they could hear the roar of engines as the vehicles made their way into the clearing. Crawling on their bellies, the three ATF agents watched as the jeeps made a half-circle at the far end of the meadow. It reminded Jared of an old western he had once watched, when the settlers had circled the wagons to fend off an approaching Indian attack. The box truck pulled up to the edge of the woods, keeping to the shade.

Four men got out of the vehicles and walked over to where the two earlier men were standing.

"In position," Tyrone radioed.

"Roger," Jedi answered, never taking his eyes off the men in the clearing.

Several more minutes passed before Tyrone and Bruce reported that they were in position too. Jared and his teammates made verbal notes about the suspects they were watching. One of them was nicknamed Bubba by Jared.

Bubba was a huge man and easily topped the three-hundred-pound mark, but it wasn't fat. Muscles bulged in his forearms and Jared knew that this man would be difficult to subdue. Bubba moved like a man used to giving orders and taking out anyone who didn't comply.

Jedi must have read his mind. "Think the only way that we are gonna stop that one," he gestured toward Bubba, "is to take him down with an elephant tranquilizer."

Jared gave a derisive laugh. "We'll need two doses. Bubba, there, looks like he eats elephants for breakfast - right after he bench presses them."

Micah chimed in. "If you two ladies are done gossiping, then you might want to pay attention to the driver of the box truck. Look familiar?"

Training his binoculars to the man emerging from the truck, Jared swore as he recognized one of the biggest hit men on the FBI's most wanted list.

Russian-born Yuri "Bulldog" Vasiliev had immigrated to the United States as a child. According to his rap sheet, he had been in and out of trouble since he was eight years old. No one knew his exact age when he joined up with organized crime, but it wasn't long before he'd found a niche as the cleanup man. The FBI had been searching for him for over a decade.

"Looks like our favorite hit man is moonlighting," Jared commented. "Wonder why he's hanging out with a bunch of poachers? That's not his usual M.O. but it would explain where the hell he disappeared to."

Jedi shook his head. "I told you that this operation didn't feel right." Turning to Micah, his voice low and clipped, he ordered, "Find out who the hell that big guy is and get me Intel on the others, too. The plan has changed. We need backup. Get me more agents. This is going to be one hell of a fight."

● ● ●

Jared pulled Kyle's hat down low over his eyes. With any luck, just his mouth and chin would be showing. He wished for the umpteenth time that he had seen Kyle walk so that he could imitate it now. So much was riding on his performance to make the poachers believe he was Kyle. *"No pressure,"* he thought.

After months of searching for the most elusive criminals in the United States, it now appeared that they were part of a bigger network of underworld scumbags. This was the type of case that made or destroyed careers, depending on the outcome. These guys were some of the most dangerous men on the planet. Kyle must have kept Amanda's identity as a secret vendetta for himself. If he had told his hunting buddies about her, they would have tracked her down and killed her by now, not wanting to risk the distraction she could have created.

All Jared's senses were heightened as he shrugged into a replica of Kyle's shirt then buttoned it over the Kevlar vest. Wincing, he wiggled his shoulders around to loosen the tight garment, and then he began to unbutton it.

"You are not taking off the vest." Jedi's voice came from behind him.

Jared spun on his heels. "I don't intend to, but I can't move my arms in this damn thing. I'll be a sitting duck if I can't get to my gun."

"You'll be a dead duck if you take it off." Jedi wasn't about to be talked out of it, not that Jared had planned to.

"Turn around," Jedi commanded as he took out a hunting knife.

Jared raised his eyebrows but did as he was told.

Jedi grabbed the shirt collar then sliced two openings into the back of it. The garment immediately loosened.

"You must be hell on your wardrobe," Jared commented as he easily rolled his shoulders. It felt so much better.

Jedi sheathed the knife. "Just don't turn your back on these bastards," was all he said.

Unable to argue, Jared walked to the small deer path that led into the meadow. He had sent a text earlier stating that his vehicle had broken down on one of the fire roads so he'd be heading in on foot. Someone had texted him back, offering to pick him up, but he'd answered that he was traveling through the woods and would be there in about twenty minutes. Now those twenty minutes were gone, and it was time to make his appearance.

The sun had fallen below the tree line in the west, creating shadows deeper in the forest. The birds were twittering loudly as they flew back to their nests for the approaching evening. Jared let his mind go blank as he walked and just listened to the sounds around him. When a picture of

Amanda entered his head, he was quick to think of something else. Thinking about her was too dangerous right now. Personal emotions had no place on a mission, in fact; they could get an agent killed.

Pulling out Kyle's phone, he stopped and texted that he was five minutes away. He instructed them to tell the chopper to proceed. Holding his breath, he waited for a reply. There weren't any other numbers in Kyle's phone so he had to assume that someone else would give the thumbs-up to the pilot.

Sweat from beneath the band of the wide hat ran down his cheek. It was hard for Jared to tell if it was from the humidity or nerves. Hell, he'd rather dodge bullets than sit and wait for something to happen.

A bird startled him as it chattered from a nearby branch, giving warning to all other birds in the area that he didn't belong there.

At least it wasn't a crow, Jared thought. Not that he was superstitious, but he would take all the good omens that he could get.

Moving farther along the path, he could see glimpses of the meadow through the thinning? foliage. Switching the semi-automatic rifle into his other hand, he wiped his sweating palm on his pants. A few deep breaths cleared his mind. From here on out, his instincts would dictate his moves. They had never failed him before. He hoped to hell they wouldn't fail him now.

Pulling at the brim of the hat, Jared stepped into the meadow.

• • •

Bubba and his cohorts were gathered in a group at the other end of the field. They were all in the same general area, but as Jared studied them, he noticed they were too far apart to be talking to each other. That brought a faint smile to his lips.

They didn't trust each other. Go figure.

*"Maybe they weren't that stupid after all,"* he thought as he stood at the edge of the tree line.

Bubba was the first to catch sight of him and when he did, he pulled out a cell phone.

After a quick second of pushing buttons, Bubba put the phone up to his ear and began to gesture.

The others turned to watch him. It was too great of a distance to judge the looks on their faces.

Pretending to limp, Jared moved toward the group, slowly. His earpiece crackled to life.

"What the hell do you think you're doing?"

It was Jedi.

The microphone was on, so there was no need to push the button.

"Just giving them a little performance," he replied, barely moving his lips.

"You were supposed to just show yourself, not head closer."

Jared could feel Jedi's anger through his earpiece. No doubt Jedi would love to take a shot at him at that moment. The thought made him chuckle. "Looks like Bubba just made the call for the chopper, so if I can keep them busy for a few minutes, it'll buy us some extra time. Make them less suspicious."

Jedi's words came fast. "I already have confirmation that a chopper took off without filing a flight plan from a small airport west of the city. ETA is about fifteen minutes by calculation. How do you plan to keep them busy for fifteen minutes? They're gonna realize you're not Kyle the moment they get close enough to see your face."

Jared figured that Jedi would have an ulcer before he was thirty, if he didn't already have one. Stopping, he kneeled down as if to tie his shoe. "Stop throwing logic into my plans, Jedi, it messes them up. I want to put myself in between these scumbags and whatever is in that truck. I don't trust these bastards not to shoot the animal in there the moment we make our move."

"I KNEW you wouldn't just do as you were told."

The poor bastard really did need to take some vacation time, he was sounding so stressed out.

"I swear to god, Jared, that if you don't turn around and get the hell out of there, right now, I'm going to beat the shit out of you the minute this is all over. You could get us all killed with this stupid stunt."

Jared stood back up and started forward again. "By the time I get close enough to blow my cover the chopper should be here. I'm done talking."

Bulldog was the only one still watching Jared's progress across the two-acre expanse of grass. The Russian was leaning back on the hood of a jeep and smoking a cigarette, as if he had all the time in the world. The other men had moved over to the cargo truck and were in the process of pulling a large enclosed metal crate from the back of it. Bubba held one end of the crate easily while the three guys on the sides looked like they were struggling under its weight. They heaved it out of the truck and dropped it to the ground. A cry of protest came from the enclosure.

Jared was still a good distance away, so it was hard to say what type of animal had made the noise. Most likely whatever was inside was sedated.

"How we doin' on time for that chopper?" he asked, still limping forward.

"Around eight minutes," was the reply.

It would take him about three to four minutes to reach halfway across the expanse, and then he would somehow need to get around the vehicles to get to the crate. The tricky part was keeping the poachers convinced that he was Kyle until he could get in position. If they found him out before he could get behind the enclosure then the operation would be in serious jeopardy, never mind that he would be in the direct line of fire. What would they do if he veered off to the left and disappeared into the forest?

"Still time to bail." Jedi was reading his mind.

"Sorry buddy, no turning back now."

"Don't get killed," was the terse reply.

No doubt about it, he was going to have to buy Jedi a few rounds of beer to make up for all the stress he was putting his buddy through.

• • •

Beads of sweat ran down Jedi's back as he lay motionless in the underbrush, his binoculars following Jared's slow process across the meadow. Glancing at his watch, he estimated that they had about five minutes before the chopper arrived. Micah was in the underbrush, too, about a hundred yards to his left.

Swinging the binoculars around, Jedi watched the suspects as they walked back toward where Bulldog was still leaning against the hood of the jeep. It bothered him that Bulldog hadn't moved or taken his eyes off Jared. The hit man hadn't gotten where he was by letting his guard down. Jedi would bet that Jared wasn't fooling him.

"I think Bulldog is suspicious of you," he radioed Jared.

A few seconds went by before Jared answered. "Not surprised, word is, he's suspicious of his own mother. That's what's kept him alive for so long."

Before Jedi could respond, there was a subtle change in one of the suspect's posture. Jedi watched as one of the original sentry guards leaned over and said something to his companion who then looked in Jared's direction before straightening up.

"I think one of them just made you," Jedi warned, never taking his eyes off the two men. Raising his rifle, he sighted them in his scope; if they as so much as raised their rifles a millimeter, he wouldn't hesitate to fire.

"Yea, I see them."

Jedi shook his head as he watched Jared continue to move forward, though he had to admit that there wasn't a heck of a lot else he could do. Jared was in the middle of a field with nowhere else to go. If he headed for the sides, then the poachers would open fire and he wouldn't stand a chance. Yep, he was gonna beat the crap out of Jared when this was all over and he was going to enjoy every moment of it.

"What's the plan now, hot shot?" Bruce added his two cents.

"Same as before, take these guys out and don't get shot."

Jedi could tell that Jared was basically talking without moving his lips in case someone had a pair of binoculars trained on him. He was about to reply when the distinctive sound of a chopper reached his ears.

*Shit.*

"Jared, get out of there, now!" Micah's voice boomed through the earpiece, making Jedi wince. "You're going to be between them and the chopper. If they figure out who you are, they'll gun you down. You can't outrun a chopper."

Jedi kept his scope trained on Bulldog and his crew. They had heard the sound of the chopper too and quickly headed to different strategic spots. They probably knew that the chopper was early and wanted to protect themselves in case the approaching craft was not the one they were expecting.

Jared took the opportunity to sprint to the nearest jeep and hunker down next to it, out of Jedi's line of vision.

"Who's got the visual on Jared?" he asked.

Jedi could see the two men he had mentally nicknamed Dumb and Dumber had both hidden under another Jeep. Bubba and the three other men disappeared under the cargo truck. Jedi wondered how the hell Bubba was able to squeeze out of sight.

Gary broke in, "Check, I got a visual on Jared."

Jedi was scanning the area, but it took him a moment to realize that he couldn't see Bulldog.

"Who has eyes on Bulldog?" His voice was drowned out by a helicopter clearing the southern tree line.

The powerful blades created a down draft of wind as it hovered over the vehicles, causing leaves and debris to become airborne. Bubba extracted himself from underneath the truck and must have given a signal, because the pilot turned the chopper and headed for a landing spot on the end of the field closest to Jedi, Micah and Tyrone, who were several hundred yards to their left.

Jedi and Micah scooted backwards into the denser underbrush. The pilot hovered over the landing site for a moment before putting the chopper down with a slight bump. The blades slowly came to a stop as the passenger's side door opened and a man disembarked.

Jedi moved forward again and trained his binoculars on the newest arrival. The man was tall, lean and moved with quick, sure steps.

"What the hell is he wearing?" Micah wanted to know.

"Looks like our buyer thinks he's on safari," Jared's voice answered.

Sure enough, the new arrival was wearing an outfit straight out of the movies, white shirt, beige khakis and brown leather jacket to boot. He even had a whip hanging from his belt. The iconic fedora was pulled down over his face so Jared couldn't see any distinguishing features. An automatic rifle dangled from his hands.

Slowly rising from his spot next to one of the jeeps, Jared pulled his own hat further down his face and headed out to meet the newcomer.

"Is everyone ready to take these bastards down?" he breathed into the mic. Five affirmatives answered him. Adrenaline was pumping through his veins, making him hyper-focused. "Then as soon as I disarm Mr. Big here, you guys move in."

Again, there were five affirmatives.

Jared took a slow breath. "Okay then, let's do this."

Less than a hundred feet separated Jared and the client when all hell broke loose.

Jared was trying to figure out the facial features of the man walking toward him when shouting erupted behind him. As he turned, a large blast sounded from the back of the meadow where the crate was located. Smoke billowed up from the area and then several more explosions went off, close to where the first one had originated from. Jared had thrown himself to the ground at the first eruption; unsure if someone was shooting at him. Looking back at the buyer, he was surprised to see the man still standing and staring off in the direction of the chaos.

"Any idea, what the hell that was?" he asked, rolling to his feet, keeping his eye locked on the new arrival.

Before anyone could respond, the chopper pilot started the engine and the large blades began to slowly turn.

More shouting. More explosions. All Jared's instincts told him to look behind him but there was no way he was going to let the client out of his line of vision, never mind the chopper pilot.

Glancing at the motionless trophy hunter, Jared noticed that Tyrone was making his way through the waist-high grass, his rifle aimed and ready, coming up behind the chopper.

"It's Bulldog," Gary's voice came through the noise. "He's setting off M80's and other explosives. Can't see much through the smoke."

Jared's mind raced. Why the hell would Bulldog be setting off explosives just as the buyer arrived? Usually the customer would look over the merchandise, hand over the fee and then get ready for the hunt.

The chopper's blades were reaching lift-off speed and the noise was deafening, adding to the chaos. Tyrone had reached the door of the bird and flung it open. Jared watched as the startled pilot attempted to take off with Tyrone hanging from the open door. Tyrone easily subdued the man, causing the aircraft to thud back down on to the grass.

Through the noise and confusion, the buyer hadn't moved a muscle, as if they were transfixed to one spot. Now, he gave an audible gasp, then raised his rifle to waist height.

Jared turned to see what would have given the client such a reaction.

A white Siberian tiger trotted unsteadily out of the smoke towards them. The poor animal was emaciated and obviously under the effects of a sedative. Its eyes were glassy and unfocused, yet it managed to keep its balance and move forward.

The Siberian tiger was the biggest cat in the world and usually weighed between three hundred and six hundred pounds. This tiger's ribs were showing, and Jared doubted that it would tip the scales at two hundred pounds. Its coat was dull and dirty, yet it was still one of the most majestic animals that he had ever seen. There was a movement behind the animal.

Jared gasped when he saw another, smaller white tiger.

How the hell did Kyle manage to get one white Siberian tiger, never mind two? These tigers were the most endangered tigers in the world, thanks to poachers selling their pelts and body parts due to the myth that just about every piece of the tiger was powerful in Chinese medicine. Jared knew that there were only about four hundred and fifty of the species left in the wild, mostly in the Bikin river basin forests of Russia.

Bulldog. Now it made sense as to why the hitman was here.

Out of the corner of his eye, Jared saw the buyer raise the rifle to his face. There was no time to think, just react. Swinging his arms wildly, he let out a loud yell as he leaped at the trophy hunter. Knocking the man to the ground, the rifle discharged, shooting a bullet harmlessly into the trees.

The buyer's hat went flying when they hit the ground. Long brown hair came loose from a bun that had kept it neatly hidden under the hat. Suddenly, the man that Jared had tackled turned into a she-cat. He grabbed her wrists as she tried to gouge at his face with her fingernails. Her legs were flailing, and he moved forward to avoid getting kicked. It took him a few minutes, longer than he would have liked to admit, to subdue her. Turning her onto her stomach, he pulled her arms behind her back. Pulling a zip tie from his vest pocket, he handcuffed her hands together. too much adrenaline was searing through his every muscle as he got to his feet and hauled her up off the ground.

"What do you think you're doing?" the infuriated woman spat at him. "My father paid good money for those animals. He'll have you shot for manhandling me."

The commotion had sent the tigers veering off to the right and now Jared could see them staggering toward the edge of the clearing. The bigger tiger lay down in the long grass but the smaller one paced nervously nearby. Through his binoculars, he could see the larger tiger was breathing hard. Jared felt his anger rise on its behalf.

Looking back at the woman, he realized that she was barely twenty years old. Her long brown hair was disheveled and her brown eyes were shooting sparks at him.

"Who is your father?" Jared demanded to know.

Her eyes narrowed. "If you don't already know who my daddy is, then I'm not about to tell you. I'm not saying another word without my lawyer."

"Fine with me," Jared replied, his voice hard and cold.

The woman struggled against his tightening grip as he marched her back to the chopper where Tyrone, Jedi and Micah awaited them.

. . .

Jared, Jedi and Micah watched as Tyrone started the chopper's engine and lifted it into the air. Tyrone had been a chopper pilot in the military and took the controls easily. The original pilot and the girl were tied together in the back. The team had decided to get them out of harm's way and to also remove the chopper, just in case the remaining poachers decided to use it to escape.

There were still some occasional explosions coming from the far end of the field, but the smoke was getting thicker.

"Give me an update," Jedi asked into his microphone.

The three men crouched down in the tall grass about halfway into the meadow. Jared could see flames behind one of the jeeps and someone was yelling in a foreign language.

"There's too much smoke." Bruce's voice came through the earpiece. "Large amount of grass is burning. My guess is that these guys are going to cut their losses and make a run for it."

"Affirmative," Gary's voice followed. "They're headed for the vehicles. Using the smoke as a screen."

Jared, Micah and Jedi leapt to their feet. Gary was positioned to their left, at the entrance to the South road. Bruce was at the far end of the meadow covering the North road. Not wanting to get in the middle of any crossfire, Jedi and Micah ran along the edge of the clearing, toward Bruce and the

North road. Since that was where the poachers had made their entrance, it made sense that they would head out in that same direction.

Jared watched as his teammates disappeared into the smoke. He hesitated to follow. Something wasn't right about this whole scenario. Those tigers were extremely rare and almost impossible to acquire. Kyle and his cohorts had gone to a lot of trouble to pull this deal off so it made no sense that Bulldog would jeopardize it the way he had. Word had been that this buyer was one of the biggest names on the FBI's most wanted list. So why was the daughter here? What master billionaire criminal was going to send his daughter into a den of cutthroat mercenaries without an army to back her up? Everyone knew that there was no honor among thieves. They could have kidnapped her and sold the tigers on the black market, which would have been business as usual. What was he missing?

Even if Bulldog had known that their cover was blown, why release the tigers? They were worth tens of thousands of dollars. These guys didn't strike him as the type to just "cut their losses and run." They were the type to stand and fight. Nothing about this situation added up.

"Listen guys, this is all wrong," Jared radioed his team. "I'm thinking they knew from the start that we were going to be here. This could be a trap."

Looking back over his shoulder, Jared could see the tigers were still at the edge of the forest. Something in his gut told him that he shouldn't head into the melee that was in front of him. He should hang back and keep an eye on the felines.

"We need a fire crew up here, now," Jedi yelled into the mic, startling Jared.

The smoke was getting thicker and the unmistakable sound of crackling filled the air as the fire gained speed. Heat began to roll over Jared, causing him to retreat several yards.

What the hell was Bulldog up to?

One of the jeeps headed out of the smoke and toward the South road. There were three men in the vehicle. Dumb, or was it Dumber was driving. Hitting a rut in the meadow, the man in the back was almost toppled out of the vehicle.

The jeep was several hundred yards from the opening to the road when a shot echoed through the meadow. It was immediately followed by the sound of a tire blowing. The auto weaved erratically for a few seconds before the driver regained control.

Jared watched as the driver gunned the engine and continued toward the fire road. Gary fired another shot and took out the other front tire.

This time, the jeep did not respond to the driver's maneuvers but stopped abruptly, sideways, grass and dirt flying.

The three men abandoned the vehicle and tried to run for the tree line. Again, Gary's gun sounded and the lead man fell. The others ducked down in the tall grass and fired some shots in the direction that they thought Gary was hiding. Several more shots and then silence.

Multiple shots rang out in the direction of the North road, but Jared stayed back in the middle of the field. For several moments, there was no other sound but the crackling of grass and the whoosh of fire as it climbed the dry branches of a tree.

Then the shouting began again.

Jared could feel that something was about to escalate. The tension in his gut was getting stronger. Stepping backwards, he inched closer to the tigers. He was about five hundred yards from them when the hair on the back of his neck began to tingle. Spinning around, he came face to face with Bulldog.

The big man resembled the canine that he was nicknamed after, with bulging eyes, smashed-in nose and an under-bite that was an orthodontist's dream. His grey hair was thinning, and Jared figured that he had to be on the far side of sixty. Deep wrinkles on his face, mixed with a few scars, showed the rough life that he had led.

The Russian aimed a revolver at Jared's head. There was spark of amusement in the hitman's eyes, yet his hand never wavered.

"I could have killed you several times and be miles away before they were aware that you were dead," the hitman said conversationally. There was still a hint of his Russian roots in his speech.

"Well, since I'm still alive, I'm assuming that there is a reason for that."

The older man smirked. "I usually like to tell people why they need to die. Eases the pain. In your case, I have some questions."

That surprised Jared which amused Bulldog even more.

"Where is Kyle?"

Jared decided that nothing short of the truth was going to satisfy Bulldog. "Shot and killed."

Bulldog nodded. The news didn't appear to come as a surprise. "So you take his phone and pretend to be him."

It was a statement, so Jared didn't bother to answer.

"What's the girl got to do with Kyle? Why did he want her dead?"

Years of being undercover is what kept Jared from reacting, but the blood in his veins suddenly ran cold. How the hell had Bulldog found out about

Amanda? If he knew who she was, and that she had been a witness to the poachers ten years ago, then he would try to find a way to execute her. He didn't appear to be the kind of mercenary to leave loose ends.

"What girl?" Jared answered, stalling.

Bulldog waited, his gun still perfectly aimed. "You have three seconds to tell me, one..two..three.."

Jared threw himself to the right as the gun went off. Rolling, he got up on his knees and aimed at where Bulldog should have been. Instead he saw Jedi, his rifle raised, standing a short distance away. Bulldog was lying face down in front of him with blood soaking the back of his shirt.

Jedi walked forward, never lowering his weapon, until he'd turned Bulldog over with his foot. The hitman was dead.

Jared sat back on the grass and ran a hand over his face. Looking up at his teammate, he asked, "How did you know that he'd doubled back on me?"

"I didn't. I figured that someone was going to get those tigers back somehow, so I came to protect them."

"I'm glad you did." Jared glanced back at the fire. "Did any of these bastards escape? Where's Bubba?"

"He put up a fight, but he's not the brightest. He's locked in the cargo truck. We got them all."

"Thank god," Jared said, relief flooding his body.

· · ·

Within the hour, scores of firemen, rangers, policemen and anyone who could support the effort had converged on the meadow to help fight the fire. It was contained with less than an acre being burned. Bulldog's body was removed from the scene and slowly people started to head back to town.

Bubba and his gang were escorted by helicopters to the State Police station for booking. Jared doubted that there were enough charges to keep them behind bars for very long. Most of the charges would be for possession of endangered animals, arson and resisting arrest.

· · ·

Jared stood beside Jedi and the rest of their team to watch the Siberian tigers get loaded back onto the cargo truck.

Micah had made some calls while they'd waited for the local authorities to arrive. "These tigers were bought off of a small traveling zoo that couldn't afford to keep their animals anymore. Thought they were selling them to another zoo. Not for slaughter. They were pretty upset to hear about the poachers."

One of the firefighters had wrangled up some steaks for the starving animals. The tigers, almost completely recovered from their sedation, were busy chewing away at the raw meat.

"Where are they headed now?" Bruce wanted to know.

Micah grinned. "I called a friend of mine who got us permission to send them to a big cat rescue in California. The actress, Tippy Hedren, from the movie *The Birds*, started the sanctuary back in the eighties. They'll take good care of them there."

Everyone nodded their heads in approval, grateful that some good was going to come out of this day after all.

. . .

As the ATF team walked back to where they had left their vehicles hours earlier each of them became lost in their own thoughts. It had been a long day. It was dark by the time they had reached their jeeps.

Jared ripped off the confining shirt and Kevlar vest. The hat had been lost hours before. Opening the back of his jeep, he threw his gear into the back and grabbed a bottle of water from the duffle bag. Sitting down in the cargo area, he twisted off the cap and took a large swig. "Wish this was an ice-cold beer," he said, grinning. The back of his throat was as dry as the Sahara so the water tasted almost as good a beer, for the moment.

He offered a bottle of water to Micah, Bruce and Gary but they declined, eager to find something to eat and get some sleep. They climbed into their vehicles and drove away.

Jedi accepted the water and sat down on the hood of his vehicle, facing Jared. The light from the jeep's interior didn't quite reach his face, leaving most of his features in shadows.

Taking a sip, he wiped a hand across his mouth and looked at his friend. "What's the plan now, hot shot? You know as well as I do that this was just a diversion to throw us off the real deal. My guess is that something was going down somewhere else in the park."

Jared guzzled the rest of his water.

"Your cover's been blown. It's going to take years to get a lead on these guys again. Good news is they have no idea who your girlfriend is. Seems as if your buddy Kyle kept that one to himself."

Jared gave him a withering look.

Jedi tried to look innocent. "What? Isn't that good news? No one will be looking for her and you didn't get yourself killed today. I'm calling today a win."

Crushing the empty plastic bottle with more force than was necessary,

Jared turned and threw it into the jeep. "We didn't get the poachers. They're still out there. How is that a win?"

Jedi studied his friend for a moment and then, in true Jedi fashion, he continued to share his wisdom. "Tell her who you really are and how you feel about her. You're not fooling anyone. You've been crazy for this girl since the day you met her."

"How the hell would you know? You just flew in two days ago."

Jedi shook his head and grinned, his white teeth flashing in the dark. "I wasn't in town ten minutes before I heard about you and Leigh, aka Amanda. Both of you were the main topic of conversation among the customers at the Café I had dinner at last night. Seems people are making bets about the two of you and I hear the odds are better than what you can get in Vegas."

Jared looked away for a moment. He wanted to punch the shit-eating grin right off of Jedi's face. "Look, you can make jokes about this all you want, but it doesn't change a damn thing. I work undercover. It's who I am and what I do. There's no future for us together. So go ahead and laugh. I'll be ready to head back to Washington in the morning. The sooner we close this case, the sooner we can start looking for the main operation."

He turned to close the rear cargo door.

"Never thought you'd take the coward's way out," Jedi challenged.

Jared wheeled around with his hands clenched. "Coward's way out? Are you shitting me? There's nothing I'd like better than spend the rest of my life with her, but you know the risks. Amanda's been in hiding for years, afraid that one of those bastards was going to find her and kill her, like they did her family. She's been through hell. I'll be damned if I'm gonna ask her to live in fear because of me."

Jedi took a step closer. "So what, you're going to just throw it all away without even asking her what she has to say about it? How long do you think you can continue to go undercover and risk your life, knowing that you could have what all of us dream of having? It doesn't matter if you never see her again; she's under your skin, man." Jedi was nose-to-nose with him now, not letting up for a moment. "Yeah, you're a coward. You'd rather get yourself killed than put your heart on the line and take a chance on happiness. I'd give anything for an opportunity like that. Even if it didn't work out, at least I'd know that I gave it my all."

With that, Jedi climbed into his vehicle, backed up and drove away.

• • •

The ringing phone brought Jared to the surface of consciousness. The bedroom was pitch black so he had to fumble around until his fingers were able to grab the device from the nightstand. "Yeah?" he rasped into the receiver. A glance at the clock told him that it was several hours before dawn. He'd been asleep less than five hours.

He rolled onto his back and flung an arm over his eyes as he heard Billy's voice.

"Be at Gertie's in fifteen minutes. I know where the original site was supposed to be."

Jared swung his legs over the side of the bed. "I'm on my way."

Billy hung up.

Jared immediately speed-dialed Jedi's number and relayed the same command when his friend picked up the phone. Not giving Jedi a chance to reply, he dropped the phone on the bed, grabbed his gear and got dressed as quickly as he could. Snatching up his rifle and equipment bag, he was out the door in five minutes.

● ● ●

Jared and Jedi pulled up to the curb outside Gertie's diner at the same time. They parked on both sides of Billy, who was sitting on his ATV. Jared recognized another ATV as the one he had ridden from Billy's place several days before.

"Should we call in the rest of the team?" Jared asked Jedi as he rounded the hood of his jeep.

Jedi shook his head. "Not sure yet, we'll let them sleep until I know what we are up against." He turned to Billy. "Jared said you know where the original kill was supposed to happen. Tell me how you found it."

"Haven't been there yet," Billy answered. He raised his hand to stop Jedi from speaking. "I've been watching the skies. Saw the chopper headed to where you were yesterday. I wanted to make sure that no one followed and surprised you. As I watched, another chopper flew by me but it didn't follow the flight path that I had been monitoring. This one took a more southwest route. Got me thinking, so I pulled out the old site maps of the park. I know now where they went."

Climbing off the ATV, Billy grabbed a cylinder that had been attached to the rack on the back of the vehicle. Opening it, he pulled out a map and spread it out on the hood of Jared's jeep. The dim light from inside the diner wasn't enough to illuminate the map so Jared grabbed a flashlight from the front seat of his vehicle.

"This is where you were yesterday." Billy pointed to an area on the map. Sliding his finger across the map, he stopped at an area several inches below. "This is where I saw the chopper go. At first, I couldn't understand why they'd head that way. There's nothing there but forest. It's been a long time since I've been in that part of the park."

"But you figured it out?" Jedi prodded when Billy grew silent.

The older man nodded. "They're smart. Nobody patrols that area anymore. It's accessed by two old fire roads that haven't been maintained in well over twenty years." He slid his finger over another inch on the map. "This area shows a slight depression. Not as deep as a canyon, but it has high walls on three sides, so all you have to really cover is the opening. It would be the perfect place to hide out and keep something big."

"How long would it take us to get in there?" Jared wanted to know.

Billy's face was thoughtful. "Half an hour, if we went by chopper, but they'd hear us coming and disappear into the wilderness long before we got there. Three hours if we trailer the ATV's to this area," he pointed to another spot on the map. "No guarantee that the fire roads are passable though. We might have to hike in. That would take another half hour."

Jedi wiped a hand across his face. "Let's take the chopper. There's no way that we can get the team assembled and out there in less than six hours. Maybe if we surprise them, they'll screw up and leave us some clues as to who the hell they are."

Jared and Billy nodded in agreement.

• • •

There was a definite lightening of the eastern horizon when the three men finally boarded the chopper. As it rose into the air, they pulled on headphones to protect their ears from the noise of the rotors. Billy signaled to the pilot the direction they should fly in.

Twenty minutes into the flight, vultures were seen circling in the early morning light as the chopper crested a ridge.

"There!" Jedi announced into his microphone, breaking the tense silence and causing Jared to jump. Below them there was a crescent-shaped depression in the landscape like Billy had described.

The pilot quickly found an open space to set the machine down. Crouching low, Jared, Billy and Jedi exited the chopper and looked around. Billy had been right. They were in a small canyon that couldn't have been more than half a mile wide. Twenty-foot rock walls encircled the men on three sides. Jared eyed some deep gullies under the tall grass and fallen trees. He figured thawing snow in the spring would turn the canyon into a dangerous river. There were plenty of signs of recent human activity. The grass had been trampled and there were various flat spots where tents had been erected. The remnants of campfires were still smoldering. Moving slowly, with their rifles ready, Jared and Jedi flanked Billy as they walked toward a venue of vultures.

As they got closer, Jared could see that the birds were fighting over entrails. There was no carcass. Jedi tapped him on the shoulder and pointed at three other spots the vultures were fighting over.

Unsnapping a knife from his belt, Billy tried to shoo the birds away but the large scavengers weren't easily scared off. The birds squawked and flapped their wings at the human interruption, hopping just far enough away for Billy to grab and cut a piece of the bloodied flesh, which he placed into a plastic bag. He then headed to the next kill site to get another sample.

While he was gone, Jedi and Jared searched the dirt for any clues.

"Check it out," Jared called.

Jedi walked over and looked at where Jared was pointing. A paw print was visible in the dry dirt.

"My guess is a big cat," Jedi said, squatting down to take a closer look. He measured the size of the print against his hand.

"That's what I'm thinking. What kind of cat would be worth all the trouble that they've gone through?" Jared asked as he watched Billy finish up collecting his samples and start to head back in their direction. "Another Siberian Tiger? Lion?"

Billy was close enough to overhear the last part of Jared's question.

"I saw black fur on some of the remains back there. If it's a cat, then a black panther would be my guess. Endangered animals certainly seem to appeal to these bastards."

"How long ago would you say they left?" Jedi asked him.

"They were here yesterday, just like they'd planned." Billy shook his head. "The other site was a decoy to keep us all busy."

Jared scanned the area. He counted five tent sites but only three campfires. Searching the grass, he found several boot prints but not much else. The poachers had once again swooped into the park and left no clues that would help to identify any of them. Just like before; as elusive as ghosts.

. . .

The team silently made their way back to the chopper. Jedi was the one to break the silence as they approached the field that they had taken off from. "Billy, when will you get the DNA samples back?"

Billy held up the bags of torn flesh and entrails . "I have a friend in the lab. I'll make sure he runs them as fast as possible."

Jared knew that once they were able to identify the species that the entrails had belonged to, the cyber unit could get on the deep web and try to track down where the animals had come from. With any luck, they could find out who had bought the animals and have some sort of thread that could lead them to the gang they had been tracking.

Dr. Davis finished writing in Amanda's chart and placed the file under his arm. He studied her for a minute as she awkwardly sat up in bed. A nurse had removed her IV catheter earlier that morning. It was still painful to breath and the throbbing in her head had only calmed to a dull ache. She was unable to open her right eye to more than a slit but, according to the nurse, the swelling had begun to subside.

"I'm going to release you from the ICU and put you in a regular room." Dr. Davis grinned at her. "I'd like to keep you in for several more days for observation."

Amanda pasted a smile on her face. This good news did not make her feel any better. She was still as helpless as a baby and had no place to go. No one had visited her in the ten days since she had been admitted. Dr. Davis had explained that only immediate family members were allowed in the ICU but mentioned that the nurses had turned away several visitors who were anxious to see her.

It wasn't the good doctor's fault that she was feeling sorry for herself.

The news that Samantha had been found safe had lifted her spirits until she'd realized that no one seemed to know what had happened to Kyle. She had no news about Shadoe, either.

She'd had plenty time to think as she lay in bed. Even with Kyle's disappearance, there was still a band of poachers operating in the area. They may have finished with their dealings in the park, but that didn't mean they wouldn't be back to try to finish the job that Kyle had started, with or without him. Did they think that she was still a threat to them? If so, then nothing had changed, and she would still be looking over her shoulder for the rest of her life.

Dr. Davis left the room and a nurse took his place. Moving efficiently, she removed the heart monitor clips and released the brakes on her bed. "Are you ready for your new room?"

Not having much say about the process, Amanda nodded, too preoccupied with her own misery to pay attention to the whirring sound that passed by her door.

• • •

Jared must have fallen asleep somewhere around midnight. He had spent the last five days filling out reports and debriefing his superiors, who wanted to send him to the staff shrink to 'decompress'.

"You know how these situations can lead to PTSD," his commanding officer had warned him. "I can't let you back out in the field until you're cleared by the doctor."

Jared made an appointment for three months in the future, then took the next flight out of Washington. He had almost wept with relief at hearing Jessie's voicemail, "Amanda has come out of the coma and has no sign of a brain injury." The thought that he might have been too late to save her had been tearing at him. He'd never felt fear for his own life like the fear he felt when he saw the rifle butt slam into Amanda's head as she faced down Kyle.

He arrived at the hospital just before 10 p.m.

Jared's chair creaked as he tried to shift into a more comfortable position. The way his muscles ached, he figured a team of masseuses couldn't get out all the knots. His own pain was nothing compared to Amanda's battered face and black eye. Thanks to pain medication that the nurse said she had been given earlier, Amanda was sound asleep.

Grinding his teeth, Jared wished that Kyle was still alive so that he could kill him all over again, this time with his bare hands. The nurse had tried to make him leave, but he flashed his badge and told her flatly that he was staying; she had smiled and backed off.

Ignoring the protests from his own body, Jared leaned forward to hold Amanda's hand. Her left eye opened and sought him out. She was groggy, but she managed a small grin.

"Hi," she said sleepily.

"Hi yourself," he answered in a whisper.

The medication must have dried out her mouth because she kept trying to swallow.

"Do you want me to get you something to drink?" he asked.

She shook her head. "No thanks, I'm having the nicest dream that you're finally here," she said before she turned toward him and fell back to sleep.

Jared pulled the chair closer to the bed. He brushed Amanda's hair away from her face and leaned down to kiss her cheek. Without letting go of her hand, he put his head down on the bed and fell into a deep, peaceful asleep.

• • •

Jared was sitting in the chair next to her bed when Amanda woke up the next morning.

"So, it wasn't just a dream. You're actually here." As soon as the words were out of her mouth, she wanted to snatch them back. Of course he was there.

He'd taken a shower and looked clean shaven. She could have sworn that he'd had the start of a beard last night. She felt absolutely grubby in comparison.

Jared gave her one of those grins that said he'd noticed her comment but was going to let it slide. "Yeah, I got in late last night. You woke up and spoke to me for a moment. Figured that with all the pain meds they have you on, you probably wouldn't remember." He pulled his chair closer to the bed and turned it so that he could face her.

So many emotions were going through Amanda's head; relief that he was okay, guilt that she had dragged him into her past and sadness that with all that had gone on, it had changed nothing.

Taking her hand, he looked solemn. It was the look of someone who had bad news to share but didn't know how to say it. She would know that look anywhere.

"What?" she choked out when the silence became unbearable. "You have bad news, don't you? Kyle got away and he's still out there, waiting to come get me?"

Jared rose from the chair and sat on the edge of the bed. He lightly cupped both hands on either side of her face and forced her to look at him. "Kyle is dead," he announced. "I shot him, just after he hit you with his rifle."

At first his words didn't sink in.

"Kyle is dead," he repeated. "It's over. He can't hurt you anymore."

"The poachers?" she asked in a whisper.

Jared looked away for a moment before meeting her eyes. "They got away."

Amanda started to shake. "Then it's not over. I'll never be able to be me again. I'll always be wondering who's coming for me next."

Somehow, even though it was what she had expected all along, the reality of the situation hit her hard. She wanted to be Amanda Whittier again.

Wanted to be free to do as she pleased, without worrying who and when someone would try to kill her.

Despair must have shown in her face because once again, Jared cupped her cheeks.

"Listen to me. It's over. No one but Kyle was looking for you. He had a personal vendetta against you for getting away from him. It was something that his ego just couldn't handle. Now that he's dead, you're free to take back your life, Amanda."

She reflected about what he said for a moment. Then a thought occurred to her. "How long have you known who I am?"

Jared looked angry for a second as he slumped down in the chair. "Not long enough. I put a listening bug in Billy's cabin and heard you two talking. You should have told me sooner. I could have protected you better, had I known the truth."

*He blamed her?*

"Why should I have told you?" she asked defensively. "You weren't forth-coming about who the hell you were, either. A listening bug?? It never made sense to me that you were just a photojournalist, but you're some sort of agent, aren't you? FBI or something?"

Standing up, Jared turned and for a moment. Amanda thought that he was going to walk out the door but instead he began to pace back and forth at the end of her bed.

"I can't tell you much, except that I do a lot of undercover work. This was just supposed to be a fact-finding mission. Because I'm from the area, my bosses thought people would open up to me. Get some new leads on these guys, since the trail had grown so cold." He ran a hand through his hair. "I had no idea that you had survived, ten years ago. I always wondered what had gone down on the mountain that day. The murder/suicide story never felt right to me. Not sure why, considering I had never met your father or your uncle. Anyway, I got a call several months ago about this assignment, so I jumped at it. It was a chance to try to solve something that has always bothered me."

Crossing to the side of her bed, Jared once again sat down on the edge of the mattress. "I should have figured out who you were much sooner and protected you. I'm sorry."

His words made her anger disappear. "Don't be sorry. I had no idea who to trust. It seems that everyone else in town knew exactly who I was. I guess it was just my bad luck to fool the one person who could help me."

Jared was about to say something when Jessie knocked on the open door, interrupting him.

"Mind if I come in?" she asked.

"No, not at all." Rising from the side of the bed, Jared moved back so that Amanda could see her visitor.

Jessie's smile was tentative yet warm.

"Glad to see you're okay," she said to Jared before turning to face Amanda. "I've gotten permission from the doctor to get you into a wheelchair and take you outside. There are a couple of visitors who would like to see you. I thought you might enjoy getting out into the sunshine for a little while. What do you say?"

Amanda glanced at Jared before smiling. "Sunshine sounds great."

• • •

Jessie had brought Shadoe to the hospital. Billy was holding the canine's leash as he stood beside Gus in the manicured garden. Shadoe almost turned himself inside out when he locked his eyes on Amanda.

No one had mentioned Shadoe to Amanda, and she had been too afraid to ask, convinced that Kyle had killed him. There were no words to describe the relief at seeing her best friend again. Burying her face in his fur, she sobbed. She wore her emotions on her sleeve lately. Having been dormant for so long, they would not be contained. When she was through hugging and kissing him, the shepherd settled down at her side.

Amanda couldn't believe she was sitting outside in the sunshine with her dog, Jared, Billy, Gus and Jessie. It all felt so normal. The conversation was light, allowing her to relax.

Jared shared stories of some of the mischief he had gotten up to as a child, making her hold her ribs against the pain when she laughed. Jessie commented on pieces of local gossip but Billy and Gus didn't say much, which was usual for both of them. It took Amanda a while to notice the odd looks the men were giving Jessie.

Glancing back and forth between Jessie and the two men, Amanda finally asked, "What's going on?"

Jessie cleared her throat before getting up and moving to the bench next to Amanda's wheelchair. "We have something we need to tell you, now that you're stronger."

In that moment, Amanda didn't feel so strong, but she held on to Jessie's gaze.

Jessie looked up at Billy, who nodded to her, and then she turned back to Amanda.

"There's no easy way to say this so I'm just going to blurt it out." Closing her eyes for a brief second, she opened them, took a deep breath then announced, "Your uncle Peter is alive."

Amanda's mind went blank. Not a thought, feeling or memory came forward. In fact, right at the moment, she wasn't even sure she was breathing. Jessie's words had stopped everything. If the birds were singing, she couldn't hear them. Shadoe nudged her hand but she didn't notice.

It was Jared who brought her back.

"What do you mean that her uncle is alive?" His tone was guarded but firm. "There's no way he could have survived that fall."

Jared rested a hand lightly on Amanda's shoulder. She was grateful for the contact, which grounded her, as she let Jessie's words sink in.

Jessie took Amanda's hands in hers. "I know this is a real big shock to you, honey. Peter has been here every day since you were admitted. He's been worried sick about you. "

Shadoe whined and Amanda automatically reached out to pat his head. After everything that she had been through, she wasn't sure what to believe anymore. "He was alive, all these years?"

"The doctors warned your uncle to stay out of sight until you'd had time to heal and get stronger." Jesse glanced nervously at Jared and then back to Amanda. Bowing her head, she seemed unable to continue.

Gus spoke up. "Your uncle suffered life-threatening injuries from the gunshots and the fall over the cliff. He was in bad shape when we found him. It took us over two hours to get him airlifted off the side of the Gorge. We weren't sure if he would make it to the hospital."

Amanda struggled to take his words in. She was still stuck on "Your uncle Peter is alive." Jared's hand felt reassuring as he pressed gently against her shoulder.

"He'd lost a lot of blood from the gunshot wounds," Gus continued, "and his spinal column was severed in several places. His coma lasted for over three months. When he finally came to, Peter was paralyzed from the chest down and had to relearn everything again."

"What do you mean relearn everything?" Jared quizzed, the investigative reporter taking over.

Billy answered this time. "Everything. He had lost all knowledge. He couldn't recall the alphabet, numbers, colors, how to speak or dress himself. Nothing. It was like he was a newborn all over again."

Amanda glared incredulously at Billy. "You knew about this?" Her voice cracked under the deep disappointment that he had also lied to her. And for so long.

Jessie's eyes glistened with tears. "It's been a long road for your uncle, Amanda. Years of therapy did help him to regain his memories. He does remember most of what had happened to him now. He remembers you and wants to see you very badly."

"Where is he? Why isn't he here?" Amanda whispered, afraid that this was just a dream again.

"Give yourself some time to process this. You've been through so much already." Jessie smiled as she sat back a little against the bench. "We asked him to wait until we could tell you that he was alive. I thought it best that you heard this news from us."

"I saw him." Amanda spoke slowly. "I thought I'd died. I thought he was an angel waiting to bring me to heaven. I was so disappointed that it wasn't my dad who had come for me. I wanted to see my dad."

Shadoe whined and nudged her hand again. She stroked his head without taking her eyes off Jessie.

"I'm okay," she told her dog. "I'm tired, Jessie. I'd like to go back to my room, now."

Billy spoke quietly. "We'll bring Peter to see you tomorrow."

Amanda hesitated before looking up at him to give an affirmative nod.

None of the others said a word as they watched Jared wheel Amanda back to her room.

# CHAPTER TWENTY-FOUR

After a restless night of trying to process the news of her uncle, Amanda was once again in the courtyard with Shadoe lying at her feet. She let her head rest against the back of her wheelchair and closed her eyes. Jessie, Gertie, Gus, Billy and Jared had all shown up to support her as they waited for Peter to arrive. They were sitting on benches in the shade of a massive oak tree, making small talk. When the chatter abruptly stopped, Amanda opened her eyes to see an older man in a motorized wheelchair moving up the path towards them.

The whirring sound of the chair was familiar, but it took Amanda a few seconds to remember where she had heard it before. On the day that she was released from ICU she had heard this sound outside her door. Why hadn't he come in to see her? She was filled with so many thoughts and emotion at seeing her uncle that she wasn't sure exactly what she was feeling. Fear, joy, anger, hope and something else she couldn't put into words were all warring inside of her.

Jessie took Shadoe's leash and gave Amanda a half-smile before turning to walk over to another set of benches, a short distance away. Jared leaned down, kissed Amanda's cheek then squeezed her hand. He joined Billy, Gertie and Gus, who were now sitting with Jessie, leaving Amanda to meet her uncle in private.

As Peter got closer, Amanda could see that he had aged dramatically in the past ten years. His blond hair had wide streaks of gray and his forehead was creased with wrinkles. She noticed several deep scars on his right cheek.

Her uncle's resemblance to her father was uncanny. His wheelchair stopped several feet in front of her. They studied each other, neither one speaking, unsure of what to say. They were virtually strangers.

Peter was the first to break the silence. "I've thought about this moment for so long, Amanda." He gave a slight grin and his voice was husky with emotion. "I rehearsed what I was going to say to you a million times, but right now, I can't seem to remember one word of it." His grin faded as he regarded her for a moment. "You've grown into a beautiful woman. In fact, you look just like your mother did when she was your age." His voice broke so he paused.

Bowing his head, he took a deep breath. "I know I have a lot of explaining to do," he finally managed to say.

Amanda glanced over to Jared, but he was in deep conversation with Billy and Gus. Looking back at her uncle, she tried to think of something to say.

Before she could respond, he continued. "I was working undercover at the park, trying to get evidence on Kyle for the murder of Joan Kent. We didn't have much on him so we figured that if we could catch him poaching, then we could arrest him." His eyes were becoming moist and Amanda saw his hands begin to tremble.

"If we could get some leverage over him, we could use it to get him to confess to tampering with Joan's brakes. There was an operation in motion to catch Kyle and his gang on the morning that you and your father showed up. I should have made you leave before it got out of hand. I'm so sorry."

Amanda felt a lump forming in her throat as Peter's voice cracked.

"The poachers were supposed to have some big client come in to shoot a black bear. The claws alone are worth thousands of dollars on the black market but Kyle somehow found out what I was up to. So they set up the hunt somewhere else in the park and set a trap for me. I had made sure that your dad had that day off since he didn't know anything about our operation. They weren't supposed to be anywhere near the gorge."

Peter paused to take a deep breath as he struggled to gain control of his emotions. "I tried to talk Mark out of going out there. He wouldn't listen. He must have been suspicious that something was up and didn't trust me to handle things on my own."

When he raised his head to look at her, Amanda saw the pain in his eyes as he took in her beaten face. Without thinking, she reached out her hand.

Peter moved his chair forward and grabbed her hand like it was a lifeline. "You need to know that I had no idea we were walking into a trap. I would have stopped both of you from coming to the gorge that day if I'd had any idea what was waiting for us."

Amanda started to speak but her uncle put up his hand to silence her.

"Please, let me get this out. You must understand." There was another heavy pause. "I was in a coma for so long. It was years before I started thinking clearly again. I thought about coming for you a million times but the guilt kept me away. I didn't want to upset your world after you got settled in with your new family."

"But you're my family," she replied, tears spilling onto her cheeks.

He squeezed her hand. "I got an apartment in Washington D.C. About two years ago, the head of the Wildlife and Game Commission came to see me. They wanted my help to get Kyle and his team so I created a task force to take Kyle down. I'm the reason that you're here.

"I kept seeing your requests for a job at the park but I turned them down. It was only after I realized that if we put the right safeguards in place, you could lure Kyle back to the area." Peter's eyes were now begging for forgiveness. "My stupid idea put you right into his hands. I underestimated him and that almost killed you."

Amanda leaned forward to wrap her arms around her uncle's slim shoulders. "Kyle almost killed me, not you. And I would have found another way to move back here. I don't blame you for my dad's death, or anything else for that matter."

Peter pulled back from her. He glanced over to her friends, then returned his gaze to her. "There's something else you need to know."

The anguish on his face made Amanda's heart skip a few beats. "What's that?"

"Your father's not dead."

Amanda's world shifted on its axis for the second time in two days.

"Your father was rescued from the gorge, but he suffered major injuries, especially to his brain." He paused. "Severe bleeding from the fall starved his brain of oxygen."

"Where is…?" Amanda began but Peter cut her off.

"A facility in D.C. I live close enough to keep my eye on him."

"Facility?" Her words were soft.

Peter glanced again to where Jessie and the others were still talking. "His memory was badly damaged, but he remembers you, Amanda."

"That's good," she replied, her eyes brightening a little.

"He has no concept of time passing. Every day, he expects you to come home from school, just like you did when you were fourteen."

"What do you mean?" she asked.

"Your father can only remember you as you were on that day. It's like his memory got stuck at the moment of impact."

"But why did they have a funeral for him? There's a grave." Amanda was trying to comprehend that her father was alive. Her mind raced. What kind of relationship could they have now if he didn't recognize her? She had fantasized that he might still be alive, but these notions had always consisted of her father knowing exactly who she was.

"Gertie, Gus, Jessie and Billy all wanted to make sure that Kyle was convinced that Mark was dead. They didn't want him tracking your father down and finishing the job."

The implications of this statement hung unspoken in the thickening air between them.

"Why didn't anyone arrest Kyle if you all knew it was him?"

Peter looked over her shoulder as if gathering his thoughts before looking back at her. "Kyle was in league with some of the world's most wanted criminals and some of his contacts are trained assassins. All Kyle had to do was say the word and they would have murdered all of us, Celeste and Roy included. It would have been made to look like accidents and no one would have been the wiser. Kyle knew the heat was on and that there were warrants out for his arrest, so he went underground for several years but eventually he kept coming back to this park." He paused. "I think he was looking for you and knew that someday you would eventually make your way back here. Unfortunately he was right."

Her head snapped up. "You still should have told me." She pierced her uncle with a hard look as anger replaced surprise. "I've been in hell for over ten years, believing that both of you were dead. You had no right to keep this from me!"

Her voice was sharp, and it carried over to the other bench. Shadoe whined and pulled on the leash, trying to get back to her. Jessie reached down and patted the canine's head, reassuring him, but she made no move to come closer. Jared took a step in her direction but was stopped by Gus' hand on his arm.

Peter lowered his head for a moment and then looked at his niece. "You were put in grave danger by coming back now. Can you imagine what would have happened ten years ago? My brother couldn't take care of himself, never mind raise a teenage daughter. You deserved to have a life."

He paused. When she didn't answer, he continued. "You would have raced to your father's side and become his fulltime caretaker. That's not the life your father would have wanted for you. I hope you understand that I did this for you."

Of course she would have gone running to her father's side. Amanda had been a scared teenager who'd believed for years that she'd lost her whole family that day. In some ways, she had. Now she was a grown woman and she was in charge of her future. "You didn't have the right to send me off to live with Celeste and Roy. I didn't even know them!"

"I didn't send you to live with them. Decisions had to be made so Billy stepped up. As soon as Celeste heard about Mark's accident and realized that I was in coma, she offered to take you in. It was Billy who got you safely out of Ramsey and he found your dad an assisted living facility where he'd have round-the-clock care."

Rubbing his hand over his face, Peter took a deep breath.

"It was years after I emerged from my coma, that I was able to make decisions again, for both of us. I thought about taking you to D.C., but you'd settled into your new high school and had plans to go to college. You were making a life for yourself." He lifted her chin so that she had to look at him. "I know that you love your father, but he is not the same man you remember."

Amanda held his gaze as tears ran, unchecked down her face. The future seemed dimmed with so many questions, yet she felt a little flicker of hope. Her father was alive! She could see him again. She could hug him and spend time with him.

"I want to see him," she said, firmly.

Her uncle sighed and then nodded. "Okay. I'll make the arrangements as soon as you're well enough to travel."

• • •

Jared sat staring at the computer screen but he wasn't focusing on it. He couldn't help but admire the irony behind Peter's hiring him for this job and all the while, he had had no idea who Peter was. Maybe if he had known, he could have kept Amanda safely out of Kyle's way.

Now, his commander was making a lot of noise about having him get back to work. The chief wanted Jared to get more evidence on Bubba and his associates. The hope was that they could find some information that could lead them to the bigger operation. So far, all they had on the decoys were misdemeanor charges. Without evidence, the justice system would be forced to set bail and release them. The question was, did he want to go back undercover and forget about Amanda?

Jared leaned back in his chair. He'd dealt with the deadliest people on the planet, criminals who had no respect for human life. Men like Kyle. Jared's job was to infiltrate these organizations, to move among them, and gather enough evidence to put them all behind bars for good.

Amanda had been a surprise. He had left Ramsey not too long after she did. Her uncle and father had been declared dead and she hadn't known that it was all a cover up. It took a hell of a lot of guts for her to come back here and face what she faced.

Peter hadn't blown his cover, but Jared was going to have to tell Amanda something before he left. He owed her that much. She was leaving in a few days for D.C., to be reunited with her father. Jared planned on flying with her to Washington and saying goodbye to her there. Jessie and Gus would drive Shadoe out to join her once she got settled in.

He took a swig of beer. It was so easy for him to picture himself married to Amanda. They'd have a nice house and a couple of kids. Grow old together. He smiled at the thought of her with children, and then eventually grandchildren, then his smile faded. He could also imagine the terror he would feel if one of his old enemies found him. They wouldn't hesitate to kill them all.

"No," he thought out loud, "I can't take that chance."

Setting his beer to the side of his laptop, Jared typed a reply to the email from his commander, assuring him that he would be ready to leave in a couple of weeks. He felt a piece of his soul break off as he hit the Send button.

• • •

Shari held a party for Amanda several days before she was to leave for D.C.. Amanda couldn't be sure, but it felt like everyone in the town was there to wish her goodbye and good luck. As she suspected, most of the people who had known her as a child hadn't been fooled by her disguise.

Looking around, she realized just how much she had missed being a part of this community. These people had helped neighbors for generations through births, deaths, and anything the elements had thrown at them. Amanda was proud to be from this stock and felt guilty that she had put any of them in danger. It had been foolish to come here and think that she could have taken Kyle and his gang down by herself.

She still had nightmares about Kyle taking Samantha. Amanda smiled as she looked across the room at the six-year-old who was rolling on the floor as one of the two new puppies tried to lick her face. Samantha had been so brave. Despite the horror of her abduction, she seemed to have recovered much of her innocence. Amanda hoped the child could move on from her experience as unscathed as possible.

It had been two weeks since Amanda had been released from the hospital. Her facial bruises were fading, and the doctors were happy with her progress. She was forced to use a wheelchair because her foot was encased in a large cast and her ribs were still tender, so she was unable to get around on crutches.

The wheelchair was bulky and hard for Amanda to maneuver so Shari had insisted that she move in with Shari and her family. Amanda was struggling with being reliant on others when she was so used to doing everything for herself.

She wondered how her uncle had managed to handle his debilitating injury all these years.

Turning the wheelchair around, Amanda saw that Cole was standing behind her. He was dressed in a brand-new pair of jeans and a light blue button-down shirt. His shoes were polished and he looked like he had stepped right out of a high society magazine.

Taking a few steps toward her, he held out a bouquet of summer flowers.

Shari swooped in from behind Amanda and whisked the flowers away, stating that she would find a vase and water for them.

"You seem to be recovering well," Cole noted as he sat on the end of the sofa, facing her.

"Yes. Dr. Davis said I could be released from physical therapy soon. I should make a full recovery."

"That's good to hear." Nodding his head, he lapsed into silence.

Searching for something to say, Amanda remembered the last time she had seen him, when he had been destroying her father's house. Moving her chair a little closer, she said, "I never thanked you for finding Samantha and bringing her home."

It could have been her imagination, but she thought he looked a little uncomfortable.

"How did you happen to be at my uncle's house that morning anyway?" She paused, giving him a chance to answer. When he didn't, she decided to catch him off guard. "I'm guessing that you didn't find what you were looking for at my father's house, the night before, so you headed over my uncle's place."

Cole took a deep breath and averted his eyes. She watched as he absent-mindedly twirled a ring on his right hand.

Just when she thought he wasn't going to respond, he looked back at her and cleared his throat.

"For as long as I can remember, nothing I ever did was good enough for my father. He made me grovel for any bit of affection or money that he might throw my way. My brother," he spat the word, "was a bastard, yet he demanded all of my father's attention and got it without even trying."

Amanda noticed that he didn't confirm or deny that he had been at her father's house.

One of the servers that Shari had hired for the party stepped in between them with a tray full of drinks. Taking two glasses of wine, Cole offered one to Amanda. She declined with a shake of her head.

Placing one of the glasses on the end table to his left, Cole took a gulp from the other glass and continued. "All my life, all I ever wanted to do was raise horses and prove to my father that I was the better son, a son that he could be proud of. I thought that if I could get the ranch off the ground, have the best breeding stock in the state, then maybe I could finally make him proud of me. Of course, I needed money for the startup and I was damned if I was going to ask him for it." Another gulp of wine. "A colleague told me about the legend of the Ramsey silver mine and how no one had been in the old mine for years."

"What legend?" Amanda interrupted.

Cole looked surprised. "You don't know?"

Racking her memory, Amanda couldn't remember ever hearing about a legend attached to the mine. As far as she knew, the mine had closed because of safety concerns and because the silver vein had played out. She said as much.

Finishing his first glass, Cole reached for the second. "There were always some questions as to why the mine closed. I heard that a cave-in was inevitable, due to the condition of the beams, but someone else told me that it was closed because the owners made a lot of bad investments and couldn't pay the workers anymore. I prefer the legend, which claims the miners were on the verge of hitting a large vein of silver and maybe even some gold, when the owner suddenly closed it." Cole leaned in closer and lowered his voice. "I paid a private investigator to find out everything I could about the old operation. He came back with news of a map that supposedly recorded where the new vein would have been. The problem is that no one can find the bloody map."

Now Amanda was beginning to understand. "So, you thought my father and uncle might have a copy hidden somewhere in their houses? That's why you were pulling up the floorboards and making holes in the walls? Didn't it occur to you that you were trespassing and destroying someone else's property?"

Cole shrugged his shoulders, and then finished the second glass of wine. "No one had been to those houses in years, except for kids who would party out there. The places should be condemned." Leaning forward he spoke in earnest. "Obviously you don't know where the map is, but if you would give me permission to open the mine and make some tests holes, I'll give you a forty percent share of everything that is brought out of it."

Blinking at his audacity, Amanda couldn't tell him that her father still legally held the deed to the property. No one else had been told that her father was still alive. Even if she could reveal this, it seemed that he wouldn't be up to the task of making any legal decisions anyway.

"It's very generous of you to offer me forty percent of my own silver, if there is any down there of course, but no, thank you. I won't be opening the mine." Although Amanda had emphasized the word generous, she had tried not to sound sarcastic. While Cole wasn't exactly a friend, she didn't need him as an enemy.

Cole opened his mouth to argue but must have thought twice about it because he excused himself. Walking across the crowded living room, he smiled and nodded to a few people before walking out the front door.

Amanda watched Cole leave, then she searched the crowd and found Jared, who was in deep conversation with Billy. She recognized that stubborn look on Billy's face; he wasn't buying anything of what Jared was saying. Did Jared know that he was wasting his breath? He looked like a cowboy in his white shirt, jeans and boots.

God, she was going to miss him.

Amanda had spent the last ten years building walls to keep people out but somehow Jared had managed to get in. He had been annoying as hell at first, but somewhere along the line she had fallen in love with him. Unfortunately, he didn't appear to feel the same way about her. He had just announced that he was accompanying her to the capitol but would then be flying to Asia for a new assignment. Her heart had felt like it was breaking but she had just smiled at his news.

Why wasn't she brave enough to tell him that she loved him? Brave enough to face the rejection that her honesty could bring?

She would just have to move on. Again.

The private plane's tires hit the tarmac with a jolt, causing Amanda to grip the armrests on her seat. She hated flying. No matter how many times she flew, she was always convinced that the plane was going to crash and kill them all. Even though she acknowledged that it was the safest way to travel, it was impossible for her to shake the feeling of dread.

Jared covered her hand with his and, for a moment, she forgot about the landing. Wishing that she could read more into the gesture, she knew that it was only meant to comfort. She gave him a slight smile and let his hand rest on hers, treasuring every moment she had with him, storing each memory in her heart.

Never again would she take anything for granted. *Then tell him how you feel*, an inner voice nagged. *For what?* she reasoned with herself. She was sure that he did care for her, in some way. She was also sure that she couldn't handle the rejection if she were to hand him her heart and he handed it back. It was old- fashioned, but she was a big believer in the fates. If it was meant to be, then someday, it would happen.

Peter was seated in his wheelchair in a special spot behind the co-pilot. His chair was tied down with straps so that it couldn't move around the small cabin. He was facing forward and paying no attention to Amanda and Jared.

The plane had landed and was taxiing slowly toward the gate.

Jared started to let go of Amanda's hand but she grabbed onto it. He looked at her inquiringly. She tried to form the words that would change his mind, and make him want to stay with her, but all that came out was a weak, "Thanks."

He smiled and leaned over to kiss her cheek. "No problem, that's what friends are for."

She searched his face for any clue of his feelings. "Is that all we are, friends?"

His expression never changed, "That's all we can ever be."

Knowing the answer didn't lessen the feeling of disappointment. Amanda schooled her features to match his. "Then friends it is," she smiled, telling the biggest lie of her life.

Jared looked relieved and it took every ounce of energy she had not to break down and cry.

Her uncle chose that moment to make an appearance.

"Are we ready to go?" he asked, looking back and forth between them. His gaze rested for a moment on their clasped hands before looking back at Amanda.

"Yes, I'm ready," Amanda said, dropping Jared's hand.

Jared stood up and before she could protest, he lifted her out of her seat and carried her from the plane, leaving her uncle to follow.

• • •

Two cars with drivers were waiting for them at the foot of the stairs. A handsome man with blond hair was leaning nonchalantly against the trunk of one of the cars. Amanda had no idea who he was. He grinned when he saw that Jared was carrying her. As the chauffer was busy placing their bags into the trunk, and her uncle was talking with the blond stranger, Jared gently placed Amanda onto the back seat of the limo.

"This is where I say goodbye," he said quietly as he crouched down next to the car. He didn't look directly at her but at a spot just past her right ear.

Amanda had known this moment would come and had been preparing for it all day, but now that it was here, she felt blindsided. She wanted to throw her arms around him and ask him to stay, but that wouldn't be fair. He had a life of his own and she would just have to accept that. She tried to console herself by feeling grateful to him for helping her learn how to let people in. He had pried open her heart to love even though that heart was now breaking.

"Thank you seems so inadequate for what you've done for me," she said with a sad smile. "I love you and I'll miss you."

Not trusting herself to say anything more, Amanda held out her hand. To her surprise, he reached in and pulled her close. For a moment, she thought he was going to say something, then his gaze turned to her lips and he crushed them with his own.

Jared was the one to pull away. Staring at him, she knew that was not a platonic kiss between friends. It was so much more.

"Goodbye," he rasped, and then he turned and disappeared into the other waiting car.

The blond stranger looked her way and nodded before joining Jared.

She stared until his car was out of sight.

* * *

"You are one stupid son-of-a-bitch, I'll give you that."

Jared stared out the car window and tried to ignore Jedi's scolding but that was impossible. When Jedi had something to say, he usually said it.

"What the hell would you have done? Given up your job to settle down? Have a few kids? How long do you think it would take your enemies to find you and your family, and if you were lucky, kill you all?" Jared's voice was shaking. "If you were unlucky, they might keep you alive long enough to let you watch your family get tortured. I'm not selfish enough to take away Amanda's life now that she finally has it back."

"Are you shitting me right now? Is that what's stopping you? This isn't some Hollywood movie where the bad guy plots revenge on the good guy. Half of these criminals are morons. They can't even wipe their own ass without directions."

Jared remained silent.

Jedi gave a long-suffering sigh. "How long are you going to stay in the agency? At some point, you're going to want to have a life, a house, wife and kids. Are you going to deny yourself those things because *maybe*," he emphasized the word, "someone will figure out who the hell you are and come looking for revenge? Like I said before, I never knew you to take the coward's way out."

Jared ground his back molars together and was surprised when they didn't turn to dust. "I'm not taking the coward's way out. Amanda deserves to live a normal life without worrying about another psycho out there, waiting to take everything away from her again." He narrowed his eyes at Jedi. "If you're such a believer in family and all, then why the hell haven't you settled down with a decent woman and started a clan of your own?"

Jedi grinned. "If I could find a decent woman who would have me I'd settle down with her in a heartbeat." He became serious. "You have a choice here buddy, and if I were you, I wouldn't take a hell of a lot of time to figure it out. I don't have to tell you that life is full of risks, but some chances only come around once. Are you willing to live with the regret of letting her go?" Jedi leaned back in his seat. "From what I understand, we don't regret the things we've done; we regret the things we didn't do."

Jared stared out the window, but he couldn't get Jedi's words out of his head.

. . .

Looking out at the lights of Washington D.C. from her uncle's spare bedroom, Amanda leaned her forehead against the cool glass. Jared was gone but she was going to meet her father in the morning. She had gained yet lost so much in such a short time. Her mind wouldn't stop racing and sleep was the last thing she wanted. Amanda had to steel herself against the possibility that her father would not know her. Perhaps he would never recognize her again. They had been so close. That thought brought some consolation in the quagmire of her life.

Amanda had arrived with her uncle Peter to the small apartment just before lunch. She'd been amazed at how self-sufficient he was. Everything in the apartment had been adapted to allow him to easily maneuver his wheelchair through the rooms and cabinets had been modified so that he could reach items with ease. The rooms weren't set up for two wheelchairs, so she maneuvered gingerly around on crutches, as her ribs still ached when she used them for too long. Peter had prepared them lunch and then served it on the balcony that had a breathtaking view of the Capitol.

Looking at all the concrete had made Amanda homesick for the mountains and forests of Ramsey. She had spent the rest of the day flipping through the photo albums that her uncle had set out on her bed. It was remarkable how life had changed in the blink of an eye. One moment, she'd been a teenager with no greater concern than which boy she liked, the next moment had made her an orphan and left her worrying about everything. The photographs captured all the happy moments from a childhood that had been cut way too short.

Tomorrow would dictate how Amanda was supposed to move on. Closing her eyes against the unbidden tears that pressed against them, she took a deep breath. She was afraid to meet her father knowing that she wouldn't be able to bear it if he didn't know her. Where did that leave her in his life?

. . .

The assisted living complex was made up of rambling brick buildings, located several miles outside the Capitol. Manicured lawns and lush gardens were interrupted by brick-lined concrete walkways that led to brightly colored doors. As Amanda glanced around, she could feel herself relaxing in the peacefulness of the setting. She had been afraid that her father lived in some type of institution and had pictured concrete walls with sterile hospital corridors, but this place had the look of a country club. She took note of the tennis courts and beyond them, the glimmer of a pool.

Pulling into a handicap spot next to one of the walkways, her Uncle Peter parked and turned off the engine before giving her a sideways glance. He seemed to understand that words weren't going to be enough because he gently took her hand and squeezed it.

Amanda got out of the van and let her mind take in the surroundings a little longer. Peter unlocked his wheelchair from behind the steering wheel and backed up into the van. Pressing a button, the side door opened and a ramp slowly glided into position. He rolled his chair onto it then pressed another button. Effortlessly, the ramp brought him down to the pavement, where he navigated over to where Amanda stood leaning on her crutches. She followed him slowly up the path to where her father was waiting.

* * *

The door to her father's apartment was opened by a woman who introduced herself as Patricia. She was a large woman that Amanda guessed to be in her early forties. Her black hair was pulled back into a neat pony tail and she had a smile on her face. Peter had already explained that Patricia was Mark's home health aide. Instead of the utilitarian room Amanda was anticipating, the apartment was a good size with an open floor plan and was lightly furnished with several recliners and a couch in the living area. Set to the side of the room, easily accessible to the kitchen, was a small dining table, a bowl of fruit in the center, two wide upholstered chairs on each end.

Amanda was relieved to see that her dad was being so well cared for, but she was also a little sad as she recalled how independent he had always been.

"Mark is waiting for you on the patio," Patricia informed them before she disappeared into the kitchen.

Amanda followed Peter through the living room and then through a slider on the far end. She felt a sudden jolt of energy in her chest the moment she saw the profile of her father, who was sitting at a glass table. Her eyes drank in the sight of him while her brain tried to categorize the changes. His blonde hair was covered by a baseball cap but she could see that it was turning gray with the passing years.

Mark turned to face them as they made their entrance. He smiled as he recognized his brother.

His face was fuller than Amanda remembered it to be, but it was his eyes that revealed the biggest change. They were dull and hard to read, with no sign of the sparkle she had loved so much. It took her a moment to realize that he was sitting in a wheelchair, just like Peter. This observation brought tears to her eyes. They had all paid a terrible price for one man's greed and a world of corruption.

"Hello Peter." His voice was flat and halting.

Amanda knew this was a classic sign of head injury. There was no spark of recognition when his eyes swung toward her, making her heart sink, and for a fraction of a second, she wished that she had never found out that he was still alive. Then the guilt set in. Of course she was happy to see him! This was her father. For better or worse, she would rejoice in that victory. The rest would have to be followed on faith. She wasn't a little girl anymore. Amanda was strong, capable and resilient. She bowed her head, then inhaled deeply before raising her face to him. "Hello, I'm Amanda."

Stepping forward, she struggled to balance herself on one crutch before offering her father her hand.

The seconds hung in the air before Mark smiled and wrapped his warm hand around hers.

"Amanda," he repeated, smiling. "I have a daughter named Amanda."

"Yes, I know."

Peter cleared his throat, excused himself and then navigated his wheelchair back through the living room, toward the kitchen.

After her father released her hand, Amanda sat at the table, unsure of what to say. She and Peter had agreed that they wouldn't lie to Mark, but they would keep information to a minimum. They would take their clues from him.

"How did you hurt yourself?"

She had been expecting this question. "I had an accident a little while back, but I'm doing much better now."

He rubbed his right hand with his left fingers and looked bewildered for a moment. "I had an accident too. It makes it hard to think sometimes." He was stealing glances at her, as if trying to make up his mind about something, and then he leaned closer. "Are you a therapist?"

The question took Amanda by surprise. "Um, no, I'm a forest ranger. I lived in Massachusetts for a while but I just moved back to Idaho."

The mention of Idaho brought a look of joy to his face. "I was raised in Idaho. I was a forest ranger until my accident. Did I know you? I don't seem to remember…"

She was saved from a reply when Peter reappeared, closely followed by Patricia, who was carrying some glasses and a pitcher of lemonade.

Amanda listened carefully as the two brothers talked about being rangers, just like old times. She was amazed at the amount of information that her father remembered from the past. It was more recent information that confused him. He seemed to think that his accident had just happened and that he would soon recover and go home to his old life. Amanda began to understand what Peter had meant about her father having no concept of time passing. More than once, he wondered aloud when he could go back to Idaho to see his daughter.

Amanda felt her whole body relax as they talked. For all his injuries and deficits, her father appeared to be happy. With prompting from Patricia, he was able to outline his daily routine, which included some swimming, watching movies and weekly cribbage games.

"I love to play cribbage," she announced. "I can never find anybody who wants to play with me."

Her father smiled, wistfully. "I have to wait 'til Friday. Everyone is too busy the rest of the time."

"I'm not busy," Amanda heard herself replying. "Would you mind if I come over to play cards with you. I could also bring a movie that we could watch together."

She had mixed feelings of joy and anxiety when he nodded in agreement.

It was a start.

•  •  •

Amanda met with her father every day for the next two weeks to play cribbage and watch old movies. Memories flitted through her head of the two of them talking while playing cribbage before his attempted murder. She hadn't realized how lucky she had been to have had her father's undivided attention as a child. He'd shared stories from his childhood and taught her so much about life during a simple card game.

Since Amanda was still using crutches and hadn't been medically cleared to drive, they hadn't ventured very far from the facility. She doubted that she would try to navigate the busy D.C. traffic even if she had been physically fit to drive.

Now, as she sat on the patio across from her father, she came to the realization that her uncle had been right. Had she known her father was alive ten years ago, she would have given up everything to take care of him.

Mark didn't understand that she was his daughter, but Amanda could see from his demeanor that he looked forward to her visits and enjoyed her company. Deep down, he was still the father she remembered and loved. There was a tentative bond between them that she hoped would grow until he remembered her for who she was. Amanda knew that he might never recognize her as his daughter, but she hoped to create a new place in his heart; one that came as close to being a family as possible. If that was all he could manage, then it would have to do.

. . .

As grateful as she was for these daily visits with her father, Amanda was homesick for Idaho. The noise, traffic and overall bustle of D.C. were wearing on her nerves. She longed for trees and fresh air. It didn't help that she was unable to get around on her own. But how could she go back to Ramsey and leave her father behind? He was happy in D.C., and his routine gave him stability and comfort. Amanda had nothing in Idaho except for a decaying house and an abandoned silver mine.

Her father was finishing pegging the points from his crib when the apartment doorbell rang. Amanda heard Patricia answer the door.

Grabbing the cards, Amanda started to shuffle the deck when she heard the sound of toenails running across the floor. Before she could turn around, Shadoe had nosed her arm out of the way and placed his two front legs onto her lap. Laughing, she hugged him as he tried to lick her face.

"Oh my gosh Shadoe! I've missed you so much buddy!"

There were no words that could describe how much she had missed the exuberant canine. To have him here meant the world to her.

Leaving Shadoe had been her biggest regret about moving to D.C.. Both she and her uncle would have been unable to take care of him, so it had been decided that Jessie would care for him until plans could be made.

Jessie and Gus were standing in the doorway, both wearing enormous smiles.

"He missed you," Jessie said, smiling as she leaned down to give Amanda a hug.

Gus moved forward and shook hands with Mark.

Shadoe, satisfied that he had greeted his mistress sufficiently, turned and gently nudged at Mark's hand.

Amanda watched as her father grinned, and then patted the sleek shepherd's head.

"Who is this?" he asked, rubbing the dog's ears.

"Shadoe," Amanda spoke up. "My best friend."

As if on cue, Shadoe lifted his paw and offered it to Mark. After a brief pause, Mark laughed and shook the paw.

Amanda watched the two of them together for a moment, before turning to Jessie and Gus. "When did you get to Washington?"

They took seats at the glass table.

"We flew in yesterday," Jessie replied in her booming voice. "And before you have a fit about the dangers of pets in the cargo hold, Shadoe was in the cabin with us. It took some fancy talking, but the crew allowed it, since he is a therapy dog and all."

Amanda looked at Gus. He grinned. She turned her own grin to Jessie.

"A therapy dog? Since when did he become a therapy dog?"

Jessie's eyes sparkled with mischief. "Since I'm scared to fly. I needed him right next to me if they didn't want to listen to my screaming for the entire flight."

Amanda's eyes grew wide and she clasped a hand over her mouth. "You didn't?" she asked, trying not to laugh.

"You bet I did! No need for him to travel steerage when he could be comfortable in the cabin with us." Jessie reached out and patted the dog's head. "Shadoe lay down on the seat between us. Slept like a baby for the whole flight. Good as gold. It was as if he knew we were coming to see you."

"He's a good dog," Gus added.

Shadoe sighed and sank to the floor, resting his head on Amanda's feet.

"He's the best." Amanda felt blessed to be surrounded by almost everyone she loved, with the exception of Jared. He was a loss that she would eventually have to accept, but for now, having her father and uncle back in her life, and Shadoe, was more than she had ever dreamed of. It was more than enough, for now.

• • •

After lunch, Amanda and Jessie sat at a table enjoying the shade of an umbrella, next to the pool. Mark and Gus were sitting a few tables over, playing a game of poker with some of the other male residents. Shadoe slept soundly under the table. He opened his eye every time someone moved, as if to make sure that he wouldn't be left behind, again.

"Too bad that Cole is selling and moving," Jessie commented as she took a sip of her drink.

They had been talking about trivial things, so the sudden change of subject took Amanda a moment to digest.

"What do you mean he is selling and moving? Why would he do that? Ramsey is his home."

"It seems that Cole is tired of living in his brother's shadow. He finally decided that he wants to become his own man." Jessie took another sip before continuing. "From what I understand, he cut ties with his father and left politics to pursue something else. Dean made a lot of mistakes in the past. Tried to overcompensate to Kyle for giving him up (he didn't, only Gertie did). Unfortunately, Cole suffered because of it, as did you."

She sighed. "Cole tried to be the good son but Dean was just so consumed by Kyle that it was never going to be enough. I guess Cole finally realized that he needed to find out who he is. Start over, in a new place, where no one can compare him with anyone else."

"I thought the property was Dean's?"

Jessie smiled. "It was Catherine's. She left it to her children. With Kyle dead it became Cole's."

A picture of the Langford kitchen popped into Amanda's head. Would the new owners keep the character of the room intact, or would they be like Cole, and want to remove all traces of the house's roots? "So, who bought the place?"

Did she really want to know? Why did she feel as if she had lost the house, when she had only seen it once?

Jessie studied her a moment. "No one has even looked at it yet. I asked Cole to wait a while before putting it on the market. I wanted to talk to you first."

"Talk to me?" Amanda was surprised. "Why would you have to talk to me about Cole's ranch?"

Jessie took a long, deliberate sip from her drink. It was all Amanda could do not to reach across the table and shake her. The suspense was killing her.

"Because I was hoping that you would take over the place. Maybe you could restore it."

Amanda's mouth fell open. "Are you crazy? I don't have any money to do something like that, and besides, what would I do with a ranch?"

Jessie just watched her with those unreadable eyes as a glimmer of hope and possibilities started to pop into Amanda's head.

"It's time you came home, Amanda. Think about the future. You don't want to live in Washington. Idaho is in your blood. All you've done since I arrived is talk about going home."

Amanda glanced over to her father.

Reaching across the table, Jessie grabbed her hand. "I need you to listen to me and don't say anything until I'm finished. Dean has agreed to buy Cole out of the ranch and to give it to you." She held up her free hand to silence Amanda as she started to protest. "Let me finish. He wants you to have the ranch, with one condition, though he is aware that you don't owe him a damn thing. You're to use the ranch as some kind of healing center to help kids. Dean knows he failed you, Cole and Kyle, all those years ago. This is his way of trying to make amends."

"What about my father? I can't leave him."

Jessie squeezed Amanda's hand. "You'd also have a place for your father to live. Just think of all the good you could do with a ranch like that. All I'm asking is that you think on it."

With that, Jessie leaned back in her chair and left Amanda to her thoughts.

Amanda glanced around the renovated kitchen and smiled. They were on schedule to open next month. It had been a long six months since Dean had signed the ranch over to her, but she was feeling excited. Running her hand over the scarred oak table, now waxed and polished to a shine, she let out her breath before inhaling the clean smell of wax and fresh- cut wood. The floors had been sanded and polyurethaned bringing back their original beauty, and the old wood stove was blackened with its chrome accents polished. New appliances were tactfully hidden behind cabinetry that kept the original character of the room. This was the kitchen that Amanda had envisioned that first day, when she had walked through the ranch with Cole. It was perfect.

With Jessie, Gus, Billy, Gertie and most of the townspeople's help, the whole ranch had been transformed. Each room was given a fresh coat of paint, windows were replaced and the plumbing and electrical updated. A handicapped ramp led up to the front door.

Once the word had spread that Amanda was going to open a horse ranch camp, geared to helping handicapped and at-risk youth, offers of help had poured in from across the country. One man had offered rehabilitated horses that had once been abandoned and neglected. There were funds and grants to help cover the cost of much-needed equipment. A large animal food company had sent an eighteen-wheeler truck filled with bags of grain to help defray the cost of feeding the horses and a promise to also cover the cost for the first year's food. Money and donations were sent from as far away as Australia. Every fence post had been replaced and trees had been cut down to create more fields and pastures.

Amanda had lost count of the offers of generosity. It was hard to believe that there were evil people in the world when she was surrounded by such wonderful, caring people now. Her father had moved into one of the suites in the back part of the house, bringing his aide Patricia with him. Her aunt and uncle were coming from the Cape next week to help get ready for the opening. Everything was falling into place. Well, almost everything. Amanda refused to let her mind go further than that.

• • •

The sound of a car engine coming up the driveway made her smile. It was probably her father and Patricia coming home after going to the senior center for Mark's weekly cribbage club.

Exiting the kitchen from the side door, she made her way around the corner of the house, ready to help unload Mark and his wheelchair. Amanda stopped dead in her tracks when she saw a black jeep with its top rolled down parked in front of the house.

Even though it was late April, there was still a bite to the air. She shuddered as a man climbed out of the driver's seat. A black cowboy hat was pulled low over his face but she knew by the set of the shoulders and the way he moved who it was.

Jared.

Anger was her first emotion. Amanda hadn't heard a word from him since the day at the airport.

Nothing.

And now he just drives up her driveway without so much as a phone call or text?

How was she supposed to act with him? Kiss him on the cheek and pretend that he hadn't broken her heart?

Jared was so busy taking in the front view of the house that he hadn't noticed her yet. She could turn and run. Hide from him until he left. Mentally shaking off that thought, Amanda had vowed to never to run from anything or anyone ever again. She straightened her spine, inhaled the cool air and walked toward him.

• • •

Jared looked at the house and swallowed hard. It had taken nine excruciating months, but now that he was here, he didn't know what to do. How would Amanda react to seeing him? Would she give him a chance to explain or throw him out on his ear?

A movement to his right shifted his gaze to see that Amanda was bearing down on him. God, she was more beautiful than he remembered. The haunted look was gone from her face. In its place was a woman ready to do battle, and for some reason, that cheered him up and bolstered his courage. She must still have feelings for him, if she was this pissed to see him. He offered her a dazzling smile and then watched her halt several yards away. She crossed her arms in front of her chest and waited.

"Jared," she finally acknowledged with a nod of her head. "I didn't hear that you were back in town."

Pushing his hat back off his face, Jared looked at her for a moment before he replied. "I just flew in. You're the first person I came to see."

She looked surprised.

"Why would I be the first person you wanted to see? I seem to recall that you couldn't get away from me fast enough, last time we talked." Amanda was unable to keep the bitterness out of her voice.

Taking a step forward, he stopped when she took a step back. Pulling off his hat, he ran his hand through his hair, giving him a minute to think. He didn't want to scare her. He needed her to listen. "Look, is there somewhere we can talk? I have a lot of things I need to say to you. I'm hoping you'll give me a chance."

Amanda straightened her spine.

"Please," he pushed his advantage, "just hear me out."

Relaxing her stance, she nodded and strode toward the front porch.

• • •

*Was she out of her mind?* Amanda wondered, opening the front door and leading the way into the living room. A small fire was burning in the fireplace and the heat was welcome after the chill of the outdoors. Next to the kitchen, this was her favorite room. Gone was the heavy, dark furniture, bar, pool table and gloomy walls. Tables with chairs had been spread around the room, some with chess boards and board games on them.

Crossing to the fireplace, Amanda added a couple of logs to the small flames and stirred the ashes before sitting in one of the upholstered chairs that flanked the hearth. She tried to appear calm. Seeing Jared again had caused all her senses to go haywire. Her eyes feasted on his face, looking for any clue of what he had to say, while she breathed in the clean male scent of him. Her skin tingled in response to the electricity now building in the room.

Jared sat down on the couch, facing her, and then cleared his throat. "I've practiced what I'm going to say to you a thousand times, but now that I'm here, I don't know where to start." He took a deep breath. "I know I hurt you when I left, but you have to understand that I had to go. I had commitments. There were people waiting for me. Yet you have to also know how much I wanted to stay. This is home."

Suddenly, Amanda didn't want to hear what he had to say. Was this some confession to ease his guilt so that he could move on? Standing quickly, she moved back to the fire, her back to him, and poked at the logs. The flames danced along the fresh wood, eager to feed off it, reduce it to ashes.

"I'm not sure why you came here, Jared, but I'm okay, really. You don't need to explain anything. I've learned a lot of things about myself since I saw you last." She moved across the room, putting some distance between them. "I've got some semblance of my life back and though dad doesn't recognize me as his daughter, I know that he still loves me and that's enough for right now. I have Uncle Peter, and friends that know me and care for me." Her voice cracked but she cleared her throat and continued. "I want to thank you for all that you did but you didn't need to come all this way to check in on me." She gestured to the room. "We're all set to open a riding camp for handicapped and underprivileged kids in a few weeks and I couldn't be happier."

The fire crackling was the only sound in the room for a few seconds. Jared started to speak but she stopped him. "I've put the fear behind me, Jared. I'm living for myself and in the moment and I'm not taking one single minute for granted. I refuse to have any regrets and that includes you. You made it very clear that you didn't have any feelings for me and I've accepted that so let's just part as friends and move on." Amanda knew that she was babbling but she couldn't help it. Tears were threatening to fall down her cheeks and she was damned if she would cry in front of him. She had shed enough tears for him already.

Jared stood up and looked at her like she had lost her mind.

"What the hell are you talking about? Of course I have feelings for you." He crossed the few feet between them and gently grabbed her by the upper arms. "I've made a lot of enemies, Amanda. I was so afraid that someday they would find me, and if they did, they would certainly go after anyone I love. I couldn't take the chance I'd put you in danger so I just left."

He placed his forehead against hers. "I was all set to go undercover again but couldn't get you off my mind. All I could think about was coming back here, to you. I've spent the past nine months setting up my undercover persona's death so that no one will try to find me. Find us."

Uncertainty flickered in Jared's eyes. His grip tightened around Amanda's arm when she didn't respond. "Say that you care for me, even just a little. Give me some hope that I didn't lose you in the process of trying to do the noble thing to protect you. I love you and want to spend the rest of my life with you."

Tears glistened in Amanda's eyes and she couldn't speak for a moment. He loved her? He had given up his job for her? With a strangled sob, she flung her arms around his neck.

Amanda could feel the tension leaving his shoulders as he pulled her close.

"Does this mean that you like me?" he teased into her ear.

Pulling back, so that she could look into his face, she swiped at her tears and then swatted him on the chest. "I love you too!" Closing her eyes for a moment she gave a silent prayer of thanks.

Jared flashed his devilish grin. "Then marry me," he whispered before he kissed her.

•  •  •

Billy was sitting outside his cabin, whittling on a stick, when Jared came through the trees on the Appaloosa. It was an unseasonably warm autumn day. A light breeze rustled the leaves as sunshine filtered through them.

Dismounting, Jared tied the horse to the fence and hailed a greeting to the old man. "At what point did you know I was coming?" he asked, as he took a seat on the bottom step.

Billy grinned. "When you left the ranch. Amanda called to say that you were on your way. She asked me not to shoot you."

Jared chuckled at that.

It had been six months since he'd proposed to Amanda. Five months since they had been married. Even though he had given up his undercover work, he was still tracking the bad guys, but from the cyber unit.

Following the money and shipments of illegal animal parts was the only way to really find out who the money men were. They hid in the shadows of the dark web, letting others do their dirty work. It was poachers like Kyle, who took all the risks and paid the consequences when and if they were caught. Jared knew there would always be some impoverished hunter, struggling to survive in a third-world country, who would step forward. A tiger pelt alone was worth a five-year paycheck to someone desperate to feed his family. That's what made poaching so hard to stop. Money meant more than any animal's life. The more endangered the species, the higher the cost to the client, but also the greater thrill.

Jared's current case focused on the illegal shark trade in China. Shark fins were in such high demand that in one area, poachers were catching up to twenty-three thousand sharks a day, cutting off their fins and then throwing the live sharks back into the ocean. Without their fins, the sharks would drift with the current until they starved to death. It sickened Jared to think that this was why the shark population was in danger of extinction.

"I talked to Jedi this morning. Kyle's old gang is poaching again, somewhere out in Washington State."

Billy looked out over the scenery. "They'll make a mistake one of these days. They always do. We'll get them." He sounded sure of himself. "How is Amanda holding up?"

"What do you mean?" Jared hedged.

Billy gave him the look that said he didn't deal with fools lightly. "She must be very busy these days, what with her being pregnant and running the ranch?"

"How did you know she was pregnant? We haven't told anyone yet. Amanda wanted to wait until the first trimester was over before she told you, Mark and Peter."

Billy looked down at the horse he was whittling. "Let's just say that I heard it on the wind."

"Oh, right," Jared replied, "and I assume that the moon told you what sex the baby is and the sun told you the color of its hair?"

Billy kept moving his knife through the wood, expertly carving the face of the horse. "Your son will continue our mission of protecting the Earth's creatures. I am hoping that he has his mother's good looks and pleasant disposition."

Somehow the way Billy said that the baby was going to be a boy felt like a prophecy.

Jared didn't care if it was a boy or girl, as long as it was healthy, with ten fingers and ten toes. "A boy?" he mused out loud smiling. That had a certain appeal considering the thought of raising a girl who might be as strong-headed and as beautiful as Amanda was terrifying.

"Besides," Billy continued, "since it's such a secret, I'm sure that Jessie, Gertie and the whole town already know."

Jared laughed.

Damn. It was good to be home.

THE END

# ACKNOWLEDGEMENTS

I have been blessed to have so many creative people help me throughout the years. I wish I could acknowledge them all.

Thank you to Nicola Burnell and Joan Graham for their guidance and editing and to the amazing Kristen vonHentschel for the cover art and helping me format it all!

A huge thank you to  Gail Nickerson, Nancy Nicol, Paul Fasano, Rick Paris and all the others that sat around Nicky's table over the years and helped me with this story.

 Special thanks to my numerous beta readers for their support and invaluable feedback – Carol, Glenn, Kristen, Nancy, Pam, Maria and David.

Of course I need to thank my husband Steve, and my children, Brendon and Madison for giving me the peace and quiet to sit down and write.